STORIES FROM
JAPAN

PAST TO PRESENT

STORIES FROM JAPAN

PAST TO PRESENT

Toward Reconcilation
in Japan Missions

Al Hammond

STORIES FROM JAPAN, PAST TO PRESENT

Copyright © 2008 by Alvin D. Hammond

Direct requests for information to:
Al Hammond Publications
P.O. Box 20096
San Jose, CA 95160-0096

Printed by: **Bethany Press International**
Bloomington, MN 55438

Scripture quotations marked NASB are from the New American Standard Bible. Copyright © 1960, 1962, 1963, 1968, 1971, 1973, 1975, 1977, by The Lockman Foundation. Used by permission. (www.Lockman.org)

Scripture quotations marked NIV are from The Holy Bible, New International Version Copyright © 1973, 1978, 1984 by International Bible Society. Used by permission of Zondervan Bible Publishers.

Library of Congress Control Number: 2008907095

Hammond, Alvin D.
Stories From Japan, Past to Present
(Toward Reconciliation in Japan Missions)

1) Missionary Autobiography, 2) Intercultural Communication

ISBN 978-0-615-22112-0

To
Audrey West

She left a successful College Career

And went to Japan in 1953

To serve for 55 years

She is still there

At age 100

FOREWORD

The following stories from a 16-year veteran missionary and 34-year professor of mission are more than factual accounts. They are subtle explorations into lessons for those who see missions as kingdom business. And yet the stories are delightful and lighthearted at times because Al Hammond is not afraid to laugh at himself, his own social blunders, and odd situations in which he finds himself as he willingly immerses himself in a diverse culture with his wife and growing family. Like every missionary, sometimes this immersion is a baptism by fire and he feels he is way over his head. But his seasoned years of experience in Japan give way to walking on firm ground which can help all of us do the same.

Now an octogenarian with a spring in his step and a youthful smile arising deep from his heart, Professor Emeritus Hammond expresses some of the lessons we wished we had known early in our intercultural communication encounters. Though we all best learn by committed experience, this volume will be helpful to all those who are considering crossing cultural borders, have just begun the journey, or those who have been involved in intercultural activity for a long time. In the last chapter, he digs up his ten-nugget summary to encapsulate principles of truth we have encountered along the way in our reading.

Hammond grounds his stories in the culture of the land he adopted long ago, but the lessons he reveals will help all of us consider our own intercultural experience and mission. Most missionaries today ease into the experience through short-term missions, but this is not how Hammond began. He began the traditional way—on a ship with a one-way ticket and a commitment to learn the language, culture, and melt the typical Japanese reluctance to become followers of Jesus. Though success in Japan has been meager compared to African, Brazilian, or Korean responsiveness, Hammond's commitment to work closely with national leaders and missionary colleagues brought a turnabout in the lives of many Japanese people.

As a continual student, teacher, writer, editor, and practitioner of mission, the author's mission continued after he returned to his native California. He regularly taught college classes and seminars, led short-term missions, and encouraged many to devote their lives to lifelong intercultural missions. Even in his eighth decade, he took the humble position of a peer in a 5-month mission with novices a quarter of his age.

This book is purposely written in story form so that you can gain the insights of missions without wading through theoretical principles and strategies. It may surprise you how easily you will learn some important insights from these first-person accounts. Don't hesitate to take these lessons to heart so God Himself can use you in the process of changing the hearts of people outside your cultural circle.

Roger Edrington, Ph.D.

Senior Pastor, Central Christian Church, San Jose, California
Former Executive Vice-President of William Jessup University

PREFACE

The following accounts are my own experiences and are therefore limited in their perspective. I describe mainly those missionaries and Japanese nationals with whom I had a personal working relationship. God has given me awareness over the years of the other workers, who were devoting their lives to Him. Their labors fill in the larger areas of the total picture which is only known by the Master Painter.

The focus of the stories we are telling about Japan is not primarily on the missionaries, the culture or its people. I highly enjoy relating accounts of both culture and workers, but I wish mostly to point out to the reader the underlying theme of *what God is doing* in a very tradition-bound culture through weak human vessels. Having reconciled us to himself through Christ he has given us a ministry of reconciliation (II Cor. 5:18-19). As I write on Japan, I experience a felt need for reconciliation in three sensitive areas: (1) between missionaries and national leaders, (2) between those of a free-church position and traditional denominational leaders, and, (3) between evangelicals and charismatic believers. Happily, our true stories give examples of the healing touch of God in each of these contexts.

I am indebted to Japanese nationals and field based missionaries for helping me update the records. I have bounced many questions off respected veteran missionaries, Walter and Mary Maxey in the south and Paul and Rickie Clark in central Japan. Pastors Hideo Yoshii and Yoichi Muto, especially, have given helpful input on Japanese culture and theological perspectives. Mickey Richards, and her husband, Charles, Bible translators in the Philippines, were very gracious in giving positive affirmation and suggestions. Pastor Clay Baek gave me insights on Korean culture which helped me compare fairly their church growth to that of Japan.

Stateside friends were most encouraging also. Veteran missionary, now retired, Harold Sims, and Frank Higashi, an American Japanese, who served as an interpreter for the U.S. military during WWII, gave me helpful input on the chapter on Japanese religion. Betty Patton, and her husband, Andrew, helped jog my memory about the work and whereabouts of former missionary colleagues. Retired business man, Tetsuo Domen, gave me clarification to insure the accuracy of the accounts concerning his conversion and later marriage to Hideko Yabiku, renowned gospel singer.

Roger Edrington, a former colleague at William Jessup University, who has a doctorate in Missions, graciously consented to painstakingly work through the entire manuscript to correct my spelling and grammatical lapses, and offer helpful insights. My wife Beverly put her English language training to good use as she helped remove bumps for the potential readers. Other family members and innumerable friends gave me constructive feed-back on the sections that they read. I am very grateful to each one for their participation.

To help retain a feeling of the cultural environment in which the stories take place, I have sprinkled Japanese language expressions in numerous places. For the most part, the context conveys the meaning. It is my prayer that the Lord, who led me to share these stories, will also help each reader to understand what He is doing in Japan.

Al Hammond

San Jose, California

CONTENTS

INTRODUCTION

A Story Teller Approach

My children loved to hear stories and that is one reason I love to tell them. I observe that the students in my classrooms pay closer attention when I've illustrated academic truths with stories from life's experiences. I have also noticed that when I amplify points in my messages given in churches with a well told story that a few more people wake up from their naps. When asked to comment on a lecture or a message I am aware that the supporting stories stand out in my memory more than the factual points themselves. As I read the gospel accounts I am impressed that some of the greatest truths of Jesus are contained in stories. For these reasons the format of this book is story telling and I believe the stories will draw interest because they are true.

The mentors that God has placed in my life helped give me interpersonal peace and greater appreciation for others by removing misunderstandings that came from cultural stereotypes. Having served in the US Navy in World War II it was inevitable that I should be exposed to ugly, negative images about the Japanese. Because God called me to serve as a missionary in Japan I also became aware over the years of the beauty and sensitivity latent in Japanese hearts even prior to their introduction to Christianity. The true stories that I am recording do not gloss over human error, either ours or others, but they do reveal the socio-historical circumstances that compelled behavior that was later regretted. In addition to bringing understanding about historical and cultural contexts I want to recount the stories of changes in the hearts of people who have encountered the grace of God.

As well as going to bat for the beleaguered missionaries in Japan by relating accounts of their patience and faithfulness, I look forward to sharing many stories of dedicated national church leaders. In the process, honesty dictates that we reveal the tensions that arise at times between missionaries and their Japanese coworkers. Thankfully we can also tell of the healing and blessings that God brings when we mutually lay our problems before Him.

It has been fun to retell stories of living in Japan to my five offspring, three of whom were born there. Without discounting Catholic strengths in the focus on celibate workers, I want to affirm the testimony of the Protestant missionary family as one of the most effective witnesses in missions. My wife and children opened doors that would have remained closed to me. Our bonding experiences with Japanese families led to mutual understanding that would not have come as easily by the verbal teaching of an adult male alone. The age spread in our family prevented a generation gap in our witness. Our visible love for our growing children convinced others of our ability to love them also.

Above all I am glad that I can share true stories of the providential love of God. At times when our own efforts fell far short in communicating His message God provided bridges of understanding that closed the gaps. We were privileged to see Him change the hearts of others through circumstances of which we were unaware and did not fully understand even when we heard about them. We learned through experience that "all things work together for good to those who love God" (Rom 8:28).

There is a shift in style as I introduce provocative themes that we discussed in our open forum quarterly, **Far East Christian Missionary**. It broadens the focus as we hear from writers in different fields in Asia and other parts of the world. Topics such as, Missionary Strategy, the Role of Women, Demons, Culture

Shock, and the Unity of the Church are discussed with candor. We also include descriptive narrative about the missionary's pressure filled experiences when on furlough, and the difficult re-entry adjustments when he returns to Japan. One chapter tells the exciting story of the open window to the newer immigrants in California and the fruitfulness it brought to our college; yet we keep to our central focus and show the Japan connection.

The structure of the book is chronological. Early stories are about our Japan experiences while living there from 1954 to 1970. Later accounts are about periodic re-visits as a missions professor introducing students to the field. These short term experiences extend from 1974 to 2001. Further updating has been done through correspondence to missionaries and nationals on the field and through research sources. The account of Japan's dramatic change through the years is a fascinating story in itself.

Since the larger portion of my life has been directed by God to pass on mission insights to others, either on the printed page or in the classroom, I have an ongoing drive to share these perspectives gained over 50 years, inclusive of time in Japan and mission teaching. I have reached the age where I realize all the more that the task of bringing the gospel to the remaining unreached peoples must be passed on to the next generation. It is my prayer that our positive approach to the missionary calling to the so-called "resistant fields" will encourage others to take up the challenge. At the same time we who have reached advanced years need the reassurance of true stories that strengthen our hope for the final victory.

MAP OF JAPAN:

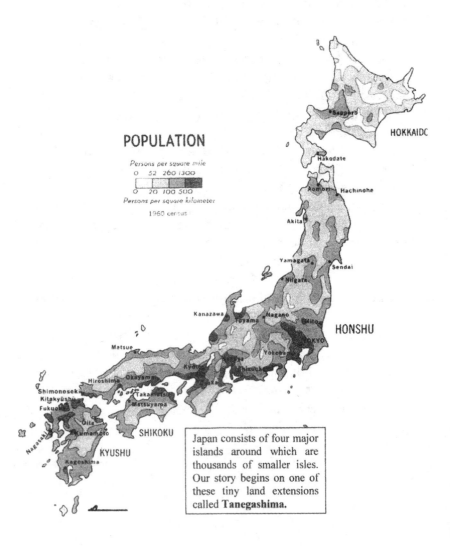

POPULATION

Persons per square mile

0   52   260 1300

0   20   100 500

Persons per square kilometer

1960 census

HOKKAIDO

Sapporo

Hakodate

Aomori Hachinohe

Akita

Yamagata Sendai

Niigata

Kanazawa

Toyama Nagano Mito

HONSHU

TOKYO

Matsue Yokohama

Hiroshima Okayama Kyoto

Shimonoseki Takamatsu Osaka Shizuoka

Kitakyūshū Matsuyama

Fukuoka

Oita SHIKOKU

Nagasaki Kumamoto

KYUSHU

Kagoshima

Japan consists of four major islands around which are thousands of smaller isles. Our story begins on one of these tiny land extensions called **Tanegashima.**

Chapter One

A PERSONAL INVITATION

Fukamachi San's Visit

"Please, I beg you, come to Tanegashima." That much of the flow of Japanese words that tumbled from her mouth we understood. At least we were given the strong impression that the elderly matriarch with the sun darkened face, who was on her knees in front of us, was making a passionate plea. But we could not grasp her dialect. She was quite small even for a Japanese, but evidently very strong. She had carried a heavy bag of rice wrapped in a *furoshiki*, (cloth wrapper) which she set at our feet as an *Omiyage* (gift). At my wife's suggestion I called Pastor Iimure to come and translate to clarify the purpose of her visit.

We had been in Japan only a little over two years and had shortened our intensive language study in centrally located Kobe to come south and replace a rural missionary who left for a needed furlough. One year of intensive language training was not sufficient to pick up rapid speech or strange dialects. We had been praying about where to locate when the missionary family returned and we wondered if this urgent request was possibly our answer.

Pastor Iimure entered with a traditional word of greeting, the gold in his teeth adding to the disarming nature of his pleasant smile. After sizing up the situation he began talking to our kimono clad visitor in an amiable manner for about half an hour. "Her name is Fukamachi San," he began, "she is from the island of Tanegashima. She is a Christian and is requesting that you come to Noma, her home in the central part of the

1

island, and preach the gospel." Gaining more information from the *Obaasan* (elderly lady) he then translated, "There had been a church there but the building was destroyed during the war and the members scattered. Only a few are left, and they need a missionary to come and build things up again. She is worried about her grown sons, who are drinking too much and know little about the Bible." Then after seemingly getting a confirmation about her request, he turned to us and said briefly, "She wants you to come with her today!"

Mark Maxey, the missionary we were replacing, had taken us to the port city of Tanegashima, once before. I remembered that it was a fatiguing six hour journey by ship from Kagoshima City. We met some of the remnant Christians, who welcomed us in the waiting room of a doctor's clinic. Mrs. Mogami, the doctor's wife, was especially cordial and pointedly stressed the need for a leader to come and build up the church. Pastor Yoshii, a young coworker of Mark Maxey, was with us and had good responses from his preaching during this short term visit. But it was apparent that full time workers were needed for follow up. We knew of the need on this small island (30 miles long and 3.5 miles wide), but there were similar needs all through Kagoshima prefecture on the main southern island of Kyushu. Was there a compelling reason for going to this more remote place?

Previous Typhoon Experience

We were informed that the low lying island of Tanegashima was directly in the path of the annual typhoons. Its topography offered little protection from winds or waves, but we had already experienced one of the most severe typhoons during which the Osumi peninsula was in the eye of the storm. Not many months after our arrival in Kanoya typhoon Louise hit. We spent a fitful night without electricity in the mission home which was a metal prefab building. The force of the wind caused the sheet metal roof to ripple and roar with deafening noise. The frame of the house seemed to groan in protest as it was buffeted by the winds. Candles flickered, went out and had to be lit again.

After a few hours of early morning sleep we awakened to the sound of hammers. Our neighbors were stoically repairing damage and picking up strewn roofing tile that covered the ground. We were shocked at the amount of destruction to the mission property. Fences were down; tile was stripped from the roofs of mission buildings. Window shutters and drain pipes had been torn off the home. The work shed was nearly demolished. After checking on our safety, the mission carpenters told us that several churches built by the mission had been damaged and one destroyed.

Hearing that the Kushira church was flattened we became concerned for the welfare of Kudo Obaasan (Grandmother Kudo). She was a widow that served as *rusuban* (caretaker) of the church and could have been inside of the church building when the typhoon hit. The carpenter and I rushed off to Kushira. A scene of complete destruction met our eyes as we came to the place where the church had been. The roof with its cross still attached lay some thirty yards from the building site. Rubble was strewn even greater distances. All that remained of the chapel was the wood platform. I was shocked! To my great relief, there on this last remnant of the former house of worship sat Kudo San calmly fanning charcoal in a cooking brazier.

"You're just in time," she announced. "Come up and have some tea." Then in a matter of fact tone with a touch of humor she said, "A bit of a blow last night, don't you think?" As the carpenter and I gratefully drank the offered tea the Obaasan related calmly how she had read Scripture, sang hymns and prayed throughout the night feeling perfect peace. Her faith strengthened our resolve to trust God in all circumstances.

Since we were only caretaker missionaries until the Maxeys returned we felt concerned about the amount of funds needed for repairs and rebuilding. We prayed and decided to write to the furloughing missionaries and also to send a report to the mission journal, Horizons Magazine. Both responded positively. Mark Maxey informed stateside churches of the need.

Horizons printed the story and put a photo of the wreckage of the destroyed church on their cover. The funds came in to cover the damage, giving us the assurance that God provides.

Reminding ourselves of these experiences, my wife agreed that it was the Lord's will that I should go with our determined visitor and check out the need in the lower part of Tanegashima. Meanwhile, Pastor Iimure convinced Fukamachi San that waiting until the next day to make the necessary bus and ferry connections was wise. This gave me time to pack and prepare mentally for the trip.

It was not an easy decision, Eleanor and I had the needs of two small children to consider, three year old Timothy, and one year old Sharon. In our first two years in 1950's Japan we had experienced frightening bouts of worms and other upsetting gastrointestinal problems. We assured ourselves that our cultural shock was waning and that we were ready for a move, but we wanted to make sure it was the Lord's will.

Following My Guide to Noma

My appreciation for the strength and determination of my elderly female guide grew as I saw her make well timed moves to get us seats on the crowded bus that made connections with the ferry that crossed the bay to Kagoshima City. Upon arrival she hailed a taxi with the wave of an arm and gave directions to the departure pier for the ship bound for the island. Once aboard ship she disappeared, but not before she made sure I had a place to rest amidst the crowded travelers on a *tatami* mat. The Tachibana Maru was an older, round bottomed ship crowded with some two hundred passengers. Once out of the bay the ground swells of the open ocean caused a great deal of rolling and the queasiness of sea sickness. Some six hours later when we were inching up to the pier at the port of Nishinoomote, Fukamachi San reappeared. Motioning to me she bounded down the gangplank and guided me through the crowd to a dilapidated bus bound for Noma.

After an hour's travel on unpaved road, we neared the edge of a town made up of aging unpainted wooden buildings. The Obaasan gave me the signal that we were getting off the bus. This was the town of Noma. Silently she motioned for me to follow and we arrived at a spacious two story home. Upon announcing our arrival two women wearing appropriate colored kimonos for their ages appeared and I was introduced to Mrs. Tanoue and her daughter, Michiko. They bowed and expressed words of greeting. Their typical polite demeanor contrasted to the eccentric directness of Fukamachi San. Apparently there was a prearrangement to borrow *futon* (Japanese bedding) from the Tanoues. A very large bedroll was produced and without any hesitation my elderly guide lifted it to her back and bid me follow to her home. In response to my request that she let me carry the heavy bed roll, she replied cheerfully, "No problem, I have legs." Her tiny bobbing figure with its very large bundle hustled down an unpaved dirt road for about a mile and finally stopped at a farm house on the town's outskirts. Pointing to the well she gestured, "You can freshen up there," and she went immediately to the kitchen. The sun was beginning to lower.

I became aware that there wasn't any electricity in the farm house when I saw the kerosene lanterns that lit up the dining room. My energetic host had quickly put together an aromatic meal of soup, rice, fish, vegetables and *daikon* (Japanese pickled radishes). Her loud call of "*Gohan*" (dinner) was followed by the entrance of three burly grown men somewhere in their forties, who plopped down on *zabuton* (floor cushions) on one side of a low lying table. Motioning to me, my host insisted I sit at the head of the table and urged me to go ahead and eat. On this cue the men began moving their chop sticks rapidly while at the same time staring at me. Speaking slowly with clearly worded Japanese so that I could understand, Fukamachi San explained to her puzzled sons, "The Reverend Mr. Hammond is going to teach us from the Bible after dinner." A growing feeling of vulnerability and complete inadequacy overwhelmed me. Inwardly I prayed for the Lord's strength and guidance.

During my first year in Kanoya, the home of the furloughing Mark Maxey family, I struggled to prepare one sermon a week in Japanese. Okabe Sensei, a partially blind minister helped me translate my English messages into formal Japanese. It was necessary for me to study the translated message for 30 to 40 hours in order to preach it with any degree of confidence in the rural churches. The pained expression on the faces of my listeners belied the kind words of appreciation by a few kindly Christians following the message. I had brought a few copies of these sermons with me to Tanegashima. The Japanese syllables were typed in Roman letters for easier reading, but my fear was that the dim light given by the kerosene lantern would not be bright enough for reading. As I glanced at the somber faces of the men sitting at the table, I wondered if anything could come from my strained efforts at reading one of my old sermons in a school book form of the Japanese language.

A few things were in my favor. In spite of their brawny size and rough exterior Fukamachi San's grown sons were obedient to her. However begrudgingly, they would sit and listen. Also, I wanted to live up to my host's expectations. She had gone to a lot of trouble to bring me to this place for this very hour. Furthermore, I believed that the Holy Spirit could work in spite of my lack of ability. Struggling to see by the flickering kerosene lantern I did my best to read with expression and meaning. Following my closing word of prayer, each of the men mumbled something, stood to their feet and left the room.

Without comment my host began clearing the dishes. Later she set the table aside and laid out the *futon* so I could rest for the night. Fatigue overcame my anxious concern as to the results of the evening. I slept soundly; arose early, thanked my host profusely and returned to the mission house the next day. It was not until a year later that I became more fully aware of how God used this sincere Obaasan's compelling invitation to further the kingdom on this remote island.

Chapter Two

FAMILY ADJUSTMENTS

Traveling With the Carpenter

"**S**ensei, you can save a lot of money going third class." The carpenter's suggestion was offered as we approached the ticket booth to board the ship to Tanegashima. Without difficulty he soon had his third class ticket in hand. As my turn in line came up I asked the ticket agent for one ticket to Nishinomote in the third class section. "You don't want third class," retorted the clerk behind the desk. Thinking that my expression of Japanese may not have been clear, I repeated the request, "Yes, one third class ticket, please." "But you are a *gaijin*," the agent stated with apparent irritation in his voice, "third class is not good." Perhaps because he had stereotyped me as a foreigner, it was my turn to be irritated. In a firm tone I made my request for third class passage one more time. He reluctantly took my 5000 *yen* note and thrust the ticket across the counter along with the change.

Together with the carpenter I climbed the gang plank and handed my ticket to the steward. He looked surprised, but waved me on to a line on the left, past the first class lounge. "Looks nice, but I don't need that," I said to myself as I saw some of the first class passengers drinking coffee in a comfortable lounge. We were directed down a short ladder to the second class level where I saw large rooms beginning to fill up with passengers sitting on *tatami* mats and drinking tea. I had traveled that way before and recalled that it cost twice as much as third class. Glancing at our ticket stubs a seaman guided us to another descending ladder. Part of our group was directed to the stern; the rest of us were led toward the bow. It was darker below decks and our eyes needed to adjust. The rounded shape of the ship's hull became apparent. Boards had been attached to the ships ribs fashioning a floor upon which we were asked to lay down on loose mats in opposing head and toe positions. A brass pan was placed by the head of each traveler.

"I'll just sleep for the six hour trip," I thought to myself, feeling pride that I was traveling in a manner that identified me more with the common people. While the ship traversed Kagoshima Bay, the drone of the engine and the easy roll of the steamer lulled me to sleep. As the vessel exited the bay and entered the open ocean, I became aware of the surprising height that the bow climbed with each wave, followed by a downward plunge and a pitching roll. Up and down over and over again. The ship seemed to shudder with each wave it encountered. I was determined not to get sea sick, but when person after person began to reach for their brass pans, I felt uneasy. Eventually the retching sound and the smell of vomit upset my system. At this point I wished I had listened to the ticket agent who wanted to restrain my purchase of a third class ticket.

This trip was important. By prearrangement with the church and mission the carpenter was going to check on the cost of building materials and initiate plans to erect a chapel on the open land south of the port town that the church had purchased. The Kyushu Christian Mission had employed Shimoda San, a Christian carpenter to build a number of these economical buildings for young start-up churches. In the 1950's the materials for this could be purchased for $500 to $750 each, a sum that the church could repay in time. Helping the churches become self supporting was part of the mission strategy.

The chapel on Tanegashima would include compact living quarters for our family. The carpenter wanted my help in planning the parsonage addition which would include two small bedrooms, a kitchenette, an *ofuro* (Japanese bath), and *obenjo* (Japanese toilet). I had explained to my wife that this would be nothing fancy but more like a camp cabin. Running water had recently been made available to this southern part of town but electricity was available only in the evening hours.

Since Eleanor had spent her high school years working in a rustic lifestyle on a ranch in the sand hills outside of Burwell, Nebraska, she assured me that she would be O.K.

Conversation With a Farmer

While the carpenter was busy talking to building materials suppliers, I visited with a farmer in the outskirts of town near where the parsonage would be built. After extensive self introduction the following is a paraphrase of what our Japanese conversation may have sounded like in idiomatic English:

Al: "What are the principal crops here?"

Farmer: "Sweet potatoes for starch, then comes sugar cane and rice."

Al: "Is making a living difficult?"

Farmer: "Very difficult. The gov'ment just makes promises but don't do nuthin' for the farmer. We don't even sell our vegetables to market 'cause it would be just givin' them away."

Al: "What do you do with your vegetables?"

Farmer: "What we don't eat ourselves we sell to the neighbors. If you need anything, let me know."

Al: "How do fishermen do?"

Farmer: "They do better 'cause when they ain't fishin', they're farmin', and when they ain't farmin' then they're fishin'."

Al: "I guess the war really upset your economy."

Farmer: "You know we was all set to kill you Americans when you came 'cause the gov'ment said you were goin' to kill us. We had some guns, sticks, shovels, just anything, and we were getting' ready to use them."

Al: "Then what happened?"

Farmer: "Why then these soldier boys came a passin' out chewing gum and acting like they was on a picnic. That's when we knew the gov'ment had been lying.

Al: "What do you think about Christ?" (My abrupt question didn't startle him).

Farmer: "Well, what I've heard, it seems like he was the god that started your history; something like Ieyasu Tokugawa became a god because he began a long part of our history. Course, we have many gods you know."

Al: "There is much more to it than that. May I give you this Bible portion …"

Farmer: "Yeah, I'd like to learn about that some more, but right now, I must go… If your kids like sugar cane to chew on, I got lots of it. You might ask the Misus if she wants any vegetables; be glad to give 'em to you. Bye for now."

Return to Kagoshima

The carpenter found out that he could get the needed building materials in the port town and didn't need to have things shipped from the mainland. He also assured me that he could add the small parsonage on the back of the chapel without problems. We were ready to return when the carpenter approached me. "Sensei, that was a rough trip coming here and I am sorry that I didn't advise you better. But we can still save money returning third class and have a pleasant voyage. We can stay outside and enjoy a cool breeze and not have to go below decks." At this point I was beginning to bond with the *Daikusan* (a term of respect for carpenter) and appreciated his guiding advice. Since it was very hot in this southernmost climate his suggestion sounded appealing and his practice of frugality was a good example for our family as we saved in order to make the move to the island following the Maxey's return.

After boarding we made our way to the ship's fantail behind the smoke stack because there was more open deck there. From the rail we could wave to the handful of Christians who had come to see us off. Gradually the ship left the pier and their friendly faces began to recede with the distance. A breeze picked up as we left the harbor; its welcome coolness was exhilarating. I was beginning to feel good that we were topside on the open deck, but then the weather began to change. In a couple of hours clouds began to accumulate, and before we could crowd into the limited shelter, a rain squall began. Following a drenching with rain, the sun came out from behind the clouds and made us feel unbearably hot. To make matters worse, for some unexplained reason the smoke stack began to belch soot to add to our discomfort. We arrived in Kagoshima sunburned and dirty. The carpenter didn't look my way when we disembarked.

Adjusting Our Lifestyle

During our first years in Japan our Willys Jeep station wagon served us well. When it slid into a ditch it provoked a humorous comment which I remember well. A farmer with a horse happened by and tying a line on the bumper easily pulled the car out of the ditch. "One horse pulled out a one hundred horse power auto," he laughed, going on his way. Yet in those early postwar years American autos had very good resale value in Japan. Since extra funds had not come in to make the move to the island, I thought of selling the jeep. A lightweight motorcycle would fit in better on the narrow roads and rough terrain in rural Tanegashima and it cost only a third of what we could get from the jeep station wagon. I had my eye on a knee action Honda motorbike. At the time I didn't realize how important it was to my wife to be able to travel with the family all together in the car. But she suppressed her objections and later purchased a bicycle with a motor attached to do her shopping. My insensitivity was overcome by her game adaptability.

Once I began making the rounds to the churches on the motorcycle there was a noticeably different response from foot travelers and other bikers. Only the very few had cars in those years and they contributed to a negative image by causing billows of dust or splashing mud on pedestrians. Smiling inquirers asked me about the size of the engine and my personal liking of a Japanese Honda. Using this mode of transportation available to the average Japanese along with gradual inclusion of expressions from the Kagoshima dialect opened doors of communication. On a few occasions, the appearance of all four of us crowded onto the small motorcycle caused curiosity and admiration. We were a little more ready to move into the more economically deprived lifestyle of the island to the south.

Goodbyes are difficult. We had bonded with Japanese friends during our two years in Kanoya. Our children felt very accepted. Sharon was held by adopted grandparents or aunts in most public and home meetings. Tim had bonded with the Toyama's son, to whom we referred to as "Toyama Chan" (polite for little Toyama). This was a little long for Tim so he settled for "To-chan," which brought laughs to adults for it means, "Daddy." Tim learned much of his Japanese language from this bosom buddy. As we parted, rather than *Sayonara*, we chose to say, *Mata aimasho*, (Until we meet again).

Family's Arrival on the Island

The carpenters, Shimoda San, and his son, Katsuo, were at the building site doffing their caps in greeting the day we arrived at the island parsonage. "Sensei, we are sorry we didn't get the *ofuro* done, the tile is not yet laid." The *Daikusan* seemed apologetic. "No hurry," we replied and thanked them as we looked over the small apartment built in the back of the chapel. Two small bedrooms were created simply by adding two plywood partitions. The floor covering was *tatami* (rice straw mats). There was a picnic style bench table setting on the kitchen's wood floor and a chrome sink with wood counters was placed under a small window. A sliding door exited onto a ground level *genkan* (Japanese entrance). This would be the way to our living quarters. We would not have to pass through the chapel during meetings.

On the opposite side of the kitchen was a small enclosed room in which a large elevated round iron tub was encased in a wood frame. On a level lower than the kitchen floor a drain had been made in the freshly poured cement floor. This bathing area would later be covered with tile for easy drainage and cleaning. Outside of the cubicle was an opening through which a wood fire could be built to heat the water in the cast iron tub. "Can we use the bath before the tile is laid," my wife asked. "Yes," answered Katsuo San with a smile, "But be sure and put the bottom boards in before getting in the *ofuro*," he cautioned as he held up the circular wood frame designed to protect the body from the heated bottom of the tub.

Four year-old Tim and two year-old Sharon had run outside while we were talking. They apparently had climbed the hill in back of the parsonage where they could see the ocean about 100 yards away. "There's a beach real close!" their voices chimed as they came back into the kitchen, "and there is sand to play in too." Their clamor was interrupted by an important question from the carpenter. "We haven't made the toilet yet," he explained. "Do you want it separated from the building or put next to it?" We came to understood that it was to be an outhouse style and that scarce funds prevented installing a septic tank with running water. "Oh please put it next to the house," pleaded my wife as she thought of the need for privacy. This request led to the digging of a pit, and the building of a frame structure adjacent to the back exit. It had a wood floor in which there was an oval hole. Later, a Japanese style porcelain squat toilet was installed and a brass water dispenser to wash hands was hung nearby.

Sensing that Eleanor wanted time to talk, I suggested that we go outside with the kids to look over the land. We discovered that although this area was yet rather underdeveloped there was a shaded park on top of the hill, and the ocean and part of the town could be seen from this vantage point. "It is beautiful," exclaimed my wife after a time of reflection, which gave me the feeling that she would overlook the sparseness and do her best to make the island our home. "We will need curtains to brighten it up," she mused as she looked back down at the parsonage. "And it would be good if you could have swings made in the yard for the kids." "And we will need a washing machine!" she exclaimed with emphasis.

"But, honey," I interjected, "they limit the electricity for each household and then it's only for a few evening hours. The kids don't need diapers anymore." I added. "We can send for a gasoline operated Maytag washer," responded Eleanor, "and when it gets here, we will need it for washing clothes for a larger family!" Her last remark reminded me that she was in a family way again.

Chapter Three

A WARM WELCOME

<u>Encouraging Fellowship</u>

Not long after the family moved to the island we were given a reception by a handful of Christians in the waiting room of Dr. Mogami's clinic in town. We learned that the jovial white haired doctor was highly respected. He was known as an outspoken individualist who opposed the expansionism of Japan's military dominated government of the 1930's. He believed that the country would have been much better off to focus their energies on the development of their own neglected rural areas such as Tanegashima and other outlying islands. Apparently many citizens agreed with him. The good doctor was chosen as mayor for three terms. Today a bronze bust of Mayor Mogami can be seen in front of the city hall.

The well read physician had a special interest in indigenous foods. During our welcoming reception he introduced the juice of the "*tokeiso*," a tasty citrus fruit found on the island. Noticing that I carefully separated the seeds out of my drink, he laughed and declared humorously, "Mr. Hammond is afraid the seeds will turn into a tree in his stomach." I hesitated to tell him my thoughts when I saw him using a scalpel to slice and eat raw chicken livers But I liked the doctor and inwardly rejoiced that he declared himself a Christian.

Mrs. Mogami, the doctor's wife, was a practicing nurse. She proved to be the one most concerned for the building up of a spiritual body of believers. The outspoken doctor expressed his wish that the mission would build a large ornate church building centrally located with a tall tower, housing a bell and topped by a cross. He reluctantly agreed to the building of the small chapel as a beginning place, and came to services on special occasions. His wife, a faithful encourager of our efforts to expand the church, especially enjoyed participating in home Bible studies. In a good natured way she loved to laugh at my mistakes in the Japanese language. At the reception she was busy serving food and seeing to everyone's needs.

Yaita Sensei, a high school teacher of English, slipped quietly into the reception with his wife. He made an effort to speak to me in English and then became apologetic about his lack of fluency. I came to understand that he was a part time realtor and had initiated the arrangements for the purchase of the plot of land upon which the chapel was built. As if answering unspoken objections, he defended the location of the chapel. "Jonohama is sparsely settled now, but we bought the land at a very reasonable price and the value will increase over time. Gradually the population must expand in that direction; there is little room to build in town."

A concern shared by Mr. Yaita and his wife was the fact that their son would eventually leave the island to attend college and to find work in one of the more developed metropolitan areas. Families on the island experienced a continuous exit of their youth to the cities in the north. Wanting me to understand the loneliness of the islanders he later asked me to accompany him to see a movie called, *"Todai Mori."* (Lighthouse Keeper). It was a Japanese drama that portrayed the loneliness of family members when their husbands and fathers were stationed in lonely outposts. Over the years I came to consider Yaita Sensei a kind friend and helpful cultural advisor.

We first met Araki San when this matronly woman came to our chapel home bringing bottles of milk. "Milk is good for the children," she affirmed, "it is pasteurized and from our own dairy." By this time we realized that there wasn't any refrigeration on the island and so we usually used powdered milk. But Araki San's gift of fresh milk was welcomed. At the reception Mrs. Araki quietly helped with the serving and talked with the children. My first impression of her was that she was a typical quiet, serious minded Japanese lady.

We later discovered that Mrs. Mogami and Mrs. Araki were very close friends. We also found out that both of them had a keen sense of humor. When they got together, these two middle-aged ladies would share thoughts that made them giggle like school girls. On one occasion when gathered in a small room, a guest speaker spoke in a very loud voice, even shouting at times. The ladies saved their comments until the guest had left. Then knowing that I had difficulty at times in hearing the high pitched sounds in the Japanese language, they asked facetiously, "Hamondo Sensei, could you hear the speaker all right?" Then they doubled over and covered their faces they were laughing so hard. I appreciated their playfulness and enjoyed laughing with them. They helped me overcome the stereotype of Japanese as inscrutable, unsmiling and serious. From them I learned the lesson of not taking oneself too seriously.

Ministry Beginnings

As Yaita Sensei predicted, Jonohama, later called, "Kamome machi," the area where the chapel was constructed, began to build up quickly. Since land was cheaper it attracted many younger families with small children. Partially because of the urging of their parents, the neighborhood children made friends with our two youngsters. The parents may have hoped that their offspring would learn English from them. But Tim and Sharon used their naturally acquired Japanese fluency to respond to their new playmates. We were warned of one problem by a well meaning parent. Our youngsters unknowingly were learning some vulgar terms from some of the kids. Along with Tim and Sharon we were taught to avoid the usage of some expressions. For the most part there were congenial relations with the growing community. W saw them as an opportunity for us to share the gospel.

Akaike San was a young student English major we met when living in Kanoya, the home of the Maxeys. We made the proposition that if he would help us work with the children during his break between semesters we would pay him a modest sum and help him improve his English. With this young man's help we began a children's ministry that filled our chapel with noisy youngsters. While Eleanor played a small pump organ I would lead them in choruses that were available in English and Japanese. Akaike San would follow up on my Bible stories in terms the youngsters could better understand. Following these learning times we had a fellowship hour during which we served their favorite *okashi* (Japanese confectionary). These youth sessions were popular with the children and their parents as well.

As we became better acquainted with the families we became aware of the post-war poverty that still existed. Cases were cited in which children had to have operations to remove intestinal worms. The Japanese economy could not yet afford commercial fertilizer and human waste was still used on the fields. If leafy vegetables were not carefully washed, worm eggs would be ingested. Medication to eradicate the parasites was expensive and the symptoms were often overlooked. Single parent families were especially vulnerable and the number of widows had increased during the war. It seemed to be the general understanding that the further north or south one moved from the central cities the lower the quality of the educational system. Youth raised in the rural areas could seldom pass the entrance exams into the prestigious universities. This contributed to a cycle of poverty that was felt on Tanegashima.

Eleanor and I were humbled by an invitation from one of the widows to come to her home for dinner. She was known as, "the flower lady," for she earned a meager living by selling flowers. Her dwelling was a small one room shack with a rusty tin roof. The *futon* was put aside and a short legged table was set in its place for the serving of the meal. She did the cooking outside using charcoal. We knew that she could not afford to feed us and felt awkward. At the same time we understood that it somehow showed our respect and bestowed dignity upon her to consent. She gave us a well prepared meal on a worn table that was graced by a beautiful flower arrangement. She then proceeded to thank us profusely for helping her teenage son learn English. Her generous hospitality motivated us to try a little harder to help aspiring youth.

Azechi Sensei, a middle school teacher was introduced to our home meetings by Mrs. Mogami and Mrs. Araki. She had recently returned from teaching on one of the small isles southwest of Tanegashima. She had a vibrant, outgoing personality and was strongly attracted to the teaching of the Scriptures that described women in positions of respect and honor. Her many sincere questions kept us all searching for appropriate answers. The story of Ruth fascinated her but she was perplexed by the familiarity Ruth showed to Boaz by laying at his feet (Ruth 2:1-11). "Is that a Christian story?" she asked us, as if doubting its morality. "Let's go back to the study of the New Testament; that's easier to understand." As the unanswered questions began to accumulate, I realized that my ability in the language was not adequate. Yet, at the same time I felt that there were a number of *kyudosha* (seekers) who were close to conversion.

Help From Our Neighbors

Our nearest neighbors, the Morita family, represented the growing middle class. Mr. Morita was a furniture maker, who ran about making business contacts on his large motorcycle. He always seemed to have a business demeanor and seldom smiled. His wife was just the opposite, a congenial and smiling person who always had something pleasant to say. She was a busy homemaker with two young sons who played with our youngsters. Through the invitation of my wife she began attending our small Sunday services and showed an absorbing interest in the teachings of Christ. She often had questions that she brought first to Eleanor. But neither my wife nor I could fully understand what she meant, so we kept repeating the basic story of God's love.

Mrs. Morita did appreciate our Sunday services and was happy that her two boys got along well with Tim and Sharon.

She enjoyed having our youngsters over at her house and looked after them during our busy times. From her husband's perspective, we had given some happiness to his wife and were helping to educate his children. Therefore in his traditional thinking he owed us something. His opportunity came when we were trying to get a taxi to the port in order to return to Kagoshima City on the mainland for an annual church rally.

Mr. Morita was alerted by his wife to our dilemma. We were dressed and ready to go early enough to catch the ship on time, but the taxi had not come. It looked like we were going to be too late. Briefly stopping by, Mr. Morita called out, "I will tell the ship to wait; the taxi should come soon," and roared off on his motorcycle. The over-scheduled taxi finally did come, but as we arrived at the pier, we could see that the ship had moved out about 30 yards towards the harbor exit. Hundreds were gathered on the pier still waving at departing friends and relatives.

Our arrival was a cue for Mr. Morita. He cupped his hands to his mouth and called out to the ship in a loud voice, "Tsubaki Maru, *Tomare!*" (a command to stop). Nothing happened. Onlookers were now staring at us. Once more in an authoritative tone our neighbor bellowed, "There are foreign guests here. Please stop". The ship's whistle blew and the Tsubaki Maru stopped just short of the harbor exit. "Now what is he going to do?" gasped my wife.

An elderly fisherman was just bringing his boat up to the south end of the pier. "Grandfather, come here!" Morita's authoritative tone underlined his request. The fisherman quickly redirected his craft to a position just below us. Mr. Morita handed Tim down to his waiting arms, then Sharon was next. He reached for my wife, but she spotted a wood ladder and headed quickly toward it. After helping Eleanor, I jumped in with my family. Prompted by our determined neighbor, the old man rowed quickly toward the waiting ship. Reaching the ship's side we found them waiting with a rope ladder. We each struggled up safely and boarded the vessel, which then immediately began moving toward the open sea. Passengers made room for us to lie down on the straw mats for the voyage. Sharon said that she felt sick. After reassuring her, Eleanor covered her eyes with a hand towel and both went to sleep. When asked how he felt, Tim declared, "I'm a good sailor," but he needed little persuasion to lie down. The excitement and effort had exhausted us so we were soon fast asleep.

An Appropriate Gift

We need to buy a nice gift for the Moritas," declared my wife as we were contemplating the return to our island home. The fellowship at the rally had been uplifting and we were in a good mood. "How about some chocolate candy," I suggested. "Yeah, that would be good," agreed the kids. "It should be something that lasts, something that Japanese appreciate," insisted Eleanor. We realized that Mr. Morita had stuck his neck out for us. If the ship had not stopped he would be a laughing stock in the community. We all agreed that the Morita's especially liked living things. Their home was graced by lovely plants and an exotic aquarium. "That pair of parakeets we saw in the pet shop would be just the thing," concluded my wife, and she won us over when we revisited the pet store.

The Moritas were delighted with the gift. The love birds added an interesting conversational topic to their home. Mr. Morita was now looked to in the community as an intimate friend of the American family. Why else would he have risked embarrassment by stopping a ship that had already pulled out from the pier? He demonstrated the courtesy of the Japanese to their foreign guests. He was a citizen for whom they could be proud. We look back on that exciting evening when Mr. Morita stopped a crowded vessel to get us on board as a turning point in our relationships within the larger community of the port town.

Chapter Four

RECEPTION & REJECTION

Return to Noma

At this point in time we could hardly say that the church in the port town was well established. It was growing and had the semblance of a regular worship schedule. We were blessed by the encouragement of the remaining believers of the earlier church. I was reminded of the Lord's words, "Others have labored and you have entered into their labor" (John 4: 38). Feeling assured about the work in the principal city, I felt it time to make a return visit to Noma, the home town of Fukamachi San (Chapter 1), located in Central Tanegashima.

Arriving on my motorcycle I thought it appropriate to stop first at the home of the Tanoue's and thank them for their earlier kindness of loaning the *futon* that my Obaasan guide had borrowed. Grapevine communication had already informed them that I had come to Tanegashima with my family for the long term. The mother and daughter were not only glad to see me but were eager to tell me about the tentative plans they had made. Michiko did the talking as her mother nodded in agreement. "Sensei, we met with Fukamachi San, who suggested that we have Bible studies in our home here in town. We are near the high school and are sure that many students would like to come; it would be convenient for the greater number of residents. The grandmother acknowledged that her home was too far out and starting meetings in our home in town was best." I was elated and agreed to come on Sunday evenings which they thought would be the most convenient for the students.

Mrs. Tanoue wanted me to know that adjacent to the large *tatami* room in which we would be meeting, her husband was suffering from a terminal illness. He could not attend the Bible studies but would be listening on the other side of the partition. I was surprised to learn that Tanoue Sensei was also a doctor, as it was with the key figure in Nishinoomote. I wondered if being the only physician in a town would cause one to seek help from God.

As predicted, the high school students did come when I arrived on the first scheduled Sunday night. Partially motivated by curiosity to see an American, and desirous for opportunities to practice English, they filled the large reception room. Older adults also came, farmers and shop keepers in the area. All seemed to enjoy the light conversation before the Bible study and the students came with rehearsed questions in English. "Where is your home?" "Do you like Japanese food?" "How old are you?" My answers were not always understood and the amusing interchange frequently caused us all to break out into hearty laughter.

After a time of friendly conversation I would request permission to lead the group into a Bible study. All were sitting on the straw mat floor in a comfortable cross legged fashion. I followed the custom for a teacher to sit a little higher in a semi-kneeling position as I directed my remarks to the group. It usually took an hour to complete a lesson in my faltering Japanese and another hour to answer questions. The respectful attitude and sincere questions were greatly encouraging to me. A source of personal embarrassment that resulted in laughter was my attempt to stand after two hours of sitting on my legs. The meeting would end on a note of good natured humor while I waited for my circulation to return. After a long full day on Sunday, the Noma meeting became an enjoyable highlight.

One newcomer to the group, called Nagashima San, changed the friendly atmosphere of the Noma home fellowship to one of tension and disappointment. In place of the polite acceptance of my mistakes in Japanese grammar, Nagashima San was rude and critical. "Your Japanese is poor. You repeat things over and over. Why don't you study more?" Instead of the thoughtful reception of Biblical truth, this 30 year old antagonist challenged the integrity of the Scriptures. "How do you know that the Christian Bible is the truth?" "Why don't you teach what the Buddhist Sutras say, as well?" His bold attacks created a different kind of interest in the meetings which tended to divide opinion. My attempt to give calm answers in truth and love may have been perceived as weakness. Some of the older farmers made remarks that appeared to agree with my opponent. In less than two months my anticipation of Noma's Sunday night meetings changed from warm enthusiasm to fearful apprehension.

<u>Further Discouragements</u>

Returning from Noma one Sunday night I found Eleanor in tears. Drunks had terrified her by banging on the front church doors and hollering incoherently. She felt lonely and frightened. Her fears transferred to the children and my reassurance that they were only drunks didn't help. The hot muggy weather of that night added to our discomfort and left us sleepless. Feelings of inadequacy and doubts about our purpose filled our minds.

A science teacher had given us a gift of a kid (a baby goat) for a pet and the children, especially took a liking to it. Unleashed dogs discovered the goat tied up behind the church and killed it. Everyone was upset including the kindly science teacher, our family and the neighbors, who also had pets.

It didn't help to comfort us when a cult leader of an off beat variety came to our door and proceeded to draw a coiled snake in black ink with a calligraphy brush on an unrolled length of parchment placed in our entry way. In a skilled manner he drew the snake without lifting the brush while chanting and shaking his body to get the effect of scales. His finishing touch was to dip two fingers in white paint to touch in the snake's eyes. Then he asserted that this charm would keep us from harm and asked what price we could pay. Much to his disappointment we politely but firmly refused to accept his drawing. He rolled it up and walked off in a huff.

Kindly neighbors, who represented the majority, in my opinion, offered words of encouragement and tried to explain that these incidences were not a normative part of daily life in Nishinoomote. A number of them came with gifts of food and offered words of comfort. We would have felt much better if they would have attended our services, for we had discovered that regular weekly attendance in a religious service was at odds with custom and community scheduling. The schools frequently used Sundays for special events such as *undo kai* (athletic events). Students, family members, and faculty alike were tied up for the day. In a six day work economy, Sundays were also used for community organized cleanup days. We were learning some of the hard lessons of missions in Japan.

A Serendipity Turnaround

On Sunday nights when I returned to the parsonage in the port town both physically and emotionally fatigued, I shared my continued disappointment about the Noma meetings with my wife. Fixed in her mind was a very negative image of Nagashima San, the cause of my pain. Consequently, we both were shocked when this same individual entered our kitchen entry way one morning and announced his presence.

My feelings of dread turned to bewilderment as I became aware of the dramatic change in my opponent's demeanor. "Sensei, I want to be baptized," he requested. I couldn't believe what I heard and asked him to repeat it, which he did. Surprise and confusion must have shown on my face as I asked, "Aren't you the Nagashima San that declared disbelief in the Bible, and kept telling me to give the Buddhist Sutras equal time?" "Why do you request Christian baptism?"

Our strangely behaved guest responded to my question by slowly removing his jacket and shirt revealing a long scar, an operational incision that had given access to his lungs. "I have been convalescing from a TB operation. The surgeons in the hospital in Fukuoka removed a large portion of my diseased lungs." He looked at us to see if we had fully understood. We nodded for him to go on. "While in the hospital a missionary's daughter came and visited me. She asked if she could pray for me and I consented. Later she revisited many times and read to me from the Christian Bible. The things she taught about God and salvation were both encouraging and upsetting. A battle began in my heart and continued after I was discharged from the hospital." Then looking directly at me he explained, "Sensei, you helped me win the battle. I was not confident of the young girl's words even though her teaching moved me to tears. At the Noma meeting I was testing you and deliberately tried to provoke you. But your Bible answers came through. I believe in Jesus Christ and want to be baptized today."

Nagashima San's convincing testimony lifted the heavy weight of discouragement that had filled my heart. "Praise God!" I exclaimed, and sat down with two open Bibles to make sure that my bold friend understood the meaning of Christian baptism. Eleanor began heating water to prepare tea. "Baptism is an expression of faith," I began, "It has meaning only as we focus on what Christ did once for all by dying for our sins." Turning to Romans, chapter six, we worked through the meaningful passage about the death, burial and resurrection of Christ as symbolized by our submission to baptism by immersion. Our guest confessed his faith and acknowledged his need following a time of study and prayer.

"I am still weak from the operation and the ocean will be cold, but I want you to baptize me today," pleaded our new convert. "Have a blanket ready and give me a hot drink and I'll be all right." We were quite ready to comply. My wife laid out a change of clothes for the baptismal candidate, put on her own sun hat, tucked a towel and blanket under her arm and indicated she was ready to help. I picked up my Japanese Bible and together we led Nagashima San down to the beach.

As we entered the cold ocean Nagashima San's frail body began to shake. While wanting to make it a memorable experience, I also felt the need to hurry so that there would be no injury to his health. Standing waist deep in water with our heads toward the rolling waves I gave him the opportunity to repeat his confession of faith in Christ. Then I stated simply, "On the basis of your confession of faith in Christ I now baptize you in the name of the Father, the Son and the Holy Spirit." I sensed a lightness of spirit in our new convert in spite of his trembling from the cold. As we emerged from the ocean, Eleanor wrapped him in a blanket and we hurriedly ushered him back to the parsonage. This was a turning point not only for Nagashima San but for Eleanor and me. We had been thinking that we did not fit in as missionaries.

We heard our new convert singing in the *ofuro* as he washed with the warm water and put on dry clothes. The man who emerged had a completely changed countenance from the rude critic that had troubled me in the Noma meetings.

Chapter Five

PROVIDENTIAL CARE

A Growing Family

The visiting missionary's prayer almost prompted us to giggle. "Oh Lord, be with the Hammonds during this trying time. Help them endure these humble conditions and keep them safe from every health hazard. Safeguard the delivery of the new infant and return them safely to their home." Assuring us of his continued prayers, our missionary friend closed his visit, concern still showing on his somber face.

Actually, we were grateful to Yaita Sensei for the use of his one room house in crowded Kagoshima City. We couldn't afford a hotel room for an extended stay and preferred the privacy of a single dwelling. There was no hospital on Tanegashima island. Dr. Mogami's clinic was only for eyes, ears, nose and throat problems. We appreciated the offer of the *sanba sans* (mid wives) to help with the birth of our third child. It was awkward to decline their kindness and then leave on the ship for the mainland. But we recalled how an incubator was needed during Tim's entrance into the world and didn't want to risk having the birth without hospital services. Yaita Sensei's offer of his vacation cottage in the big city made it economically possible to be near a hospital.

In our three years in Japan we had learned to adjust and were happy campers with the one room tatami floor, a sink with a cold water faucet and an adjacent Japanese squat toilet. We enjoyed visiting the zoo and other sights with Tim and Sharon and felt like we were on a mini-vacation. The October weather was pleasant in southern Japan. The hospital was nearby and the taxis were plentiful. We felt confident that mother and child would come through safely, which they did, but not without labor. Baby Mary was born October 6, 1957, and created a sensation when we returned to the island. Her biblical name was easily recognized, her middle name, Eleanor, was her mother's. There had never been a *gaijin* (foreign) infant in their midst and many of the island ladies competed to hold her while they cooed, *"kawaii desu ne?"* (Cute! Isn't she?).

The timing was perfect. When we returned to our parsonage home, Japan Express delivered a large crate that contained our Maytag Gasoline Washer. Throw away diapers were not yet available and the washer would make it so much easier to do infant diapers and the family-wash. I hurriedly opened the crate and assembled the ringer and other loose parts. I discovered a problem. The exhaust pipe connection had broken in shipment and it would not be easy to fix. Curious as to how it would work, I bought some gasoline, checked the spark plug and gave it a kick start. A very loud, PUT, PUT, WHIR, WHIR, began without letup. "It works!" I declared as I tried the roller ringers on the top. "But it's so noisy without the exhaust pipe," observed my wife. "We don't mind," said one of the on looking neighbors whose curiosity brought them out of their houses. *"Subarashii"* (wonderful) they declared as they watched the machine with fascination. From that day on, whenever Eleanor did the laundry a gathering of housewives came to watch. They would marvel at the confident way she gave the machine a kick start and fed the rinsed clothes through the turning rollers.

My wife didn't have privacy when doing her laundry and neither did I when I hung diapers and clothes out on the lines in the back yard. The hill above the house that led to the park was frequently a stopping place where men sat on their haunches and watched the scene below. For them it was quite a show to see an American male hanging up the diapers. They appeared to enjoy this display of a "Dagwood husband" obediently doing his wife's bidding. I believe the neighborhood wives would have a tough sell to get their husbands to buy them a gasoline washer.

All Things Work Together For Good

The Noma home fellowship came back to life. Nagashima San's conversion was the turning point. The one who had been the spoiler became the accepted Christian leader. He repeated his testimony over and over. Furthermore, he demonstrated the skills of leadership and led in outreach efforts to children. On one occasion we agreed to plan an evangelistic meeting in the town grange hall. Planning went into the project and flyers were distributed. Nagashima surprised me by agreeing that I should be the speaker. Curiosity would draw the townsfolk to come and hear what an American would have to say. At that time they were especially drawn to the news about the competition between the Russian and U.S. space programs. The Japanese reports on the island radio network spoke of the Russian *sputnik* as the first man made satellite.

Spurred on by Nagashima San I put hours of study into the preparation of my message. I had by this time improved to the place that I did not have to read the stories that explained the message outline. Since many of those with Buddhist background did not have any concept of a Creator God, I intended to use an analogy about the man-made satellite to show that planning and design is also evident in the universe that is filled with natural satellites. The hall filled up with clerks, farmers, housewives, and students. By the nodding of heads I could see that my introductory remarks were understood. Then as I began to explain about the Soviet's *sputnik*, the entire audience broke into laughter. What went wrong?

I was told that the Japanese word used for man-made-satellite was *jinko* (man made) coupled with the usual word for satellite, *eisei*. The expression "man made" came out all right, but in pronouncing the word for satellite it sounded like, *esa* (food, such as chicken feed). In a post mortem following the meeting Nagashima San explained that to the farmers it sounded like the Russians had spent millions of rubles to shoot man-made chicken feed into the sky. And at this very time it was orbiting the earth. Exploiting the rivalry of the super powers, one farmer suggested gleefully, "The Americans will probably try to shoot a chicken into orbit to get that chicken feed."

Since we had all expected positive results from this special meeting, I felt terribly ashamed of my unintended mistake. Seeing my fallen countenance Nagashima San asked, "Sensei, you came here to make us happy did you not?" I nodded. "Well we are happy," he chortled and the group broke out into laughing again. Somehow my booboo had broken the tension that existed in conservative Noma. From that time on I was greeted with smiles and genuine questions of interest. My very vulnerability was the key to changing the atmosphere to one of acceptance.

Indigenous Leadership Needed

There is a consensus in mission studies that the missionary's task is to work himself out of a job. He can be a church planter but realizes that for any permanent results there must be indigenous leadership. With this principle in mind, I contacted Tadayoshi Ikeda, a senior at the Osaka Bible Seminary, to come and help us during his school break. Ikeda San had become a Christian under the ministry of Isabel Dittemore, the sister of Mark Maxey. His Christian walk began in Kagoshima Prefecture so he would be considered home grown, indigenous to the region. He had a slim build and was relatively tall. I knew of his winsome smile and pleasant demeanor but did not yet know of his leadership ability. My prayer was that in the process of interacting with the believers they would see in him the leader that fit their needs. I was not disappointed.

Shortly after the arrival of Ikeda San a surprising request was relayed to us from a small mountain village named after the Number 16 bus stop, called, "*Jurokuban*," in Japanese. This proved to be an opportunity for Ikeda San to demonstrate his ministerial gifts. A farmer was asking for a Christian funeral service for his wife who had died. I packed a few Bibles and hymnals into a shoulder strap bag and the two of us proceeded up a narrow mountain road on my motorcycle. By counting the bus stops it was easy to find Number 16. The appearance of thatched roofs made me realize that we were in an older part of the island community.

A passer-by pointed out the home of Mr. Sakae, the man who had made the request. We learned that the widower was a farmer who had two sons. His wife had recently died after a long illness and, different from urban custom, had already been placed in a coffin and buried on his land. Sakae San was a believer and wanted to have a Christian memorial

Pastor Tadayoshi Ikeda

service. The men in the village who had prepared the grave were huddled together on the worn straw mat in Sakae San's thatched roof cottage ready to pay their respects. The women left off food preparations in the rustic kitchen when we entered and quietly sat behind the men.

Ikeda San had the gift of patiently listening to people in a compassionate way. His quiet manner and soft spoken words fit in well with the conservative rural culture. Once he had heard the details and expressed condolences he bowed his head in prayer indicating that the memorial service had begun. Although the gathered villagers were not Christians, the men respectfully removed their hats and bowed their heads. Ikeda San's remarks focused on the love of God and the reality of heaven. Everyone listened with rapt attention. Following his message he sang a song on the love of God without accompaniment. His voice was clear and strong. Everyone was visibly moved by the beauty of the hymn. Tears flowed down Mr. Sakae's face. I reached for my own handkerchief.

After this memorable meeting Sakae San's cottage became a regular preaching point. Because of the opened outside doors and the thick thatching of the roof, a cooling breeze flowed through the house. Following the Bible study, boiled peanuts and green tea were served. The meetings were quite small but it was meaningful that his sons and close neighbors were present. It was inspirational to listen to Sakae San's understanding of the Scriptures. His was a deep child-like faith. Years later we were to see the fruit of this in his sons.

Making the rounds with brother Ikeda was a learning experience. In talking to me, his Japanese was easy to understand. However, when he was conversing with the nationals he slipped into idiomatic expressions that were beyond my reach. I could fully appreciate the effect of his teaching. The ladies at the *fujinkai* (women's meeting) responded with enthusiastic interest to both his Bible lessons and his answers to their questions about his personal life. They were excited to learn of his plans for marriage the following spring. When calling on those that were sick he brought cheer and encouragement. The children found that he spoke their language and created a fun learning experience. His message on Sunday revealed mature understanding. It was apparent that he was more a teacher capable of making applications than an evangelist.

All too soon it was time for Ikeda San to return to his studies in Osaka. We had bonded into a team in the short time he had been with us. The young church rejoiced that he promised to return following graduation. As a family we enjoyed being able at times to converse with him in English. He related well with children. Tim and Sharon said they would miss him. We felt assured for the future of the work on Tanegashima. A capable indigenous leader now promised to return the following year. Meanwhile we would continue to do our best. But we had seen how the formula of having a Japanese minister come for a timely visit was effective.

Chapter Six

EFFECTIVE COMMUNICATION

Points of Contact

During our last visit to Kagoshima City a student from the nearby university came to visit us where we were staying in Yaita Sensei's one room cottage. After a preliminary exchange of greetings, he asked me if I believed that religion could help people overcome their problems. "I believe that the Bible has answers to mankind's basic problems," I replied. "What do you think?"

Seeming little satisfied with my answer, he responded, "I am a psychology major at Kagoshima University. I think psychology has some answers but I am skeptical about religion." "What human needs in Japan do you wish to heal?" I queried. He answered thoughtfully, "Underlying feelings of fear and anxiety are common. Japan is poor, especially Kagoshima prefecture. There is a great deal of uncertainty about the future." He went on to explain. "We are also troubled by feelings of shame. Are you Americans different?" he asked quizzically. "Perhaps we experience guilt more than shame," I responded.

Ruth Benedict's book, The Chrysanthemum and the Sword,[1] had been translated into Japanese and I assumed that my visitor understood the subtle difference between shame and guilt cultures. "Oh, we have guilt, too," he assured me, "but perhaps shame is a stronger feeling. We are so self conscious, you know." Aren't we all, I thought to my self?

"How does psychology help solve these painful feelings?" I asked. "That's where we run into a barrier," he said with a troubled look on his face. "Just when we get close to solving a person's problems, he denies them and projects blame on others, his parents or the school or the government." "Well!" I exclaimed, "Your problems in Japan sound very much like ours in America. Would you mind if we looked at a passage in the Bible that relates to our conversation?"

I handed my Japanese Bible to my skeptical visitor and had him read the first twelve verses of the third chapter of Genesis. I pointed out the results of the Fall and matched them with the expressions he had used in speaking of the human problems in his country. **"They knew that they were naked,"** he read. "Self-consciousness?" he queried inquisitively. "Yes, that seems to be suggested," I affirmed. Then I pointed to Adam's response to the Lord's question, **"Where are you?"** To which Adam replied, **"I was afraid....so I hid myself."** "That's fear, of course, the student responded...and shame," he added as he looked eagerly for the next point. **"The woman whom Thou gavest to be with me, she gave me from the tree, and I ate."** "Projection of blame!" he shouted, as he raised the Bible for a closer look at the context (NASV).

By finding points of contact between his major field of interest and the Scriptures I had stimulated his interest. I was versed well enough in the agnostic factors in the early developments of psychology that, had I not been cautioned otherwise, I might have mentioned and shut him off completely. As it turned out his next question was, "Can I borrow your Bible?" I gladly gave it to him along with the address of a church in Kagoshima City where he could gain further assurance from a Japanese pastor.

Tsushima Guest

"Wouldn't it be good to have a well known Japanese evangelist come to speak in Nishinoomote?" I asked the ladies who were gathered at our weekly women's meeting. "Sato Sensei ministers on Tsushima, an island the same in size, as you know, as Tanegashima. Wouldn't it be interesting if he could come and tell us about his ministry on a similar island?" "Yes, yes indeed, Sensei, that's a wonderful idea!" exclaimed Mrs.

Mogami. "We could get the large banquet room in the town inn and invite seekers." "Excellent!" agreed Mrs. Araki, and the two began from that moment to assume responsibility for planning the occasion.

I had introduced the evangelical magazine, *Hyakuman nin no Fukuin* (Gospel for the Millions) to our small flock so that they would be encouraged by the church activities throughout Japan. In one issue there was an article about Pastor Sato, a former military officer, who following his war experience in which he was wounded, went to the island of Tsushima. His hobby of sailing was helping him recuperate and he was photographed relaxing by his sailboat. Since he had embraced the Christian faith he was not just resting, but was preaching the gospel on the island.

With a special guest coming, Eleanor was glad that she had me buy some young chicks earlier. Now they were the size of fryers and would look good on a dinner menu. It was a joke on me that all of them were roosters. When the poultry salesman asked me if I wanted *"mesu or osu"* (hens or roosters); I replied, "Six of each." This had caused an eruption of laughter from the nearby shoppers. Taking advantage of my ignorance the salesman had sold me all roosters.

An evening before our guest was to arrive, my wife handed me a butcher knife. "Pick out two of the plump fryers and kill them for tomorrow's dinner," she requested. "I will show you how to clean them up." Even though the roosters were a nuisance and kept pecking at our ankles, by this time they had become pets. I couldn't follow through and butcher them. "Oh, you city boy," fumed my wife with mock exasperation, "let me show you how." Going outside and ignoring the clamor of the poultry she caught one at a time, had me help her tie their legs and hang them upside down on a fence. Then she held the heads firmly and slit their throats to let them bleed. This was done with quick dispatch and a minimum of commotion. I gained a new appreciation for my wife's farm experience.

Sato Sensei arrived at the expected time and together with the church folks we welcomed him and made sure he was made comfortable at the inn. In appearance he was tall, well dressed in a western suit, and had an engaging smile. We didn't notice until later that one hand was curled inward because of his war injury. His affable yet courteous demeanor was reassuring. He encouraged a positive expectation for the meetings, then, requested a time to rest before the scheduled dinner at the parsonage.

"*Gochisosama deshita,*" "Thank you for the feast" was pleasant for my wife to hear from our guest. She had been anxious about the dinner. Sato Sensei then went on to say, "I am impressed with your humble life style. You have adapted to the life of the people more than other missionaries I have known." "We feel comfortable," I assured him, "We have become accustomed to sleeping on *futon* and enjoy the relaxation of the Japanese *ofuro.*" And all of us, especially the children, love the beach nearby," interjected my wife. "I understand what you mean," our guest responded, "I love the island life and after the pressures of the war have finally been able to relax there. You must come and visit us on Tsushima sometime." For the rest of the evening we listened to his stories about his island home and how it compared or contrasted with the island of Tanegashima. I felt confident that this common ground experience would enhance his messages scheduled at the inn.

Harvest Time

Mrs. Mogami and Mrs. Araki, along with their helpers, had prepared well. A capacity crowd filled the spacious dining room of the inn. On each of the short legged tables that circled the room were bouquets of flowers and numerous dishes of Japanese pickles and sauces as well as tea pots. When the guests were all seated on the colorful *zabaton* beside the tables the main dishes were brought in.

The boisterous gathering became silent as we prevailed upon Sato Sensei our special guest for a word of prayer. Happy chatter punctuated the dinner hour that followed. I felt like an intruder as I stood back from the tables and took pictures. But nobody seemed to mind nor were they in a hurry. The chatter and banter slowly quieted as it became time to hear our guest speaker.

Sato Sensei knew the hearts of the islanders. His comments had the human touch as he spoke of island life in his home on Tsushima as having much in common with his observations of daily life in Tanegashima. He spoke of the simple pleasures that he enjoyed, such as fishing and sailing. He expressed sympathy and understanding for the poverty and adversities that were part of a lower scale economy. His humor was sometimes earthy such as when he compared the frequent bird droppings to military bombardments. He also spoke with heartfelt remorse about the misbehavior of some of the Japanese military that he had observed. Then he entered into his personal testimony of faith and his affirmation for the need for all to find peace in the kingdom of God. We felt the presence of God's Spirit in our midst.

Nine persons came to Christ as the result of the personal witnessing of their Christian friends and the encouragement of Sato Sensei's messages. Among those baptized in the ocean were four men and five women. Of the five women there was a housewife with a large family, a school teacher, a city office worker, a high school student and a young girl from the island's interior. Each of these had much to offer in personality and talent. It was reassuring to see Azechi Sensei among their number. Her many questions had finally been answered.

Of the four men two were farmers, one was a radio technician and one was a high school student. The latter, who was the youngest, Yoshiyuki Sakae, was the son of the farmer from the small mountain village, who had asked for a Christian memorial service for his wife. In later years Yoshiyuki was to become one of Japan's more successful evangelists.

---

[1] Ruth Benedict, "The Chrysanthemum and the Sword," Houghton Mifflin Co., 1946.

Chapter Seven

RETURN TO BASICS

Co-Workers Arrive

Tadayoshi Ikeda kept his promise. It was big news in the port town church when after graduating from the Osaka Bible Seminary, he brought his new bride, Hisako, with him to Tanegashima. Hisako was petite with brown sparkling eyes and a winning personality. The church folk gave the newly arrived couple a warm welcome.

All of us were especially pleased to learn of Hisako's training and gifts. The church mothers learned through their children that she was an outstanding story teller, who dramatized Bible stories for their youngsters. The coordinated couple quickly established regularity in the church and Sunday School schedule. Tadayoshi Ikeda filled the role of a Pastor-teacher and Hisako Ikeda took charge of the children's programs. Other couples of a similar age were now more easily attracted to the fellowship.

Our return visit to the mountain village of Jurokuban was like a homecoming. Older Mr. Sakae thanked Pastor Ikeda again for the beautiful memorial service for his wife. While eating boiled peanuts and drinking green tea, we listened again to the aged farmer's perspective on the peacefulness of the simple rural life. The pleasant breeze that cooled us under his thatched roof seemed to reinforce his views. Although the meetings were small his probing questions about the Scriptures kept up interest.

When Ikeda Sensei and I visited the Noma meeting it was apparent that the young pastor was impressed by the warm hospitality of Mrs. Tanoue and her daughter, Michiko. Their home was to be a gathering place for many Christian meetings in the future. It was clear that Nagashima San's assumed role of leadership was accepted by the Tanoue's and others who attended. Ideas for the growth of the work flowed freely through his mind and Pastor Ikeda was a willing listener.

On one occasion Nagashima San had organized a meeting of children in a classroom of a grammar school on a Saturday in a nearby hamlet. The classroom was so crowded that many had to watch from the outside, looking through the open windows. He set up a *kamishibai*, a traditional story teller's tripod with a curtained box attached on the top. The curtain was slowly drawn open across the face of the box as Nagashima built up anticipation for a story to come. Large sequential picture cards, perhaps a foot square, were inserted from the side as the biblical story of the Prodigal Son was told. Crouching behind the box the storyteller emulated the voices of the father, his two sons, and the distant foreigners. Passionate expression put into the dialogue produced rapt attention among the gathered youngsters. This was the first time I had seen this indigenous approach used to tell a Biblical story. I had seen it used by itinerant story tellers, who followed up their cultural children's stories by selling candy for a living. Later, I saw Pastor Ikeda attract large numbers of children with the use of puppets and dramatic expression.

A bond developed between Pastor Ikeda and Nagashima San. With his grass roots connections, Nagashima continued to come up with ideas for reaching out to children and adults. Ikeda was glad to help him follow up. At first, they managed to have a role for me to perform in their plans. The strange appearance of a foreigner aroused curiosity which attracted crowds. An effective team was in the making. I felt positive about the future of the work on Tanegashima.

But in a short time, tensions arose in our relationships. I was caught off guard when a projected financial plan for a kindergarten was introduced by Pastor Ikeda and Nagashima San. Why was I disturbed? While I studied in the Kobe School of the Japanese Language a respected veteran missionary spoke in chapel and expressed his doubts about the building of kindergartens by young churches. He felt that it was primarily a means for bringing funds into the church and would side track the needed focus on evangelism. I felt that this would be the case on the island. Conditions were ready for outreach, to use our energy and funds to focus instead on meeting the government standards for building a kindergarten would distract from the evangelistic opportunities.

The opposing view stated the belief that since the national educational system did not include kindergartens, a private school for youngsters would be doing a service for the community and attract adults and children alike. Legitimate fees could be charged and this would hasten the day in which the church could be self supporting. Fearful that the Japanese leaders would make a wrong choice, I didn't listen very patiently and a sharp disagreement arose over the issue. Remarks were made by both Ikeda and Nagashima that implied that I did not understand the situation in Japan. My inability to articulate more clearly my objections in Japanese added to my hurt pride.

When sharing my discontent with my wife I learned that she too, was struggling with communication problems. Pastor Ikeda and his wife had become the focus and the church ladies would go to them with their questions and problems. This, of course, was a good thing and what we wanted to see happen. But at the same time there was a feeling of displacement. Our role was not clear and both of us felt the need for more language study. We prayed about the possibility of returning to school for a period of cultural study and reflection.

The Move to Tokyo

In response to a letter of inquiry to Harold Sims, of the Cunningham Mission in Tokyo, I learned that a mission home was available in the Yotsuya district which was not far from the reputable Tokyo School of the Japanese Language in Shibuya. A response also came from the board of elders in my home church in California giving permission to finish my language training.

We had been in Japan four years, and finishing the last year of a five year term in language study would lay a foundation for more effective work in the future. A period of absence from the work would have the effect of increasing the initiative of the indigenous leaders. While feeling uncomfortable with the decision to build a kindergarten, I realized that the Japanese must be looked to as the permanent leaders and their plans should be respected. I felt I should honor their choices on method and take steps to help them.

There were Japanese Americans in one of our supporting congregations in California. They had shown interest in our work on Tanegashima and wanted to encourage missions in Japan. Their presence in the American church would make communication more effective in establishing a sister church relationship. We wrote to the Chairman of the Mission Committee suggesting that it could be an adventure of faith if they became a "sister church" to the Nishinoomote church and help them reach their goal of becoming an indigenous New Testament congregation. I explained that the term "indigenous" implied that they would be self-governing, self-supporting, and self-propagating. To my joy the Green Valley Christian Church responded favorably and asked me to explain the details of the relationship.

Mark Maxey gracefully consented to channel the funds through the Kyushu Christian Mission. It was agreed that the Nishinoomote Church, in spite of their relative poverty, would match the giving of their sister church and make every effort to become fully self-supporting. When letters came from the island thanking me for the help I replied that I was only a go-between and to write thanking the Green Valley Church in San Jose. This removed me from the misconstrued and often tension-filled relationship of "mission boss over native workers."

During this transition time I tried to correct my mistake of shipping my motorcycle to Tokyo so I could use it to go to language school. After using it for only a week in the rapid, congested traffic of the capitol, I quickly came to the conclusion that public transportation was more efficient and by far safer. It also came to mind that I had left Pastor Ikeda without this handy means of transportation that was suitable for the island. Japan Express shipped the Honda back to Nishinoomote, and it was thankfully received.

During the following years our Japanese American friends helped energize the Mission Committee and came up with specific needs in which even children could participate. One example at this point in time was the fact that Japanese crayons were too soft and didn't hold their colors. Kids from the sister church packaged and mailed U.S. multi-colored crayons as needed. The islanders typically reciprocated with gifts made in Japan. The sister church relationship became a genuine bond going beyond monetary help. Tangible goals were also reached.

Back to Language School

The Tokyo School of the Japanese Language was a mixed blessing. Their teachers were the best and the Naganuma method of teaching by sentence patterns was effective. I learned, however, that I had imprinted incorrect short cuts into my speech habits during my years in rural Japan. In order to speak on the level of an educated leader I would have to unlearn a great deal that I had assumed was acceptable. How painful! I resumed studies at the intermediate level and was quickly immersed into increasing numbers of complex ideographs. I did little else in my waking days than study to keep up with the pace of the class.

For economical reasons the Roman Catholic private school for Japanese was closed, and the priests who were being prepared to be missionaries in Japan were put into the Naganuma training program. Three of these priests were sent to my class room. One was a rigid American, who felt uncomfortable studying with Protestants. Another was a tall gregarious Belgian, with whom I became friends. The third one was a jovial priest from Ireland. The other members of the class were aspiring long term Protestant missionaries, and one short term Methodist woman.

We learned a great deal about one another although we could only speak Japanese in the classroom.

The rather tense American priest had a pride problem. It especially bothered him that the young Methodist lady caught onto new terms so quickly. He fell behind the class and was told one day to go to a room where they taught at a lower level. He left in anger and slammed the door. His superiors later made him apologize. The Irish priest could laugh at himself and made the rest of us feel more comfortable when we made mistakes. The Belgian priest was eager to learn about others outside his communion and we often had lunch together during which we discussed differences candidly. Increasingly, I felt that the Lord was teaching me to listen to others in a non-judgmental way and learn from them.

Typically, we had encountered many cross cultural communications problems in our first five year term of service. Fellow missionaries often discussed their many frustrations and were eager to hear of possible solutions. We acknowledged that part of the problems arose from our own cultural baggage. Seeing things through Japanese eyes made us more aware of our imported inconsistencies. Rubbing shoulders with other Christian communions helped remove misunderstandings and misleading stereotypes.

I was learning that one can develop bonds cross culturally without compromise of one's convictions. This principle also applies to crossing denominational barriers. In order to do a better job as missionaries, a clearer picture of the essential Christian message is needed. God was giving me a vision for an open forum in which these things could be discussed, and do much to clarify the many misunderstandings, and help put us on the road to answering the Lord' prayer for unity (John 17:22-23). These thoughts made me feel that the Lord was guiding me in a way that would affect our future role in Japan.

Chapter Eight

NEW BEGINNINGS

A Productive Furlough

Our first furlough after five years of service began in a missionary home of the Christian Missionary Alliance in Glendale, California. These were low cost rental houses nestled in the foothills above Los Angeles and completely furnished for the convenience of furloughing missionaries. Eleanor and I were kept busy with our six, four, and two year-old youngsters along with a schedule of reporting to supporting churches. Also, I was taking a full load of courses in Asian history and culture at UCLA. Feeling the pressure I bought our first television, a Sears & Roebucks black/white portable to serve as a help in baby sitting for a new family member was due on the scene.

The Presbyterian Hospital in North Hollywood still gave special attention to the needs of missionaries. We felt that our fourth child would probably be the last. If he was a boy as predicted, we would have two boys and two girls. On schedule, James Alvin Hammond was born on October 9, 1959 (his name followed the pattern of one from the Bible and one from a parent). Because he was a large baby and enjoyed robust health, he was later dubbed, *"Sumo san,"* by our friends upon our return to Japan.

During the second half of our furlough we moved to Northern California. President Bill Jessup had asked me to teach an introductory course on missions at my Alma Mater, San Jose Bible College. Since Eugene Nida's text, <u>Customs and Cultures</u>,[1] had been the most helpful to me, I taught a well attended course, "Anthropology for Christian Missions," based on his text and illustrated by my cultural encounters in rural Japan. I did not run out of material in describing my many mistakes and levels of culture shock.

My own knowledge continued to grow as I continued taking courses in Japanese language, Asian history, and philosophy at San Jose State College. I was especially pleased that the professor of philosophy was a Christian. This had not been my experience at UCLA. The professor there had announced that he did not know of any in his field of study that took religion seriously. I became more aware of the battle for the mind that took place in our secular universities. At the same time I was glad to see the growth in the Bible College. Professor Emmett Butterworth, a graduate of Phillips University and a former army chaplain during WWII, was introducing a level of apologetics that met the needs of the times. A seed was sown in my heart to keep on preparing so that I could give answer to every man for my Christian convictions (I Peter 3:15). I felt better prepared for my return to Japan for a second term of service.

Living in Suburban Tokyo

From the start the local Japanese referred to the rental house that we found in Western Tokyo as, *gaijin jutaku* (foreigner's residence). It was walking distance from the Kumegawa train station and a bus would come to take our youngsters to a school designed for U.S. military dependents. Furthermore, it was only 30 or 40 minutes away from the New Life League publishers. The location worked out well for offering English-Bible classes, and it was also convenient for the publication work I had begun.

It had been my dream for some time to publish an open forum journal in which missionaries and national leaders could share points of strategy on communicating the gospel in Japan and the Far East. We needed a forum in which we could learn from one another and pray for the much needed unity for reaching the millions. After much prayer and correspondence, I launched **Far East Christian Missionary**, a quarterly magazine published by New Life League.

Since we had come to Tokyo we had entered into a youth ministry approach and were not trying to plant a church. Fairly large numbers of high school and college students came to our home primarily to learn English conversation. I had made a deal with them. I would teach them conversational English for an hour without charge if they would let me teach the Bible in Japanese for an additional hour. "I will help you with English and you can help correct my Japanese," I suggested. This agreed with them. We also sponsored youth rallies and joined with other missionaries in sponsoring two weeks of summer camp. This approach was fruitful and converts were made, but because of the mobility of youth a church was not being planted. Furthermore, the high rent was using up scarce mission funds so when we had opportunity to receive a former military base dependent housing duplex without charge we felt God's hand was in it.

Receiving permission from our home church board we bought a plot of land that was reasonably priced. Then we contacted Mark Maxey of the Kyushu Christian Mission and asked if Shimoda San, the mission carpenter was available. His job would be to disassemble the military duplex, haul the building materials to the new site and reconstruct it. Mark's reply was affirmative. The need for the carpenter had slowed down in Kyushu. Shimoda San assented to come to Tokyo and help us for the same salary plus room and board.

For the better part of a year while the carpenter was living with us, Eleanor fixed Japanese styled breakfasts with *miso* soup, rice, soft boiled eggs, and fish. During the initial building stage of pouring the cement foundation and setting up the framing, Katsuo San, the *daikusan's* son joined in the work. These were pleasant days of renewing ties with our Kyushu friends and planning the details of our home and classroom. Part of the spacious duplex served as our home; the other half was designed for a class room and meeting place. Once finished we settled down to a routine editing a quarterly magazine and teaching English-Bible classes for youth. Two nights a week I attended Sophia University to continue my studies in Asian culture and Japanese language.

A Timely Interruption

"Gomen kudasai," (May I intrude?). Since my wife was busy helping the kids to dress in time to catch the bus and train to town, I opened the door. "Ohaiyo gozaimasu," (Good morning) greeted the short, kimono clad Obaasan (grandmother) in the entrance way. "What can I do for you?" I inquired, an impatient note may have shown in my voice. "Are you a missionary?" Her question alerted me to a possible need. "Yes, I am a missionary," I responded briefly. "Well, I have come to worship God." It was Sunday morning but we did not have services in our home, and were trying rather to get ready to go to an English speaking service in town. How was I to respond?

"We're going to miss the bus," Eleanor called out to me as she emerged from the bedroom. "Perhaps you can help explain that to our visitor," I whispered as I stepped back from the entrance way. Spotting the rotund figure in the doorway, my wife approached her in a business-like manner. "How can we help you?" she asked, and added, "This morning we don't have much time." "I heard that you were Christian missionaries and I've walked a long distance to come and worship God," replied the elderly lady in a firm, yet pleading manner. While I was checking on the kids to see if they were ready Eleanor continued talking to our early morning visitor. After a prolonged and intensive conversation she announced in a resigned manner so that all could hear, "We are going to have church services here." It was clear that the Obaasan had won.

We had looked forward to the fellowship of the English services in the Kamiochiai church. Our youngsters enjoyed interacting with other English speaking children their age. A promise of ice cream after lunch made it more acceptable to change plans and abort the trip to town. "This is Seki San," introduced my wife as she sat the Obaasan down on the sofa. After which she thrust Japanese-English hymn books in our hands and opened the small pump organ and then looked to me for a signal to begin.

It was a quaint scene. Mrs. Seki's feet barely reached the floor from her seat on the sofa. The children who were wearing their

Sunday best surrounded her on the divan Tim had the take charge demeanor of the older brother as he sat to one side in a separate chair. Sharon and Mary were making sure the visitor was comfortable. Jim was propped in a sitting position between his two sisters. Eleanor sat ready at the organ and I sat on a hard back chair in front of the small group. I announced the number of a hymn that we were familiar with and we began to sing. Thanks to my wife's training the kids kept us on key. I produced the vocal volume that kept them on the same verse, and hoped that I did not drown out the quality. Seki San appeared to participate in earnest and busied herself intently singing or turning to the announced page numbers.

After the song service my wife sat down and looked at me expectantly. Preaching in Japanese without preparation was very difficult, but I could explain a familiar passage of Scripture so I turned to Luke 15:11-32 and began to tell the familiar story of the Prodigal Son. Our youngsters were fluent in Japanese and would wince if I pronounced a word incorrectly. It had long been my favorite story of God's love and forgiveness so I preached it with feeling. After the message and a closing prayer the room was silent.

We looked toward our visitor to see what her reaction would be.

"Mottainai, mottainai..." (What a waste, what a waste) she repeated over and over causing me to feel like I had failed completely. "Gee lady, you prevailed upon us so don't complain," I thought to myself Then, thankfully, she went on to say, "What a waste to bring this beautiful service to, only one Japanese." Then she beckoned to my wife and began to relate valuable information about the people she knew in the area, who were interested in the Christian faith. Not long after this first unexpected visit of Seki San, we had not only youth in our home, but older friends of Mrs. Seki. A small house church had begun in our Kumegawa home in the suburbs of western Tokyo.

---

[1] Eugene A. Nida, "Customs and Cultures," New York, Harper & Row, 1954.

Chapter Nine

BUILDING RELATIONSHIPS

Visiting Old Friends and New

Mail correspondence convinced us that the island work was doing well. The sister church arrangement proved encouraging to both the sponsoring church in San Jose and the young island church in Nishinoomote. We were encouraged to come and visit our former place of service. By now our schedules in western Tokyo were less flexible and travel was too expensive for the entire family to go. It was concluded that Tim and I could go as the ambassadors to represent the family.

Traveling with 7 year-old Tim to visit our previous work on the island some 1,500 miles away was an unforgettable adventure in 1960. Because we needed to be frugal with limited funds for the two day trip we traveled third class on one of the older express trains. It had open compartments which could be made up into two tiers of three narrow bunk beds so you could lie down at night. Tim and I shared the bunk on top which permitted me to project my feet into a baggage area The restricted space didn't permit much sleep, but we did stretch out and arrived in time to catch a scheduled six hour ship passage from Kagoshima City's port to Nishinoomote on the north side of the island. Pastor Ikeda and friends were waiting for us as we landed.

Mrs. Ikeda's hospitality made us feel at home and we enjoyed the children's programs in the Christian kindergarten. The church folk were also warm and receptive and gave special attention to Tim, who had lived on the island as a four and five year old. After concluding our visit with the church in the port city we went by bus to Noma, in the center of the island. Our needs were taken care of by Mrs. Tanoue and her daughter in their home. A home church had begun there during our first term of service. I enjoyed teaching the small group that gathered during the midweek. The young people tried to practice their English with Tim, who chose rather to respond in Japanese. At least it showed that their English was understandable and they enjoyed the interchange.

At the time of our scheduled departure tension arose by the sudden onset of a typhoon. For two days we were buffeted by strong winds and heavy rain. During that time I made a model airplane for Tim to make creative use of the time. Michiko Tanoue and her fiance, Nagashima San, did their best to be reassuring and entertaining during the long wait. Finally, a radio message came that a plane would be leaving from the small Noma runway during a lull in the storm. When the winds abated a taxi took us to the runway and Tim and I boarded the small plane bound for Kagoshima City.

Once in the air I wondered if I had made the right choice. The plane was tossed about by the yet heavy winds; after one tumultuous hour it pounced down on the Kagoshima tarmac, bouncing several times before coming to a stop. Tim exclaimed, "Wow!" I breathed a sigh of relief. We had no trouble getting tickets back to Tokyo on the near empty trains.

"Tim, I think it best not to tell Mom about the scary plane ride, O.K.?" I suggested as we made the long trip back to Tokyo. A short time after returning home, however, wide eyed Tim gushed out the story of our wild plane ride. Thankfully, he also spoke enthusiastically of the warm fellowship we enjoyed with our friends which shortened my stay in the dog house. This was the first of many trips which I made to the island to renew ties and offer encouragement. While it was always a rewarding experience, it was good to return to the peaceful setting of our semi-rural home near the Kumegawa station in western Tokyo.

Neighborly Relationships

Raised in a Nebraskan pastoral and agricultural town, my wife knew what it meant to be neighborly. She would bake a pie in her kerosene oven and give it to a neighbor. She was puzzled about how quickly the Japanese neighbor would respond by bringing gifts in the emptied pie pan or dish. As you probably have heard, gift giving is an elaborate system of reciprocal exchanges in Japan. Mr. Masuda, was first of our neighbors to start the exchange by bringing tasty produce from his field. Since we had bought the parcel of land for our home from him, there may have been some sense of obligation in his thinking. However, we preferred to accept his gifts as genuine tokens of friendship. My wife liked to think that he and his wife and daughter had really taken a liking to her pies.

Mr. Koyama, whose tea bushes could be seen from our south windows, came bringing a bouquet of flowers. When we first came into the neighborhood looking at a lot for sale he did not know that we understood Japanese. We heard him express fears to our realtor that letting foreigners into the neighborhood would result in drunken parties and decadence. It embarrassed him when I politely interrupted in Japanese and explained that we really wanted to be good neighbors. His bringing flowers after the passage of a considerable length of time (during which we had no drunken parties) was perhaps his way of making amends for his hasty remarks.

On one occasion my wife wanted to show our appreciation to our neighbors on the north and south of our home. She relayed invitations to both households to come and visit. Koyama San was first to enter our living room and was quite pleased to have hot coffee and pie placed on the coffee table in front of him. He exchanged pleasant remarks about our children who had become friends with those of his household. The social atmosphere was one of warmth and good cheer.

Masuda San entered a little later. Having been in the home before, he greeted us with a relaxed smile and accepted the seat offered him. Suddenly he realized that he was sitting next to Koyama San. The demeanor of both men instantly changed and the warm atmosphere became frigid. Without finishing his refreshments Mr. Koyama excused himself and left. A minute or two later, Mr. Masuda, without touching the coffee or pie, also made a quick exit. My wife looked at me in bewilderment. We realized that we had a lot to learn about the background social history of the rural section in the outskirts of Tokyo in which we had made our home.[1]

Learning From Children

When Japanese are offended by you, they do not use abusive speech, but use a very indirect polite level of language. By so speaking they create social distance and buffer themselves from further pain. At a time when I thought we were finally accepted, I experienced this estrangement from my neighbor, Masuda San. I felt the sting of his formal polite greetings which had replaced the friendly insider expressions. I had been placed on the outside of his circle of cordial friends and I did not know why.

Months passed until one day the smile and warm informal greeting from this usually friendly farmer resumed. After a comment or two about the warm summer day he paid me a complement. "I like your children," he said, beaming at me. "Domo," I replied, reciprocating with the plain male speech for thanks. "Why do you like them?" I added, which was probably the wrong thing to ask. "Because they ain't thinking nothin,'" was his mystifying reply.

I knew that my younger children not only accompanied Mr. Masuda in his farming adventures in his field but also frequented his home where they received cookies and juice. Out of natural curiosity, the Masudas enjoyed the youngsters, who spoke colloquial Japanese with less foreign accent than their parents. But why did he say he liked them, because, "They ain't thinking nothin,'"? I pondered.

A reflection on my relationship with Masuda San in contrast to that of my children suggested the answer. I had approached my non-Christian neighbor as an object of missionary evangelism. From the start I was giving cues of my impatience to get the right response from him. I had subsequently angered him when I had given his daughter a translated Moody Bible Story Book without asking permission from her parents. My youngsters, on the other hand, had accepted Mr. Masuda, just as he was, as a kindly neighbor willing to teach them about farming and ply them with cookies. Their trusting approach opened his heart; my hidden agenda had closed doors (Romans 5:8).

Welcoming Students

In the rebuilding of the duplex we had the carpenter place the three bedroom half of the structure in the rear. The front half was designed with only one partition to allow for a fairly spacious class-room and a small office. The class-room was the more prominent entrance way which the public would encounter. To enter our living quarters, one would walk to a side door in the back. Students who came for English-Bible study were used to coming to the more formal classroom, but we soon learned of their desire to visit our living quarters to meet our family.

During times of inclement weather or busy school schedules only a few students might show for the regularly scheduled classes. To their delight we would welcome them into our living quarters to get acquainted and play games. The game of "Clue" was fun to play and an excellent means for helping them with their pronunciation. As you may recall, the game is played on a board which depicts nine rooms of a mansion: the kitchen, dining room, lounge, hall, study, library, billiard room, conservatory, and a ballroom.

It is a "who done it?" detective game with six possible suspects to a murder: Colonel Mustard, Miss Scarlet, Professor Plum, Mr. Green, Mrs. White, and Mrs. Peacock. A player tries to solve the questions as to who was killed in which room with what weapon: a knife, candlestick, revolver, rope, lead pipe, or wrench. The use of the English "R" and "L" is confusing to the

Japanese. Pronouncing "Clue" comes out more like, "ka-roo." The difficulty of pronunciation adds to the fun of the game and takes away any stigma in the learning process. A number of these students, by virtue of their bonding with our family, would come and visit us at other times such as during *Oshogatsu*, the Japanese New Year's celebration.

---

[1] It was intimated by Japanese friends that there had been a long standing feud between the two families.

Chapter Ten

BONDING EXPERIENCES

Visits to Western Park

Our small church was near the *Seibu sen* (Western train line) near the Higashi-murayama station. A short jumper line from there takes you to a large park that includes picnic areas, a zoo, and a miniature train leading to "Unesco Village," which displays quaint international heritage building structures. On numerous occasions the church and Sunday School would spend pleasant afternoons at the park.

Three older women, especially, Seki San, Shiroma San, and Maema San, loved getting out of their small apartments and going with us to *Seibu* park. They always made themselves useful by watching over the children and helping with picnic preparations. Their conversational exchange was encouraging to themselves and others. Words of wisdom could be gleaned from their experiential anecdotes. "Build good memories," was Seki San's advice for happy homes and a happy church. We have many good memories of our visits to the sprawling Western Park.

On one Sunday afternoon we had a guest with us from the Philippines. Pastor Diego Romulo, with whom I had become acquainted through my magazine ministry, spoke in our morning service. He also agreed to share at the park where the church had planned an outdoor picnic. On Sunday, especially during good weather, there were large numbers of people milling about on the lawns. After filling ourselves with *sushi* and sandwiches, Pastor Romulo was ready to speak and I was prepared to interpret. Diego, who is a short Asian looking man, spoke in English with a Filipino accent. My American mannerisms and accent were probably obvious as I interpreted in Japanese. The scene attracted a number of onlookers, who thought this was indeed a strange turnabout. Later, Diego remarked humorously, "This is a good way to evangelize. I speak in English and you interpret. We draw crowds this way."

Ladies' Meetings

To attract newcomers my wife had initiated a reciprocal exchange of Japanese flower arranging lessons for western baking recipes during the weekly ladies' meetings. This would be followed by Bible lessons given by Japanese ministers. Looking for something unique they asked Mrs.Haruko Takekawa to teach them how to use the Brother Knitting machine upon which she was an expert. Haruko was married to one of our faithful members, who taught Sunday School lessons to the children. The knitting class was popular and as students became proficient they could be licensed and use their skills for profit. Eleanor not only fitted me with sweaters that she made, but went on to win her license from the Brother Knitting Machine Company.

Over time the popularity of the ladies meetings extended to the new apartment complexes some distance from us. When invited by a resident, we could introduce Christian speakers to share in the club house provided on the grounds. I was elated by the breakthrough to this upper middle class neighborhood. It wasn't long before some of these ladies began to visit our regular home classroom sessions where the teaching could be more explicit.

Popcorn Evangelism

It came as a surprise to me when my wife announced that the ladies were going to make popcorn balls. She handed me a list of things obtainable in downtown Tokyo to make large numbers of popcorn balls. Picturing in my mind the ladies from the new apartment complex that always came in expensive kimonos, I voiced my objections. "Honey, you are from Nebraska, and making popcorn balls is expected there. But this is Japan, and it is a rice culture. I haven't read anywhere about a western popcorn approach to Japanese culture." In response to my emotional rationalization my wife gave me a condescending kiss and began going over the things I needed to buy for making the popcorn balls.

As directed I did find cans of "Made in America" popcorn and also bought the sugar and ingredients to make the tacky syrup to hold the popped corn together in a ball shape. Since this was a group project it involved purchasing large pans and rolls of cellophane wrap to follow through with the manufacture of large numbers of popcorn balls. My heart wasn't in it, but I felt that since this was my wife's leadership area I should go along with her plans.

In mid-December the scheduled day for making popcorn balls commenced. Our classroom was filled with ladies who had tied aprons over their clothes. I was cast in the role of a relay person to bring the popped corn and the syrup from the kitchen to the classroom. This seemed normal to the Japanese who were accustomed to the Shinto priest taking part in the religious ceremonies. Since I had never made popcorn balls before, I felt very awkward and kept burning myself on the hot sticky syrup.

An awesome scene met my eyes as I entered the crowded classroom. At my wife's instruction the ladies standing around the ping pong table were applying the sticky syrup and fashioning balls with the popcorn. Because of their natural dexterity they were learning quickly and actually competing as to how many they made. "I made twelve," declared elderly Mrs. Seki proudly as she wrapped her last creation in cellophane and reached for more. The room was filled with laughter and sheer expressions of delight as the large pans were filling with their finished products.

All took part in the next phase of this cultural venture by loading the popcorn balls in a vehicle bound for the orphanage. Booklets telling the Christmas story were given out along with the candied popcorn. The children basked in the special attention of these visiting surrogate mothers and grandmothers as they gobbled up the sticky sweet treats. It was a unanimous decision of the ladies that they must practice this exciting American custom again.

At a later time it was both enlightening and embarrassing to me to read in a book dealing with anthropology for Christian missions a principle that my wife had discovered. It said in effect, that if you could find an activity that was similar to one of the nostalgic religious celebrations in a foreign culture, yet pointed in the direction of the Christian message, you would communicate successfully. The making of the popcorn balls was similar in many ways to the Japanese custom of making *omochi* (tasty rice cakes) during their New Year's season. To prepare for this special holiday the ladies were kept busy with their hands preparing treats for pleasurable extended family get-togethers.

Permission From a Wine Merchant

Whenever we walked to the Kumegawa train station from our house, we passed by a public hall. We knew that this would have been built partially with tax money and was used for local political meetings. Japan's postwar Constitution assuring the separation of church and state was often interpreted to prevent the use of such public halls by churches. But this was often left to the local authorities, and when on the island of Tanegashima, we had used the public grange halls for our special meetings. I learned that the prominent authority over the use of the Onta Public Hall was Takeda San, a leading Sake dealer.

"Mr. Takeda", I began, "I understand that I must have your permission for the use of the public hall by our small church on Sundays." The stern faced wine merchant looked hard at me and queried, "Don't you teach against drinking sake?" I swallowed hard and responded, "That is an individual choice that members make, our focus is on teaching good news that brings people into greater happiness." Not understanding my meaning he answered back, "Drinking our sake brings pleasure." I felt that the door was closing and decided to use a different tactic.

"I noticed that the inside of the *kaikan* (public hall) is often dirty. Those who use it are not cleaning the building. Refuse and cigarette butts are strewn about and dust has gathered on the tables and floor. Our church folk can keep it clean if we can use it once a week, and I notice that it is empty on Sundays." Takeda San blinked at this and I detected a softening in his attitude. "You will clean it every week?" He wanted to be sure of this. "Yes, every week, and we will do a good job," I affirmed. "Very well, you can use it on Sundays."

Permission to use the public hall came at the right time. Our home classroom was too small for larger gatherings and we wanted to sponsor youth rallies and meetings that were open to other churches. We also needed the room to expand Sunday School. Mr. Takekawa and Miss Endo offered to teach regular classes, which they could do on the second floor of the building. The location of the hall was more convenient being right on the road leading to town and closer to the train station than our home. The lavatories were Japanese style and more acceptable to the public. One drawback was the small shrine on the outside of the building which was dedicated to an agricultural deity. We ignored it, getting reinforcement from a passage the Apostle Paul wrote.

> We know that an idol is nothing at all in the world and that there is no God but one. For even if there are so called gods, whether in heaven or on earth (as indeed there are many 'gods' and many 'lords,') yet for us there is but one God, the Father, from whom all things came and for whom we live; and there is but one Lord Jesus Christ, through whom all things came and through whom we live (I Corinthians 8:4-6 from NIV).

Our family was coming home on the train when we were approached by Takeda San, the wine merchant, who apparently was tipsy from drinking his own product. His speech was a little incoherent but his attitude was friendly. "Thank you, thank you, for keeping the building clean. It is really clean... never that clean before. Nobody took time to clean it. Now it is nice... nice and clean. You kept your word. And did you know, my daughter is going to your Sunday School? She likes it. She likes it very much." This last statement caught us by surprise. We knew a bright middle school student named Takeda was in one of the classes, but were not aware that she was the wine merchant's daughter. We felt that the Lord was working in our community.

Chapter Eleven

BOOSTS FROM FRIENDS

A Gifted Missionary

We first met the Reverend Foxwell aboard a ship of the U.S. Lines returning to Japan. He was putting on a magic show in the first class lounge and the invitation to attend was extended to passengers in the tourist section. Later we learned that Phil Foxwell had help to pay for his tuition at Wheaton College by performing his magic. Over the years his act became quite professional and by scheduling a show on the ship, his passage and that of his family would be paid for. Going to the first class lounge, itself, was a privilege so our family looked forward in anticipation to the program.

Early slight of hand tricks were followed by his making a cake in the jacket pocket of an unsuspecting volunteer. He put a funnel into the lower side pocket of the gentleman's suit coat and proceeded to put flour, eggs and milk into the funnel, which we assumed went into the pocket of the well tailored jacket. It all looked very real and gave the appearance that there would be a dry cleaning bill following the act. Then he stirred the ingredients with his wand and *abracadabra* he pulled out a small cake from the side jacket pouch of the surprised victim. As the volunteer returned to his seat he pulled the pocket lining inside out revealing to himself and the rest of us that it was clean and dry.

Tricks with cards, colored bandanas, and ropes were made the more interesting by the endless and often humorous commentary of the magician. The evening was quite relaxing until it built up to the highlight of sawing a woman in two. As they were setting up a large box, about the size of a coffin, the Reverend was flexing a fairly large tree saw which looked quite real. He then asked for a volunteer and I suspected that the ready response was from a cooperating partner. Nevertheless, we did not feel comfortable with the idea of seeing a person sawn asunder, make believe or not.

Suspense was built up as the lady was assisted into the box. Her blonde head protruded from one end and her feet appeared to stick out of the opposite end of the container. Expressing mock concern that he might make a mistake, he yet persisted in inserting the saw into a slot in the middle of the coffin-like apparatus. It truly appeared that the saw traveled from top to bottom as it was pulled in a business like manner by the somber faced magician. Then the curtain was pulled momentarily, and the next moment as it opened again, we were staring at a very much alive smiling volunteer standing beside the showman.

Magician Featured At Youth Rally

Although Foxwell was a busy professor at a Presbyterian Seminary in Tokyo he would occasionally use his magic skills at youth camps and rallies. After a typical performance he would explain that, although he would not divulge his secrets, all of his tricks had logical explanations. He would then go on to witness to the miracle of the new birth in Christ and speak convincingly in Japanese of his own personal faith.

We were collecting a lengthy list of the names of young people who had come or were coming to our classes over a period of several years. The idea hit me that it would be ideal to have a youth rally in the Onta Public Hall on a Sunday afternoon to gather many of these youth at the same time. The Rev. Phil Foxwell, Magician, would be the drawing card. They would see an exciting illusionist perform and hear a convincing testimony of faith in Christ that followed. I called the busy professor on the phone right after the idea came to mind and he gave me an affirmative answer.

We were somewhat relieved that he did not have the equipment available to perform the "sawing in half" illusion. But he had a bagful of more portable tricks and promised to do the humorous one where he made a cake in someone's pocket. We sent out invitations to those on our mailing list and also made many phone calls. On the day of the rally a number of church folk stayed over to help with setting up chairs and greeting people. The hall began to fill and the magician showed up on time with his magic wand.

A Well Dressed Volunteer

Akira Takekawa wore a new tailor-made suit that Sunday. Although he made a good living in his company, he did not often dress in a suit with such high quality. I complemented him on his apparel and I think that Phil Foxwell also noticed the gentleman in his Sunday best. When it came time to perform his illusion of making a cake in a volunteer's pocket, he suggestively looked directly at Takekawa San, who was sitting near the front. Akira promptly obliged and sheepishly went forward to stand beside the magician.

Although the members of my family had seen this act before, it was even more humorous to know what was coming and to see the perplexed expressions on Takekawa San's face. Remember he was wearing a new suit and for all-the-world it appeared that flour, eggs and milk were being poured through a funnel into his pocket. Akira looked at me with almost a sick look on his face as if to say, "How do I get out of this?" The boisterous crowd, of course, was unsympathetic, and for the most part was openly laughing. Then the magic moment came when the master showman pulled out the finished cake from the victim's pocket. Mr. Takekawa looked very relieved but puzzled when he discovered that his pocket was dry and spotless. Later he was smiling and perhaps proud that he had been the center of attention.

Pastors Gifted With Wisdom

Hideo Yoshii, pastor of the Kanoya church where we served two years, preached for us in a special spring meeting. We thoroughly enjoyed his fellowship in our home and in special services in the Onta public hall. Fairly large numbers of our English class student contacts were present. Although many had interest, only one new visitor came as a result of the 6,000 handbills that were distributed. Those present were inquisitive non-Christians and it called for a tactful approach. During the question and answer periods Yoshii demonstrated wisdom and tact that only comes by living close to the Lord. Many difficult questions were answered and there was one new confession of faith.

Masahisa Iijima first came in contact with Christian missionaries in prewar Japan. As a young student he heard the gospel message at a street meeting during a rainy night in Tokyo. Attracted by the message and drawn by the Christian love of Owen and Shirley Still, young Iijima became a Christian. "Mother Still," as Masahisa called her affectionately, gave him the Bible name of Stephen. Prior to that fateful day when war was declared between Japan and the USA, foreigners were ordered to leave the country, and when the Stills sailed away, young Stephen felt like an orphan.

A bright student, Stephen passed the rigorous examinations and entered the university in Yokohama and went to live with his aunt. As a graduate he was mobilized into officer training for the Japanese army. "It seemed like Babylon to him. He had no chapel to attend, no opportunity to talk about Christianity, and no Bible to read. Everything was forcing him to forget about Mother Still, to hate America and to hate Christianity, the religion of this enemy country."

During those turbulent years Iijima was censored for his friendship with an American by the Japanese people, and criticized for his refusal to identify with the cooperating churches which permitted Emperor worship. Just before he was to be sent to Okinawa orders came that retained Stephen and four others as instructing officers in the Academy. Most of his fellow class members in the Signal Corps Academy were either killed en route to the Philippines or sent to Manchuria. Reflecting back on the events of this dark period, Iijima felt that God was sparing him for future service. The events that followed proved Stephen's intuitive thoughts to be true. (FECM, Summer, 1961).

On August 15, 1945, the war ended and peace was declared. Perhaps a larger number of the Japanese population was fearful as the American occupation forces entered. The dreaded B29 bombing raids were fresh on their memories. However, Stephen retained his memory of Mr. and Mrs. Owen Still and hoped for opportunities to mediate between his countrymen and former enemies. Those opportunities came when American officials discovered Iijima's ability to speak English. He was transferred to Allied headquarters where his services as a translator were put to good use. In the process he came to appreciate the democratic spirit of the U.S. personnel.

An ad from the Christian Pastor's Association in the city in which he lived came into Stephen's hand which offered classes in the Greek and French languages. To his delight Iijima discovered that it was New Testament Greek that was taught. He enrolled in the class and soon bonded with the dedicated Christian teacher, Taijiro Yamamoto. At last he was experiencing the opportunity to firmly found his faith on the New Testament, and it was being taught by a man who evidenced the fruits of the Holy Spirit in his life. A few years later Stephen once again made contact with Owen Still which eventually led to ministerial service. He became the pastor of the Minato Church and a professor of New Testament Greek in the newly formed, Tokyo Bible Seminary.

Because of this dramatic background Pastor Iijima is a much sought after speaker. A number of times he was our guest speaker of choice at camp and in rallies held in the Onta Public Hall. He related especially well with the college students. An example of how he answered a personal question from a skeptical student illustrates his gift. "Since you graduated from a name university, why have you chosen to become a Christian?" The tone in the student's voice indicated something of the low view he had of the Christian faith. Let me paraphrase Stephen Iijima's response as follows:

"Making the choice to become a Christian," stated the Pastor calmly, "Is like climbing aboard a train on which the passengers are given a meaningful purpose and goal. The high priced ticket is already paid for and the Engineer knows where he is going. The journey is not without its problems, but help is given to overcome the difficulties giving a sense of peace, and the ultimate destination is described convincingly in words of breathtaking beauty." The clarity of the analogy and the credibility of the speaker motivated students to learn more about this gospel train.

Chapter Twelve

STUDENT ENCOUNTERS

Challenges of College Students

A 45 minute crowded express train was my transportation from our Kumegawa stop to Yotsuya station near Sophia University. At the time I boarded the train in the early evening there was usually standing room only. Because I was often approached by college students who sought an opportunity to speak English, I kept a few name cards in my upper shirt pocket. On the front was a schedule of our home classes and on the back was a map to reach our house. Because such a meeting on the train was a chance encounter a good number of students interpreted this as providence of a sort and did come to attend my home college class. They were impressed that I, too, was attending college and felt a sense of comradeship.

Sophia University is a Catholic institution established by the Jesuits, but taught by other orders as well. I focused on further improvement in the Japanese language and a better grasp of Asian history. Also, since I was always struggling to better communicate cross culturally, I had a strong interest in philosophy and the social sciences. The three hour evening courses were both challenging and interesting. Challenging because there were viewpoints expressed at times that were in opposition to Protestant perspectives. For instance, I had never before heard that Martin Luther was the cause of all the modern wars in Europe. Interesting, because I heard some professors honestly acknowledge the grave mistakes of the medieval Catholic church. Summing up the plus side, one's faith in the

Creator would be strengthened at Sophia, and naturalistic materialism would be rejected.

Probably the greater number of students that I met on the trains was conditioned in their secular colleges to accept evolutionary naturalism as scientific reality. The questions they asked in my suburban home Bible class were often asked in a challenging manner. "Do you believe in miracles?" "Did Jesus really walk on water?" "Did God create the world?" My affirmative answers would trigger more questions. Finally, "Do you believe in evolution?" would be the question that tempted me to preach an anti-evolutionary sermon that would discredit their teachers. Silence would follow, and they would not return. I discovered a better way.

"What do you mean by evolution?" I would inquire and then go on to add more details to my question while throwing in a little humor. "Biological evolution in which life began with single celled organisms that gradually developed over time into all of the species we have today including handsome, intelligent ones like you?" "Well supposing this theory of the gradual transformation of life is true," I would continue, "that progressive change has taken place until we have such species as the modern human, who can reflect on himself and ask questions about life and build skyscrapers and compose symphonies. Can we conclude that such a process began by mere chance?" A thoughtful silence would follow before discussion resumed.

It is interesting that when the question is put this way, most of the students conjecture that there had to be something to start things. We could then enter into a fruitful discussion as to what that "something" was. My goal was to get them to accept the plausibleness of a Creator, not to win an argument about how creation came about. They might come to faith through the door of theistic evolution and later, as they came to accept biblical authority, modify their thinking. At this initial encounter with the biblical worldview the important thing was to give them options. Meaningful insights only come from within the individual as he or she has thought an issue through. Imposing our convictions upon someone often offends and closes the door to further fruitful communication.

Patience Required

Saito San[1] was a graduate chemist who enjoyed Bible study. I sensed that he had not found fulfillment after graduation in his job with a cosmetic company. The biblical worldview that stressed purpose and goal in life seemed to fill that void. Over a number of years Saito San attended my English and Bible classes. Although he was mentally sharp, he seemed to lose hope in gaining fluency in English. That may have been because of his tendency to perfectionism. To learn a language one has to murder it, so to speak. If you hold off saying anything until you get it just right, you will never arrive at fluency.

But Saito San kept coming to my classes and also attended special events, even bringing his young family. He stayed with the Bible teaching as we went through the highlights of the gospels and moved on through Acts and into Romans. On one very rainy day he was the only one that showed up for class. We were studying some of the faith building passages in the eighth chapter of Romans when a thought came to me. Since no one else was present, it should not embarrass him if I asked him a personal question. "Mr. Saito, I consider you a friend and I respect you for your family values. We have been studying the Bible together for almost three years. Why is it so difficult for you to make a decision about its message?"

The prolonged silence was almost unbearable. Traditional Japanese are not accustomed to directness. It was easy to see that my question had made him feel uneasy. One tendency in their culture is to do their best to please you. Another compulsion is to conform and not change the traditional pattern of things. Saito San finally cleared his throat and sat up straight in his chair. "Mr. Hammond, it's true that you have been teaching me the Bible for almost three years. But I have been raised in the Japanese religions all of my life. Please be patient."

Polite Postponement

I remember Minami San [2] as a bright student whose major in college was in education. Eventually he did go on to become a High School teacher. He attended my classes and became a friend of one of our faithful church members. A number of times he also went to our Christian camp at Lake Motosu behind Mt. Fuji. He not only was exposed to my Bible teaching but heard some of the most effective Japanese ministers. He was a likable youth with a big smile. We continued our friendship through the years and patiently prayed that he would make a decision to accept Christ.

I was caught off guard the day that he stated the reason he could not change. There were a number in the Bible class with whom I had carefully answered several of their key objections to accepting Christ as the Son of God. Minami San spoke up in a somewhat defensive manner. His argument went something like this. "My parents are good people. They have cared for me and helped me go to college. It would hurt them for me to step away from our family traditions. I cannot make such a decision unless they also assent and we do it together."

I felt very vulnerable and inadequate and did not know how to answer Minami, even though his allegiance to his family was a typical response. Perhaps I should have done my best to start with the parents, I reflected. But my experience was that these aging people were staunch believers in the Japanese way of doing things. One was married in a Shinto ceremony, guided by Confucian values, and buried in a Buddhist manner, following the path of one's ancestors. Young college students were more receptive to change as possibly good; oldsters resisted it as disruptive of peaceful relationships. I didn't reach an easy answer then, but continue now to pray for my friend, Minami San.

Joyful Acceptance

Vivian Lemmon asked me to hold an evangelistic meeting in her church in Wakayama. She had heard of my interest in science/faith issues and needed some of these answers for her young people. I was glad to go to this coastal community in Central Japan because of my high respect for Vivian. This elderly missionary had such a Christ-like demeanor that the missionaries nicknamed her, "Sweet Lemon." Vivian had nourished a crop of young Japanese through teaching and motherly counseling. She felt it was time for a harvest.

The series of messages that I prepared included answers to the type of questions asked by the high school and college students in my Tokyo classes. I stressed the coherency and adequacy of biblical answers, and quoted well known scientists who held to the Christian world view. Perhaps more importantly, I emphasized the love of God as demonstrated in scriptural narratives and contemporary life examples. I shored up truths that Vivian Lemmon had taught them bringing them closer to a decision of faith. After prayer, I quietly requested that if anyone wanted to accept Christ to please stand. Five young people stood to their feet. Tears came to Miss Lemmon's face.

Tetsuo Domen was one of the young people who accepted Christ that evening in Wakayama. He was a tender hearted young man who had compassion toward any with a physical handicap because of one such member in his family. He had struggled with science/faith issues and appreciated my affirmation that there is no necessary discrepancy between the facts of science and scripture. Tetsuo defied the odds and passed the entrance exam into Keio University after first attending a college prep school. Few are those from remote rural areas that make it into this prestigious university.

Domen San is known as a joyous witnessing Christian. He has a happy, thankful disposition and loves to sing. When he met Hideko Yabiku, a blind Okinawan with a beautiful singing voice he wanted to know her better. She had been converted by the

Harlan Woodruffs and had a radiant faith. Tetsuo and Hideko began singing duets in the churches and were well received. Tetsuo's compassionate heart toward Hideko because of her loss of sight and his love for music was drawing this talented couple together. When he proposed marriage, his family objected. In their mind a graduate of Keio should marry only a person of class who had all her faculties. How could she hold receptions for her husband who had become a business executive? How could she possibly raise children? In spite of these concerns, Tetsuo felt that he was obeying the voice of God and he accepted Hideko as his wife and blessings followed.

Tetsuo and Hideko were married and over the years had five well behaved children. Because of her special training for the blind and her sweet Christian disposition, Hideko Domen was an excellent cook and a loving wife and mother. The Domen family became known throughout Japan's evangelical community. Our suburban church was happy to hear that the Domens were going to begin attending with us in Kumegawa.

Our ladies recalled the earlier time when Mrs. Paul Pratt had guided the yet unmarried Hideko to the Onta Public Hall and introduced her at a special ladies' meeting. Hideko's beautiful piercing voice, along with her expression of complete devotion, had tremendous effect on those gathered there. Tears came to my eyes as I thought of those hearing the Gospel in song for the first time. A middle-aged visitor sitting next to me offered words of comfort as she wiped her own eyes. The pagan lady caretaker of the hall ducked into her room hastily, and Eleanor saw her feverishly saying a Buddhist chant over and over as if she were in panic. The ladies poured out their thanks after the service for the spiritual sight they had received from a blind believer

---

[1] A pseudonym to protect privacy
[2] A pseudonym

Chapter Thirteen

VISIT TO SHIKOKU

Workers For the Harvest

Each year an invitation would come from Pastor Ikeda to visit the island work. I sensed that he not only wanted me to see the progress of the church and kindergarten, but also to become better acquainted with his growing family. At the time of my current visit he and his wife, Hisako, had two children, a boy and a baby girl, Shin Chan and Nozomi Chan, (Faith and Hope). Growth in the work was already evident in their first few years of leadership. The kindergarten had 80 children enrolled, and the Nishinoomote Church was attracting other young couples. In spite of very busy schedules the Ikedas extended warm hospitality during my short stay.

The big change in Noma in the center of the island since my last visit was that Hiroshi Nagashima and Michiko Tanoue had become man and wife. An interesting name change took place at the time of their wedding. Nagashima San took the surname of Michiko's family and the two became Mr. and Mrs. Hiroshi Tanoue. This was not an unusual custom, but was practiced on the basis of continuing a preferred family line. Hiroshi had married into a doctor's family.

The exciting news was that Hiroshi and Michiko were contemplating going to Osaka Bible Seminary to better prepare for Christian ministry. Pastor Ikeda had been nurturing their faith and led them to this conviction. The problem was that since her father had died, Michiko did not want to leave her mother alone. "Hamondo Sensei, would it work for Mother

Tanoue to go with us to Osaka?" they asked. "Let me write to President Martin Clark and find if there is housing and a place of service for Mother Tanoue," I responded. Upon hearing this suggestion, Mother Tanoue shed tears of relief and her children gave her reassuring hugs.

The flow of events seemed to pass rather quickly. Hiroshi, Michiko and her mother were welcomed in the facilities provided by the Osaka Bible Seminary. They were together during these formative years of preparation. Mother Tanoue filled an important niche as dorm mom and endeared herself to all the students. Eventually the Tanoues graduated from the seminary and Mother Tanoue graduated to her heavenly home. On March 20, 1965, I traveled to Osaka to take part in her funeral and testified how a church was nourished in her home and led to her children entering the ministry. Others added their testimony to mine that we had never heard Mother Tanoue speak one word of discouragement in spite of her long illness.

Shikoku Ministry

"Hamondo Sensei, come and preach for us." The request came over the phone from Shikoku, where Hiroshi and Michiko were then serving. "Why ask me all the way up here in Tokyo? There are many good Japanese ministers that are closer to you," I responded. "But your Japanese is more humorous and a funny *gaijin* attracts more attention." Tanoue San had not lost his ability to speak bluntly, I thought to myself. "More seriously," he went on to say, "we are beginning a new church with the *Burakumin,* an outcast group, and you would be better received.

Shikoku is one of Japan's four main islands and lies southeast of Honshu and north of Kyushu. I had never been there but heard that it was more of an agricultural region than the main island of Honshu. This was one of the reasons that Hiroshi thought he would fit in better there. Also, I was not familiar with the *Burakumin* and at that time was unaware that Japan had an outcast population. I was sensitized to racial tensions in the U.S. that were brought out during the Civil Rights movement and was now confronted with another example of irrational bias by the human family.

Apparently the stigma that blocked marriage to persons of the accepted majority was associated with the ancient Buddhist sanctions against those who worked with dead animals such as butchers and tanners. Newspaper accounts wrote of marriages that were cancelled when *Burakumin* background was discovered by one of the betrothed. Learning these things about a covertly segregated people in Japan, I was proud of Hiroshi and Michiko that they were bringing the gospel to them. I agreed to come and looked forward to renewed fellowship with the Tanoues and Don and Norma Burney, their missionary coworkers.

Hiroshi & Michiko Tanoue after graduatig from Osaka Seminary.

The trip to Kochi on the far side of Shikoku involved travel by train, ferry boat and bus. In many ways Shikoku looked similar to Kyushu with its neatly sectioned off patty fields and rural farm houses. Numerous *torii* gates, field gods, and temples reflected the dominant traditional culture. Occasionally I saw a church cross projecting from a modest sized building. Our bus also traveled through growing towns with many recently built houses, busy shops, and bustling traffic. Hiroshi and Michiko's smiling faces greeted me as I arrived at the designated stop.

It had been a long journey so my hosts made sure that I had a relaxing hot *ofuro* and a leisurely meal before bed time. They lived in a modest but new house that Don and Sarah Burney had originally intended to use as their own. But when the Tanoue's agreed to come and work with them they generously turned over the new house to them and remained in their old residence. The Burneys had always impressed me with their humility and I was glad that our friends from Kyushu had joined their team. We had a good visit that night before retiring.

I spent the next day in prayer and preparation. That evening we were to begin preaching at the newly formed church for the *Burakumin*. Of course, I understood that we were not to refer to them with demeaning labels, but rather to show them open acceptance and Christian love. Pastor Tanoue described them as a humble and gentle people. I looked forward to the challenge and anticipated warm receptivity because of the preparation that had been made.

Sharing With the Outcasts

Gradually the small living room designed for a single family was filling up with people. All items of furniture had been removed. Everyone sat on the tatami mat floor and kept moving closer together to make room for late comers. They represented all ages and a number of them appeared to have family resemblance. I noticed that their language idiom had a different sound to the Tokyo standard to which I had become accustomed. Although all were sitting, I noticed that Hiroshi had set up a small podium for me to use from a standing position. I felt relieved. I had become a city dweller and was no longer used to sitting on my legs for several hours.

There was a commotion in the back of the room as younger men helped an elderly lady sit on a cushion and lean against the wall. Everyone treated the aged Obaasan with respect and some were calling out encouraging greetings. Apparently she was blind as those helping her had to guide her hands to objects she wanted. Finally this matriarch was made comfortable and her sightless gaze seemed to be directed toward the front.

Pastor Hiroshi stood beside the podium and welcomed everyone. He jokingly referred to the crowded conditions as a means of keeping warm because the evenings had become cool. He then introduced me in a flattering way, but explained that if they didn't understand my Japanese, he would explain it later. Saying a prayer in my heart I stood to my feet and began to address the sitting audience. To accustom them to my way of expressing Japanese I told them of my family and related a few humorous anecdotes about the younger children. I was rewarded by a roomful of smiles.

My message focused on the love of God which was dramatically revealed in the parable of The Prodigal Son. The Father's love is expressed to both his younger self-centered son, and to the older self-righteous brother. Heads nodded as I affirmed that at times we have both of these tendencies – self-centeredness and self-righteousness. I then went on step by step to explain the background symbolism in this revealing account. My simple conclusion was that God knows our weaknesses, yet is ready to love and forgive each one of us as we decide to come home to Him.

An Obaasan's Confession

When I sat down I heard a sob from the Obaasan in the back of the room. She began to call out for a chance to speak, and Hiroshi encouraged her to do so. Everyone slowly turned at the same time to face the speaker. She began to tell us about when she was a younger woman she had gone to Tokyo to look for work and had been knocked unconscious by falling debris during the Tokyo Earthquake of 1923. She awoke in the care of a British missionary, who took care of her until she regained her health. During this time of healing the English lady read the Bible to her including the parable that she had heard again tonight. In addition to this kindness she paid for her ticket back to Shikoku and gave her a Bible and a Hymnal wrapped in a *furoshiki*.

Once again the matriarch sobbed and everyone in the room focused their attention on what she said next. "When our country entered the dark valley of war the authorities ordered the missionaries to return to their countries. Japanese citizens who had been influenced by them were suspect. Some of them were put in jail. I was afraid." She sobbed again. "One night I took the Bible and the Hymnal that the missionary lady had given me and threw them in the river." Then groaning within herself she cried out, "Would God forgive an old bag like me?"

A chorus of voices called out that God would indeed forgive her. They all seemed to understand that this was the point of the parable. God's love had indeed permeated the room through the confession of the oldster. The providential timing of her testimony with the events of the evening was convicting. I returned to Tokyo feeling that I had received more than I gave. Pastor Tanoue wrote me later that the elderly convert had been baptized in an outdoor pool.

Chapter Fourteen

FAMILY TIMES

Keeping Up With Family

"Won't it come out naturally with a little salve?" I asked my wife about the steel splinter that had stuck in Sharon's eye when she put her head out a window of the local train on the Seibu line. "No, you have to take her to the eye doctor and have it taken out." was the firm reply. I was as terrified as eight year old Sharon as we entered the recommended clinic and found it filled with children and parents with no partitions between the patients being treated. Several of the younger kids were crying.

I repeated my timid question to the doctor. "Won't it come out naturally with a little salve?" "No," he answered, chuckling at my naivete. Then, attaching a special magnifying piece to his eye, he asked me to hold Sharon to keep her from moving. When he affixed clamps to her eye ball I immediately learned that there was nothing wrong with her lungs. She let out a penetrating scream that startled everyone in the room. "There it is," explained the Japanese doctor calmly as he showed me the steel splinter he had deftly extracted from her eye. Finally he put the salve on her eye I had hoped for and covered it with a patch. Her vision was not impaired and her parents recovered well enough to meet the next crisis.

Children learn languages quickly. Jim from his earliest years learned that saying, "Gomen kudasai," as you entered a Japanese neighbor's home was like pushing a magic button. The wife of the home appears with juice and cookies for the visiting youngsters. At least, this was the case with our near neighbors, Mr. and Mrs. Masuda. The Masudas loved children and were delighted that Jim could speak fluent Japanese. Mr. Masuda liked to question him to find out more about his parents. Jim's answers were often creative. In response to the question, "Does your father eat eggs for breakfast?" Jim's reported answer was, "Oh yes, Dad can eat a dozen eggs easily." The fun conversation led to more cookies and juice and more imaginative stories.

Jim also cultivated friends with the children in the rural areas where we lived in Higashimurayama. He learned to catch *tonbo*, the Japanese dragon flies and other insects. He and his friends were especially captivated by the *kabuto mushi*, a very large Japanese flying beetle. They would attempt to tie a thread on the beetle to control its flight as if it was a kite. The neighborhood kids knew that Jim had an absorbing interest in bugs. When we later departed for the States one of his friends gave him his large collection of butterflies, all carefully mounted in a glass covered case.

On one occasion, in a playful scuffle with his playmates, one youngster fell and cut his leg on glass lying on the ground. Although this was an unintentional accident, Jim felt guilty about this for some time. As parents we only knew that something was troubling him. Finally it came out into the open. Our son expressed heartfelt sorrow that he had not told us about the problem. Not long after that Jim requested to be baptized. He had learned that the forgiveness of God goes deep enough to heal the inner hurt.

On another occasion the boys pulled out a shivering puppy from the gutter and a kitten was offered as a gift, but it was Mary that pleaded with her parents to have compassion on these poor lost creatures of the animal kingdom. We ended up with, "Blacky," a frisky mongrel, and, "Butterscotch," a cuddlesome kitten. Blacky was not allowed in the house, but Mary would make sure that he had clean straw in his dog house. One of the boys would get the straw from Mr. Masuda. When not on a leash dashing off with the children, Blacky's tether was hooked up to the clothes line so he was free to run the length of the yard. It was father that seemed to be left with the job of picking up droppings.

Dennis the canary was so named because he was a gifted singer named after the American tenor, Dennis Day, who sang on the Jack Benny program, which was among the reruns we heard on the Far East network. The canary's cage was right near the telephone and many a caller was given a favorable impression of our home from the sweet lilting song of our happy feathered friend. In writing an autobiographical assignment for school, Sharon wrote of the pets and included a turtle that Jimmy loved and the goldfish aquarium which was an object of conversation for visitors.

The Birth of Billy

"Get me out of here!" called my wife on the phone from the Seventh Day Adventist hospital in Tokyo. Knowing that the hospital had an excellent reputation, I asked in a puzzled voice, "Why? Aren't they treating you right?" "No meat, just glucose," was the troubled response. My wife was brought up in Burwell, Nebraska where beef was always plentiful and a regular part of the diet. We had made do on the island of Tanegashima by raising chickens and occasionally ordering meat to be brought in the refrigerator aboard ship. (No refrigeration was available locally). Leaving the island work in the capable hands of the Ikedas we had moved to Tokyo where beef is available. But my wife's hospital stay was unexpectedly prolonged and she was in an institution that served no meat.

The reward for anxious waiting came with the birth of William Joel Hammond. Born on February 16, 1963, he was given a biblical middle name and the first name of one of his uncles. "Billy" was our surprise baby, our fifth child. Perhaps because of the four doting siblings that preceded him, he grew up a more care free youngster with a love for music. My response to my Japanese friends as to the meaning of "Billy" was, "the very last one." I later learned that this humorous meaning actually corresponded with the Japanese word, *biri*, (bee-ree) which was the way that they pronounced the English name.

School Days at CAJ

Schooling at the Military Dependent's school where the kids were first enrolled became less accessible. It had been less expensive but was not without its problems. The Christian Academy in Japan (CAJ) was located near the Higashikurume station on an upper Seibu train line reachable by bus. The children would have to take the bus to the upper train line and ride the train to the Higashikurume station, and walk from there to the school. Big brother, Tim, assumed the responsibility to get them on the right bus and train and off at the right stop. Since the transportation vehicles were marked with Japanese ideographs and not English, initially this was no small responsibility.

CAJ is an evangelical school designed for missionary children, teaching grades 1 – 12. It was and is, academically sound and all subjects are taught by Christian teachers. Although a few of the teachers had their idiosyncrasies, for the most part the learning environment was enjoyable and the children felt safe. Some of the teachers had lovable personalities and bonded with the students. Others were tough but balanced and kept the school's scholarship high. High School basketball teams from the military bases complained that CAJ usually won in the competitive games because they prayed about it. "Not fair if God is on their side," their opponents were heard to say.

Since our daily contacts were primarily with our Japanese friends and neighbors, the social events at CAJ for parents gave us opportunity to meet fellow missionaries. This put faces on some of the names we had only seen in the Japan Harvest magazine or the handbook for the Evangelical Missionary Association in Japan in which we were members. Some of the parents served in distant areas and could only come for infrequent visits to their children who were housed in dormitories. Their sacrifice made us realize how fortunate we were to have our children at home with us.

Family Bonding

Missionary life had drawn us together into a close knit family. Our youngsters attended the same school and helped us with the church activities in the home and the public hall. The girls helped their mother in the kitchen and took part in serving guests. Preparing for Sunday services, the boys would borrow Mr. Masuda's farm cart and load it with the needed extra chairs, Bibles and song books. All pitched in to set up the hall for the morning services. Periodically the older youngsters helped me prepare the mailing of some 3000 copies of my quarterly magazine.

Breakfast might be eaten on the run, but at supper time we were all together. I would read a passage of scripture and each would take turns to offer the blessing. When he was old enough to take his turn, young Billy's prayers were refreshingly honest such as, "God forgive me for not liking the spinach, but thank you for Mom's chocolate cake, Amen." This was a family time when we would listen to the experiences of the day and give supportive encouragement.

At bed time Eleanor loved to read Old Testament stories from a book which had been simplified for children. Her expression reinforced the moral values that they would take throughout life. The Chronicles of Narnia by C.S. Lewis were my choice and I became as interested as my children. Even the youngest seem to understand the symbolism in the initial story of "The Lion, The Witch and the Wardrobe." The wicked witch caused it to become winter in Narnia, but the narrative gave us confidence that Aslan would come and change things. Aslan's death was a shocker but somehow the children knew that He would ultimately triumph. They just needed to make sure that their father did not read too far ahead after they fell asleep.

Chapter Fifteen

CONCERN FOR UNITY

Working Toward Understanding

Clear marks of character are chiseled in the facial features of some individuals. Yoichi Muto's square jawed, elongated Lincoln-like countenance (without beard) gives a lasting impression of integrity. I first met Pastor Muto when Bob and Audrey West took us to the Mabashi Church of Christ on a Sunday shortly after our arrival in Japan when I knew no Japanese. During the service, which was entirely in Japanese, I tried to pick out identifiable words. I kept hearing, "*Watakushi*," and "*Watakushitachi*" repeatedly, and came to find out that they were merely expressions of the first person, "I" and the plural pronoun, "we." That such short words in English expanded into rather lengthy terms in Japanese was discouraging as I thought of learning the language.

Much is learned by observing the demeanor of a person and how they interact with others. Although at that beginning stage of my Japan experience I could not understand the verbal message, I was given the strong impression that Muto Sensei was a committed Christian leader who dealt with others in truth and love. Over the years that first impression has been strengthened by first hand knowledge. For over fifty years John Muto has proven to be a faithful and trusted friend.

Our mutual interest in Stephen Iijima's journal, the *BOKKA*, (Pastoral Song) brought us together. John Muto was a close friend and colleague of Iijima Sensei, whereas I was only a new admirer of this expressive journalist.[1] In the ongoing quest to find an indigenous form of the Christian faith for Japan, it seemed to me that articles in the Pastoral Song came close. The growing number of Japanese readers seem to confirm this. The problem was that busy missionaries could not, or at least, did not read the *BOKKA*. There was more distrust than understanding of the indigenous approach of Iijima Sensei. I felt that an English edition would help bridge the gap.

Providence brought Muto Sensei and I together. He lived in an apartment of the former Tokyo Bible Seminary. By permission of the Yotsuya Mission I was using an upstairs room of this same building for the office and mailing address of my quarterly magazine. I approached John Muto about the idea of translating the *BOKKA* and putting it into corresponding idiomatic English. His native knowledge of Japanese and fair grasp of English might have been sufficient. By adding my experience with English idiom we could smooth out the translation. With Iijima's blessing we began regular meetings to hash out his meaning of the idiomatic Japanese into contemporary English.

The Mukyokai Connection

References to Kanzo Uchimura and the Mukyokai (non-church) movement by both Iijima and Muto put them under the shadow of suspicion by a number of the missionaries. The deceased Uchimura was one of Japan's most effective, yet controversial Christian leaders. Converted by an evangelical missionary, when 17 years of age, he confessed the need for a close relationship with Christ throughout his life. Part of his education was received in America. Through the influence of Dr. Julius H. Seelye, the president of Amherst College, he overcame doubts and disappointments in American Christianity and was enabled to grasp firmly the faith in the forgiveness of sins through the shed blood of Christ on the cross.

Uchimura became outspoken against missionary methods that, in his view, attracted ministerial leaders with shallow convictions. The propping up of leaders and programs with American dollars was preempting the work of the Holy Spirit in the Japanese churches. A number of missionaries might agree with him, but his under-emphasis on the ordinances of baptism and the Lord's Supper, and his criticism of the existing denominations made them wary.

In 1961, the 100th birthday anniversary of Kanzo Uchimura, Muto Sensei wrote an article for FECM entitled, "Uchimura's Search for New Testament Christianity." This gave a balanced perspective of the Japanese Prophet who founded the so-called, "Non-Church Movement." That same year the publication of Uchimura's complete works, nearly 50 volumes, was undertaken. Dr. William Axling, veteran missionary to Japan stated that, "These volumes are found in the libraries of more Japanese ministers than any other book except the Bible."

While thrashing out the meaning of Iijima's colorful expressions, Muto Sensei and I were both learning more about comparative language study. At times we had to choose functional substitutes for terms that had no direct correspondence. The work was hard, and I recall one warm day when our tempers flared. For a brief moment we exchanged harsh words. Then John Muto leaned back and laughed. Frustrated, I asked, "What are you laughing about? We just had an argument." "Yes, that's the point," Muto responded, "Now we are friends." Seeing my expression of bewilderment, he went on to explain, "It is like marriage, you have to have a fight to really know one another." Perhaps this is also true regarding differences in missionary methods.

Bread Without Price

The same year that the Christian press focused on the centennial birthday of Kanzo Uchimura, I wrote an editorial in FECM entitled, "Bread Without Price." I used the prophetic text from Isaiah 55:1, 2. "Ho! Every one who thirsts, come to the waters; And you who have no money come, buy and eat. Come buy wine and milk without money and without cost. Why do you spend money for what is not bread, and your wages for what does not satisfy?" I brought out that the foundation of respect for ministers in America was laid by the early pioneers who often farmed their own land for a living and preached the gospel without charge. The paid pastor system came much later with the development of urban jobs with its pattern of hourly based wages and the growth of the churches with specialized needs.

My application of this past American history to Japan was twofold; first that we missionaries should make sure the churches were free to choose their own leaders. Secondly, that we accept the principle of pastors following the Pauline approach of tentmaking, if able to do so, until the church was large enough to support them. I came to understand the great time demands on those who are leading a small, struggling church, while at the same time are working at a job to support their family. Only a few tentmaking jobs seem workable in Japan. Yet, I am glad that Pastor Ikeda overcame my reluctance and began a Christian kindergarten on the island of Tanegashima. It met a need there and utilized the pastor's skills, though it may not be workable elsewhere.

Uchimura did not consider himself a professional pastor, although he taught the Bible to growing audiences for set lecture fees. His popularity was due, in part, to his refusal to accept foreign funds. This gave him freedom to speak out against errors in the established denominations and the approaches of the western missionaries who were perceived as imposing a western form on the church. His approach was more identifiable as indigenous and therefore appealed to Japanese sensitivities. Uchimura's basic search was to grasp the spiritual essence of the New Testament. Muto Sensei summed up his article about Uchimura with these words:

> Perhaps if we all search for New Testament Christianity as did Kanzo Uchimura, that is, to seek it in application to our own spiritual needs, then we may find that we are all Christians in the same brotherhood, and beyond Denominational differences.[2]

Our Own Subtle Sectarianism

In the Fall 1962 issue of FECM, I prefaced the editorial with the words, "Yes we should boldly point out the weaknesses in denominationalism, but are we also aware of our own subtle sectarianism?" Over the years the Lord was teaching me humility and I had come to appreciate the genuine faith evidenced in other communions. My interaction with other missionaries and my exposure to wider points of view was tearing down my stereotypes. I realized that over the centuries Jesus was still building his church. I typed the following words to sum up my changing perspective:

"For most of us we are thankful that the sleep of the Dark Ages was awakened by a disturbing personality called Luther. We are rather thrilled that a formal English Church playing too much cricket with corrupt government was challenged to accept her spiritual responsibilities or lose gigantic portions of her membership to two methodically devout Christians named Wesley. We are also compelled to admire the provoking simplicity and continuity of the rather tenacious Mennonites and Baptists who both claim origin in the earlier Anabaptists. And was it not in keeping with this same type of development, i.e. men of God rising to answer particular needs of the church of their day that a group of men gathered in Scotland and passed on this passion for truth to a young member of their following named Alexander Campbell?"

"The question that we must face in our day is, has not the vigorous and growing Restoration movement spontaneously started in Scotland and America reached a place of inertia in which change is little tolerated? Has not the attitude become with too many that 'We have arrived,' rather than, 'Lord, lead us onward'? With some the term 'plan of salvation' now only refers to the initial steps one takes to become a Christian rather than God's great plan through the ages consummated in Christ" (FECM, Vol. 2, No 3).

Pastor Hideo Yoshii, one of our more mature leaders serving in Kanoya, Japan, received his graduate education in the U.S. at the Cincinnati Bible Seminary. He wrote a two part article that was printed in FECM entitled, "My Impressions of America." One of his insightful criticisms has bearings on our ministry in Japan. "A basic weakness seems to be in the danger of being satisfied with restoring only the outward 'pattern' of the church revealed in the New Testament. But not only the pattern but the real spirit of the New Testament must be restored first of all" (FECM, Vol. 2, No 4).

Through the years others have faced up to inconsistencies in Christian practice and have sought to restore the "real spirit of the New Testament." During the year 2006, the **Christian Standard**, a representative journal of the Christian Churches, published articles from outstanding leaders that revealed major progress toward unity with other Bible believing communions. They contained humble acknowledgements of our own attitudes that have blocked the oneness for which Christ prayed. The words of David Faust, the President of the North American Christian Convention (NACC) in 2006, were highlighted: **"For 100 years our actions have contradicted our plea."** This kind of reflective honesty will do much toward answering our Lord's prayer for oneness.[3]

---

[1] Stephen Iijima's conversion and role in the church is described in Chapter 11, pp. 82-84.

[2] Uchimura was a rare Japanese man who had a deep sense of sin, and referred to himself as a "baby clinging to the cross." FECM, Fall, 1961, Vol 1, No. 3, p. 120.

[3] David Faust, "Together In Christ," Christian Standard, September 17, 2006, pp. 4–12.

Chapter Sixteen

MISSION STRATEGY

Comraderie in Sharing

The "indigenous church" theme became a flash point in the Open Forum section of our magazine. Articles came in from our field editors representing the struggles to plant indigenous churches in Burma, India, the Philippines, and Thailand. Their problems were similar to those we faced in Japan. Letters came in that indicated that the struggle was worldwide. We shared a common burden to find answers that would enable the planting of indigenous churches that would spontaneously grow,

Tom Rash, our field editor from India, penned honest reflections in his article, "The Dilemma-Fraught Road to Indigenization."

Tom Rash, FECM Editor for India

He gave us a definition to start with. "Indigenous Christianity implies that a native people must support the church, guide the saved and win the unsaved. (Be self-supporting, self-governing, and self-propagating)." Tom writes that for sixteen years he has been trying "to find the Lord's way…to give the message in such a way that when I leave for another area the local Christians will be equipped to carry on the work and witness with no help save that from Above and the Book. He and his coworkers felt that starting India Bible College to train national leaders was the logical place to begin. But, he comments in retrospect, "Its very name set the students thinking of professional ministry --supported by the mission, of course."

Mel Byers, wrote from Chiengrai, Thailand, introducing a hard-hitting article called, "The Enigma of Indigenous Churches." He writes, "These are my convictions on the matter and with God's help we have been endeavoring to do something about it here… This is probably the basic problem of our current problems and behind it all are the ideals of New Testament Christianity."

Mel Byers, Editor from Thailand

Mel goes on to suggest that within the Church of Jesus Christ are "the mysteries of spiritual law, intrinsic power and latent ability to grow and reproduce after its kind –in any culture--in any heart. It does not reproduce just a mere man—but a new man; not just a new culture, but a peculiar people."

Byers then discusses what he believes are the specific hindrances that block indigenous growth. The first are the forms and distinctives of westernized denominations that seek to establish their own brand of the faith. He concludes, "Until we are free from denominational concepts and become single in our thinking we build and lay foundations which are but hay and stubble." He then points out the second hindrance – the missionary's use of money. He quotes Melvin Hodges in a report to the Alliance Missionary conference as saying: "our cultural overhang interferes in our work and our first reaction is to appoint a committee, then reach for our purse."

Mel's solution is radical. He advocates that missionaries become indigenous to the soil in which they serve by cutting off financial support from denominational or mission boards. In answering the question, "how would one live without support?" He answers by relating a dialogue with a small Chinese boy. "What are you going to do when you grow up, Tao Chyen?" he was asked by a visiting missionary. "I'm going to be a preacher and preach Jesus." "But how will you earn your living?" "I will be a stonemason."

Mel goes on to say that, "If the missionary expects this kind of dedication from the native—let himself be the example! Let him prove to the native that he is not motivated by the almighty dollar! Taking this first step, one places himself in a position to receive 'new wine.'

The Swing of the Pendulum

It is not surprising that there were reactions to the suggestions of those who pointed out the weaknesses inherent in status quo missionary methods. Barton McElroy states that speaking of the church in a hyphenated way is wrong; that is, American-church, Philippine-church, Japanese-church, African-church, Indian-church, ad infinitum. Writing from the Philippines, he states that the simplest meaning for the word "indigenous" is best, as "produced, growing, or living naturally in a region." He goes on to assert that "the Church is indigenous to the world; that it was placed here and is expected to produce, grow, and live naturally."

Barton's next point is that the New Testament teaches that the "haves" must help the "have nots." In his article, "Has the Pendulum Swung Too Far?" he gives examples of churches in Ohio that have helped other churches in America to become mature and self-supporting. He then asks why can't they also help churches reach maturity in other lands? He acknowledges the careless use of funds in which the churches being helped were not encouraged to help as much as they could making them weak and dependent. He closes with the words that it is possible to give many fine examples where financial help was joyfully received and prayerfully used.

"Instant Indigenousness" – Not Available!

George Beckman, professor of Greek at the Osaka Seminary in Japan, reacted to the indigenous church discussion by giving insights on the culture of the New Testament and salient points on church history. For those who saw in the Apostle Paul an example for modern missionaries, he suggested a closer look. He reminds us that Paul was bicultural and at home with Jewish culture, and at the same time a Roman citizen, who spoke koine Greek, the common trade language of the empire. The presence of synagogues in the major cities had existed prior to his birth. Since the time of the Babylonian captivity they had helped preserve Jewish faith. (The Bible College today serves in a similar way). There may have been many receptive Gentile "Godfearers" because the Greek translation of the Old Testament (Septuagint) was available in the synagogues. This was Paul's ready source of qualified elders in the newly planted Gentile churches.

Furthermore, he reminded us that Paul exercised freedom with regard to methods. To prevent stumbling with the Corinthians he refused to accept any funds from them but chose rather to work at his old trade of tentmaking. When his co-workers came down from Macedonia he gladly accepted the offering from Philippi that he might minister full time (Acts 18:1-5).

Beckman makes several other thought provoking points. "Japanese Buddhism is often used as an example of spontaneous, vital, indigenousness that Christianity should imitate. It is pointed out that Buddhism was introduced into Japan three or four hundred years before it became indigenous and grew." He also asked if we were willing to make the drastic changes in the norms of Christianity that Buddhism made in its adaptation to Japanese culture.

After listing a number of the modern forms of western culture, that have been fully accepted into Japanese society, such as TV's, Hi-Fi sets, washing machines and refrigerators, he raises a question. "Why does the Gospel have to be hindered when these other things have such a tremendous appeal even in non-indigenized dress?" He then stresses: **"If the Christian message is presented often enough as possessing enough intrinsic value by sincere messengers, it will have an appeal equal to the above even though it may be in a non-indigenous dress!"**

Working Principles for Indigeneity

Robert Morse, amidst his busy schedule of translating the Rawang Bible in Burma, offers helpful insight on how newly planted churches can be helped without creating a weak dependency. First of all he lets the reader know that he agrees with Tom Rash and Mel Byers that "the church of the New Testament is the God-given model which it is our responsibility to reproduce." He affirms that "the outstanding feature of the primitive church of the New Testament and Apostolic days was its Spirit-given life, its vitality, its power to win converts and influence the course of world events." He then goes on to clarify the principles that produced the spontaneous growth of the N.T. church.

Non-ending dependence as criterion, is an important foundational principle in Morse's view. He points out the error of an approach that "assumes such prerogatives of power and authority as to presume complete self-sufficiency without Christ, and to precede the operation of the Holy Spirit in the program of winning lost souls." In studying the history of the church Robert sees two factors that contribute to indigenous life. First, the church's "strength and vitality have been in proportion to its rejection of a 'closed society' system," and second, "its readiness to admit its perpetual dependent status."

"A closed society system which rejected all outside help or influence would rapidly reduce the church to the status of one of those secret societies which usually die out after several generations. But as an open society the church has shown its life and strength as it continued a process of active interaction with the outside world, taking in and assimilating as well as giving out. And it is when the church has tried to deny its God-given characteristic of being always dependent on God for its resources, and tried to become too independent and self-sufficient, relying on its earthly organization that it has departed the furthest away from the ideals and vitality of the New Testament church."

Output proportionate to input as criterion is central to the life of a living organism and it is also true of the church. "It is vital that we recognize ...this principle of life, that in order to live, an organism (which the church is) must produce and give out, while at the same time receiving from the outside. It is when the delicate balance of the metabolism –the proper ratio of intake versus output—is upset and out of kilter that all manner of illnesses beset the church, no matter whether it be in the Orient or the West... Christian stewardship is not some secondary teaching to be introduced gradually, or taught belatedly after a strong congregation has been built up. It must, and can be taught and applied from the very day a new life in Christ begins."

********* ********* ********* *********

Past and Present Mail Responses

John Pemberton, Mashoko, Africa: "I have enjoyed 'Far East' very much. Your articles have been most thought provoking, especially those dealing with the indigenous church... I am sure that many of the problems that you folk deal with are very similar to ours." (Letters section, FECM, Summer, 1963)

Tom Rash, Calgary, Canada: "Fortunately, we had helped or encouraged our evangelists to learn a trade or complete their education to qualify for teaching, etc. before we left India… So, most were able to lead small groups. Julius Yafat became head of the Bible Society of N. India and traveled the country, preaching in many churches. G.M. Timothy taught in Euwing Christian College and preached in Allahabad. M.N. Luther completed a medical program in Bhopal. He now preaches in the largest church in Bhopal."

(Response in a letter after reviewing chapter sixteen, May 3, 2006)

Chapter Seventeen

WOMEN'S DEPARTMENT

<u>Where Angels Fear to Tread</u>

The courage of Mel Byers was impressed upon me before I came to Japan. He had served in China and Burma under trying circumstances and the report is that he never faltered in his faith. Forced to leave Burma, he was now serving among remote tribals in Thailand. But when I received his article entitled, "Is Mother a Missionary?" I wondered if this was courage or foolhardiness. He walked into the women's department armed only with his pen and began to criticize their perceptions of the role of missionary women. In retrospect he did a great service, for his article triggered responses from women serving throughout the world.

Mel begins with what he calls a distorted image of the professional missionary woman expressed by a missionary wife. "First and above all, I am a missionary, secondly a mother, and lastly a wife." Byers counters with the statement, "A casual acquaintance with God's Word reveals that God's order for the duties of women are just opposite the professional standards of the world which we have adopted." He then goes on to trace the source of this "distorted image."

When a young single girl in her teens, the future missionary candidate responds to an emotional appeal at a youth camp, or convention, for "full time service to missions." In her mind this ideal ranks above the roles of being a wife and mother. As the uncertain future unfolds she feels a burden to fulfill this early, emotional commitment. When, the door of service to missions opens, she is ready to put winning the heathen above all other demands including that of wife and mother.

Because of time needed to serve as a missionary, it is easy to "drift into the role of the 'privileged class' where the menial chores of home-making are relegated to a crew of servants." "To maintain this 'fashionable missionary status' several hours are required to keep one's hair done up in the proper fashion for presentation at the regular afternoon tea fellowship, a means by which everyone can keep tabs on everyone's servants."

Mel spills more hot tea when he goes on to say, "When the children reach the ripe and tender age of six, the legal machinery orders the child to be shipped out to school. Sometimes this is not the rule of the mission, but still many mothers prefer it because the 'children are happier.' Since they can no longer handle them anyway they sigh with relief when the children 'finally go back to school' for now, the mother reasons, 'I can get some missionary work done.' Of course, at the leisurely afternoon tea fellowship all of this is referred to as the 'terrible sacrifice.'"

Putting sarcasm aside, Byers goes on to state his convictions clearly about the role of the missionary's wife. "When I married my wife, I married a missionary. We entered into the marriage union with the purpose of making a home. This, if the Lord so desired, would be accomplished on the foreign field. Her desire was to be a good wife and mother, her duties would be that of making a home. I would endeavor to do the work of an evangelist. Through personal discipline she has accepted the menial chores of making a home even as women are called upon to make a home in America. She aspires to educate her own children at home, as long as possible."

"When the small child asks, 'Is mother a missionary,?' One can positively answer, 'Yes.' That woman you see washing clothes, doing the dishes, bathing the children, cleaning the house, cooking the meals, planting the flowers and a hundred other daily menial tasks, along with correcting your day's schoolwork late into the night – is in fact your mother – my wife – and in the sight of God – a real missionary."

A Rousing Good Rebuttal

"**A**t first I was interested. Then I was mildly shocked. And by the time I had finished Mel Byers' article, 'Is Mother a Missionary?' I was more than mildly indignant." So responds Helen Morse, who has lived and worked among tribal people. She goes on to correct what she believes are misconceptions that are conveyed in Mel's article. Her impression was that Mel "feels that women on the mission field should tend the home fires, and that alone." She goes on to ask the question, "Should the wife be completely deprived of any outlet for the service which she longs to perform and for which she may have had special training?"

"After all," Helen declares, "the missionary wife is actually little different from her counterpart in the homeland – the minister's wife. Many minister wives teach Sunday School classes, sing in the choir, play the piano or organ, help with the young people's meetings, take part in the women's missionary society, go visiting in the homes, etc. And while they may sometimes be criticized because they cannot attend all the meetings of various church groups, they are seldom called to task for taking too active a part." Helen then inquires, "If it is right and proper for a wife in the homeland to take part in Christian work and participate in activities outside of home and family, then is it not equally right and proper for that wife to continue such activities if her husband should be called to carry on his ministry in a foreign country?"

Mel's description of "the western white woman who comes to the Orient, acquires a crew of servants, and thus becomes a member of the so-called 'privileged class' with no further need to concern herself with the menial tasks of housekeeping!" rouses Helen's indignation. Acknowledging that she has helpers in the home, Mrs. Morse contrasts life among tribal people with that of the USA. "It is difficult for one to understand who is accustomed to going to the door and picking up the bottle of milk, putting it in the refrigerator, cooking meals on an electric or gas range after having made a trip to the supermarket for groceries, turning on the lights when it gets dark, adjusting the thermostat for controlled heat in the house, turning on the water faucet for hot or cold running water as desired, and taking advantage of the dozens of mechanical conveniences or helpers so taken for granted in America."

"I repeat, it is difficult for one accustomed to these things to even imagine a place where there are no markets of any kind, all milk must be strained and boiled before using, the wood to be burned in an old-fashioned range or open fire for cooking must first be chopped, all water must be carried from the river and that for drinking must be boiled, and all clothes washed piece by piece by hand. For one grown up in America, all these tasks - plus pounding the husks from the rice, tending a vegetable garden, as well as raising your own pigs for ham or bacon - would present a great many problems, and consume hours and hours of time. However, people who have grown up doing these things can accomplish the same tasks in a fraction of the time it takes the foreigner."

Helen goes on to conclude, "I think most missionaries in the Orient feel that it is better stewardship of the time and strength God has given them to hire someone to perform these routine daily tasks, and devote their own time to doing those things which the others cannot do. Having helpers in the home does not necessarily mean having a 'crew of servants' to do one's dirty work, while the missionary wife turns to being a social butterfly who requires several hours to 'keep one's hair done up in the proper fashion for presentation at the regular afternoon tea fellowship,' as Mel implies. None of the missionary wives and mothers I have ever met – whether in China, Burma, Hong Kong, or Japan – have fit that description."

Lastly, Mrs. Morse deals with the criticism about raising missionary children. She wants the reader to know that there are very difficult decisions to make when it comes to the education of school age children such as, whether to teach them at home or send them away to an available school. "It is something that each family must decide individually, according to their needs and local conditions."

"I have never met a missionary mother who could 'sigh with relief' when the children finally go back to school… Those mothers who have sent their children away only because they had to, or because they felt it best for the children to have an opportunity to know what school life is like… have shed gallons of tears and spent countless hours in prayer. The fact that a woman happens to be a mother on the mission field does not automatically take away her normal maternal instincts and feelings."

Helen wraps up her rebuttal as follows. "So we come round to the starting point again, 'Is Mother a Missionary?' and I ask myself, 'What am I?' First, I am a Christian, having dedicated myself to the Lord for His service. Secondly, I am a wife. Thirdly, I am a mother. And while being all these things simultaneously, I believe that I am also being a missionary."

Readers and Writers Reactions

Marianne Baughman, West African Mission

"We have enjoyed tremendously your feature, 'Our Missionary Women.' Don and I discussed Mel and Helen's articles pro and con and he went to sleep saying, 'You can't generalize.' For me the whole situation boils down to this: There will come a day – it has already come in some places – that…Americans will have to leave their fields of service or be buried there. There will also come a day when our children will have to stand on their own two feet and fight the darts of Satan. For what will the Lord hold me responsible.

Mel Byers, Chiengrai, Thailand (Field Editor)

I would like to say just a word about Helen's article which in fact was quite mild compared to what some people think! [1] Perhaps I was boldly careless by entering into the women's department. At the time, however, it was during the rainy season when the roads turn to mud and the rivers are flooded and our place is difficult to reach – so I figured I was safe. Now that the dry season has come and the area more accessible I shall be quiet for fear that a group of angry women come marching against the house. Come next rainy season however, well, who knows?"

---

[1] For an update on the role of women see: Loren Cunningham, "Why Not Women?" YWAM, 2000.

Chapter Eighteen

EXPERIENCING COMMUNITY

Summer Camp Time

Work and play can go together in a Christian summer camp. Eleven year old Timmy joined me when I held down the vesper speaker spot for the Osaka Christian Camp. There were over 100 young people who attended consistently throughout the week. The preachers in this central Japan area had prepared well for the camp season. All who attended received solid teaching in the many classes, and experienced the richness of Christian fellowship and play together. It was a joy to see five young men accept Christ. Timmy and I especially enjoyed swimming in the Nosegawa River, and found it good sport to try and swim up stream against the current.

Inspiration at Lake Motosu

Twenty-four of our local people from suburban Tokyo joined our family in the tiring trip up into the mountains behind Mt. Fuji. Once there at beautiful Lake Motosu we greatly appreciated being out of the sweltering heat and smog for which Tokyo summers are often remembered. In this camp there were also over 100 registrations and a well trained faculty including dedicated Japanese pastors and acclimated missionaries such as Andrew and Betty Patton and Harold and Lois Sims.

The vigorous schedules of our two week camp sessions are good for the health. An early breakfast of miso soup, rice and dried fish, and daikon radish, with the option of a hard boiled egg, is set before us each day. Boisterous choruses expressing thanksgiving are sung prior to eating this indigenous fare. Turns are taken by the different crews for kitchen duty. The dishes are washed in cold water that is channeled through bamboo from a mountain stream above the dining hall. Following breakfast, Bible classes formed under shady trees are taught throughout the morning.

Various rice dishes such as curry or *hayashi* rice are served at lunch. *Pan*, the thick sliced Japanese white bread introduced by the Portuguese, is available with jam to fill up the corners of hungry campers. The good news is that camp fare along with the vigorous exercise of afternoon activities causes one to lose from ten to twenty pounds during two weeks of camp. The afternoon free time offers soft ball, volleyball, hiking, and swimming. Since there are no showers or bath houses the latter sport is a hygienic necessity. When mother nature calls there are squat toilets located in wooden outhouses in several locations.

In the evening we gather with our tired bodies and sunburned faces in the wooden dining hall for supper, fun skits and vespers. Supper might include such variations as spaghetti or a meat dish with boiled potatoes and cooked vegetables. At this point in time, everything is ravenously consumed and the cooks are praised. During the free time following dinner, American missionaries introduce fun skits and Bible dramas. Also, Japanese innovations have been very creative, either hilarious in nature or impressively inspirational. After such relaxed sessions we are ready for reflective thoughts at the vesper hour. This year we had a special treat.

Oda Sensei, the New Testament Greek professor from Osaka Bible Seminary was our special speaker. He brought the evening messages with clarity and power. On one special evening we were ushered to a beach area by the lake. It was a beautiful night with moonlight reflecting on the quiet water. We sang hymns reverently, inspired by nature's witness to the presence of the Creator. After a time of prayer, a lantern-bearing boat appeared from behind an outcropping of the shoreline. As the boat came across our vision from the right, we could see that Oda Sensei was standing erect, his white shirt visible by lantern light contrasted to the night sky. Two students in the lower shadows rowed it into a position about 20 yards from our gathering. With the natural acoustics aiding, Brother Oda then gave an awe inspiring message based on the text depicting Christ speaking from a boat (Luke 5:1-11).

Return Visit to Tanegashima

Taking a ten day chunk out of September, Eleanor and I took four year old Jimmy, and one and a half-year old Billy with us on an evangelistic trip to our island work. This was an

The names of the five Ikeda children are: Shinichi, Nozomi, Ai, Eiko, & Motonobu. (In English: Faith, Hope, Love, Grace, &, according to the parents, "the Very Last One")

eventful journey in which we experienced the warm nostalgia of old friendships. I had returned to the island many times, but this was the first time they had seen Eleanor in over six years, and they had never seen our two little boys. When last on the island, little Mary was born. Additional babies made Eleanor's earlier return difficult to schedule.

Pastor and Mrs. Ikeda warmly received us and we stayed as guests in the crowded parsonage in the back of the church sharing with them in the daily work and preaching nightly in the meetings. We both marveled at the workload they carried. Endeavoring to save money towards their permanent church building and parsonage, they have only one hired teacher in the full time kindergarten. Pastor Tadayoshi Ikeda acts as principal (referee at times) and his wife, Hisako is a one woman show – she does everything! Right along with this heavy responsibility of seventy-five kindergarten youngsters they have their own small ones to care for. Their children's biblical names seem appropriate: Shinichi (Faith), Nozomi (Hope), Ai (Love), and Eiko (Grace). (After returning from furlough we learned that the fifth child was named, Motonobu, which they declared meant, "the last one").

The nightly evangelistic meetings were well attended. Because of the hot and humid September on the island, we met in the concrete kindergarten building which is much cooler than the old chapel. On Sunday, after bringing a message to the Nishinoomote church, I accompanied Brother Ikeda to go to the mountain village where we met with the church that meets in elderly Sakae San's home. It was heart warming to hear that Brother Sakae would like to attend the Osaka Seminary for a year so that he could witness to his village neighbors better. His wish must have been passed onto his oldest son, who eventually became a well-trained Christian leader.

Typhoon Wilma's arrival made us feel nostalgic again. Southern Japan is known as "typhoon alley" and we would have been surprised if there had not been some indication of rough weather. Pastor Ikeda got the warning in time and pulled a quick switch, as he had planned beforehand. The meeting was to conclude with the 23rd, upon the day I was to speak to the combined churches of Kagoshima prefecture. According to the alternate plan, with word of rampaging Wilma on the way, the convention was changed to Kanoya on the mainland. Saying hasty farewells, we boarded the last ship and made the rough crossing to Kagoshima City.

Crossing the roughening bay from Kagoshima's ferry port, we then took the bus and completed the two hour trip to Kanoya. Stopping in at Mark and Pauline Maxey's home we renewed old ties and saw all of the Maxeys including his sister, Isabel Dittemore, who was visiting Japan on her way through to starting a new work on Taiwan. This was like old times!

Gathering at the Kanoya church the convention began in spite of the approaching storm. The numbers, of course, were few, but the old faithfuls were there. It was difficult to speak at first as I looked at the aging faces of old friends. They had welcomed us as part of the family, and were especially happy to see Eleanor and the little ones. A few of these dear brethren are in their eighties and we may not see them again this side of eternity. I preached as if the expected large crowd was there, and with the knowledge that opportunities do not always repeat themselves.

We had looked forward to engaging in the informal discussions in the afternoon, after which we were scheduled to re-cross the bay and catch our train leaving from Kagoshima City. But Wilma was too close! The ferry boats had stopped running. We had no alternative but to go all the way around the bay – a three hour bus ride on a very rough road. Also, it meant we had to leave immediately after the morning service or we would not make our connections. We left in haste, regretting the shortness of time.

The Importance of Community

The importance that the Asians place on community was impressed upon us again when our neighbor, Mr. Masuda's wife died. We felt the loss of this gentle neighbor as much or more than many in the Japanese community. By this time her daughter was in regular attendance in our weekly Bible school with her parent's permission. But the fact that Mr. Masuda had requested a Buddhist memorial service in his home, according to the accepted local custom, presented a dilemma.

What should I do? Those who attend Buddhist funeral services go through a process of bowing to an altar upon which the ashes of the deceased in a square wooden box are placed by a recent photo. They also give a prepared envelope containing cash in new yen bills to offset the funeral costs. Bowing to the altar is considered an act of worshiping the dead and Christians who do so are subject to criticism by certain people in the Japanese church and the missionary community. It would be a safer course not to attend, but this would surely be construed as a lack of concern.

I decided to go. I purchased the type of gift envelope for such occasions and placed a generous amount of cash inside. I dressed appropriately in a dark suit, rehearsed the Japanese phrases to indicate sympathy for a deceased family member, and walked over to my neighbor's house. I went directly to Masuda San, himself, expressed my deep sympathy, extended the monetary gift, and quietly returned home. As a foreigner my bypassing of customary steps was overlooked. I had been there and expressed my compassion. The bonds with Masuda San and the community were strengthened.

The Communal Needs of Lepers

It was surprising to learn that there was a leper colony a short driving distance from our suburban Tokyo home! Our experience of visiting Keiaien, the leper colony in the rural south had conditioned me to expect an isolated area. I remember being shocked when Mark Maxey first introduced us at the leper church. Many had missing ears and noses and their facial expressions were distorted. We weren't permitted to sit with them, but my heart was warmed by their heartfelt singing and testimonies.

My earlier connection with the Keiaien Leper Colony opened the door and they set up a date for me to share in the leper church near our home. However, during the interim their church building was damaged by fire. It was raining when I arrived and they asked if I was willing to hold the Bible study in the Buddhist Church. I consented and we sat in a circle on the tatami mats, unmindful of the disparate surroundings, and blessed by the warmth of our fellowship. What a paradox! Those who have been shunned and rejected by society through the centuries are the most receptive to the teaching of Jesus and eager to love and fellowship with their fellow men.

Chapter Nineteen

DEMON ENCOUNTERS

Demons and Psychic Phenomena

Toward the close of our second five year term of service I wrote an article called, "How the Christian Looks at Demons and Psychic Phenomena" (FECM Vol 5, No 4). It triggered responses from Burma, Thailand, and Africa that helped me to understand the differences from what I was experiencing in urban Japan. I quoted C.S. Lewis from his book, "The Screwtape Letters:"

> There are two equal and opposite errors into which our race can fall about the devils. One is to disbelieve in their existence. The other is to believe, and to feel an excessive and unhealthy interest in them.

I went on to say, "To go along with the basic assumptions of naturalism which undergird the Western scientific mind would do away with all that is non-matter. It would eliminate demons, but it would also eliminate man's soul and the God who made it. On the other hand, to accept all psychic phenomena as supernatural, and to equate all the symptoms of abnormal mental behavior to 'demon possession' is no different from the primitive animism of aboriginal peoples." This last remark along with my tentative conclusions may have stirred up the writers from animistic cultures.

Eyewitness of Demon Possession

Betty Morse had written earlier from her experiences among the Lisu and Rawang tribes of northern Burma affirming emphatically her witness of demon possession. "I remember thinking that I must be the crazy one when I saw my first real case of demon possession. There was Yintang tied up in the church at Tilliwagu. I was indignant, and demanded that he be released and sent home. Then the family showed us the ropes that he had broken effortlessly and the terrible injuries he had inflicted on his wife and children. Then I spoke to him and saw the terrible look in his eyes. I was there when many voices spoke from his throat at one time… I would have gladly welcomed the men in white jackets and the refuge the asylum offered if I could have been at home. But I was on the mission field in the middle of… Satan's stronghold!"

Mrs. Morse went on to tell us that she joined the missionaries in prayer and fasting. After which, "preachers from nearby villages were called and after a few days all laid hands on Yintang and prayed for God, in Jesus' Name to cast out the foul spirits who were tormenting the possessed man. Then and there he was delivered, and from that day to now, I have never again doubted God's ability to act, even in our day… Yintang has never had a relapse, and is a deacon in the Dukdang church."

"I don't say that missionaries have all the answers," Betty cautions to say, "I know of two cases where demons were definitely involved, yet prayer did not seem to help, and we were not able to cast them out. Another man (who chased me with an axe) seems to have been shell shocked in battle down country, and has a real mental condition… We know that germs cause disease, and our mission spends thousands of dollars a year on medicines for the churches up here. But we also know that in some cases where medicines didn't help, prayer did."

"Our Lisu and Rawang Christians could fill a book with accounts of plain day to day experiences with demons as they go about their work of witnessing to the world that Jesus is the Christ, the Son of the Living God. In some places opposition to the Gospel died a natural death when many Christians moved into a new area. In some areas the demons have been effortlessly driven out simply by singing of hymns and prayers of the Christians in their daily devotions at home" (FECM Fall, '65).

Demons as 'Angels of Light'

Mel Byers reacted to the notion that "the mission fields" are the place of Satan's strongholds in contrast to the "civilized" west. He writes, "I doubt if the missionary's position is any more precarious or susceptible to satanic attacks than Christians anywhere else in the world… The mumbo-jumbo of the African voodoo, or the hocus-pocus of the Oriental shaman is nothing compared to the eerie light which bathes the west in its artificial glow. It is the irresistible siren which calls forth every satiable lust and passion; a bewitching sweetness which demands pleasure and things; an enchanting light which is always (perceived to be) proper and right."

"True spiritual insight and a proper orientation in the New Testament might reveal that the missionary instead of stumbling into the very 'stronghold' of Satan has actually left it! Encountering satanic forces in their more elementary form should not blind us to his more devastating cunning and modern approach. We need not be ignorant of his devices. Any spiritually wide awake minister in America could easily demonstrate that the demons which grip, pressurize, torment and heckle the believer in America are trained specialists compared to the 'foul spirits' of the Orient" (FECM Winter, '66).

Demons in Africa

John Kernan, writing from Africa, affirms, "Certainly there are demons today. For those who have had experience of them, there is no doubt that they do live…Most missionaries in primitive areas believe in demons. Missionaries in Rhodesia and South Africa have experience of them, and so throughout Africa."

"Demons in Africa, the doubter says, and in other primitive countries, but not in the United States. I used to have that idea, too," says Kernan, "and resolved the problem by postulating the theory that as mankind advanced in civilization, he grew increasingly immune to onslaughts from evil spirits. Now I rather doubt the truth of this theory. It seems much more likely that if there are demons at all, there are demons everywhere. And it does seem likely that there are demons in the U.S. and other 'civilized' countries. Perhaps some cases diagnosed as insanity could better be treated as demon-possession."

"But this is one of the difficulties of diagnosis and treatment: some types of insanity, such as the manic phase of manic-depressive, resemble demon-possession. It's possible that only a person very skilled in psychiatry and demonology can tell the difference. Yet isn't this very fact –that it may be difficult to tell the difference –an indication of a sad lack in both psychiatry and Christian thought?. How can our ministerial schools continue to send graduates into the ministry and mission work, who are so totally unprepared to do battle with these powers of darkness?"

"The need for more research can be exemplified in another way. Betty Morse states that in one case when she and others prayed to cast out a demon, they put their hands on the head of a demon-possessed person. Corrie Ten Boom declares emphatically that one must never touch a demon-possessed person, and describes cases where people were knocked unconscious as by an electric shock when they touched such a person. Who is right – Betty or Corrie? Or are they both wrong and there is really no such thing? Or are they both right and there are different kinds of demons that need to be dealt with in different ways?"

"Demons are a problem in our day. We don't solve the problem by regarding belief in them as ignorant or childish, but by accepting them as a fact and learning how to deal with them in the way of Christ" (FECM Summer, '66).

An Effective Approach in Thailand

David Filbeck, writing from Pua Nan, describes the nature of the tribal society in which he labored. "In Northern Thailand we are not faced with a nominal Christian population divided up into so many denominations. We are faced with a Buddhist society undergirded by a firm layer of animism, which includes bloody sacrifices to demons. When we preach in a new place our message is not a treatise on cosmological arguments for the existence of God, or on the Deity of Jesus...These things, if pertinent at all (to the animist) are merely stated as true. Our teaching is more parabolic:

> Q(uestion): When you offend a spirit, what must you do?
>
> R(esponse): We must sacrifice an animal to the spirit.
>
> Q: When you do not sacrifice, what happens?
>
> R: The spirit eats us until we finally die.
>
> Q: But when you kill an animal to sacrifice to the spirit you are saved from death. Therefore, that animal dies in your place, right?
>
> R: Yes.
>
> Q: When you offend God, what must you do?
>
> R: We are unable to do anything.
>
> Q: Correct. For God does not 'eat' (accept) animal sacrifices. Have you ever sacrificed an animal to God because you offended Him?
>
> R: No.
>
> Q. But, God says everyone who offends Him must die in Hell. Have any of you offended God?
>
> R: Well, yes; maybe... I don't know.
>
> Q: Have you ever sacrificed an animal to a spirit?
>
> R: Why certainly!
>
> Q: Then you have offended God for you have chosen to treat demons as more important than God. So you must die in Hell for your sins. There is nothing to die in your place before God, is there?
>
> **Yes, there is!**

"The above dialogue I have used many times in preaching in Northern Thailand. The questions asked never fail to elicit the response as written above. Furthermore, it allows by means of a dramatic reversal, to tell the death of Jesus and why He died. 'As an animal was necessary to die in your place because you had offended a demon, so it is necessary for Christ to die in your place because of having offended God.' "By presenting Christ in these patterns we make Him a part of the culture; One who knows what the people are up against and can offer them a way of escape" (FECM, W. '67-68).

Note: David Filbeck sent an Email update in June of 2006 from Thailand on his perspective of changing tribal behavior today:

"Satan has changed tactics...and we face new enemies of the Gospel. The change of tactics I see here is the rise of secularism. Yes, we have symptoms that would be termed demon possession years ago, and they may still be so termed. But people with such symptoms are now rushed to the hospital or clinic even though a demon ceremony may still be done just in case...Modern medicine can control such symptoms to a great degree. But our basic message is still the same. To do ceremonies to demons is to place God in second place and that is sin. I also remind people that modern health knowledge and procedures are parts of God's creation (John 1:3). So to God must go the glory. To get people through the crises of health and agriculture problems while not reverting back to animism is still a hurdle. Prayer and faith are our emphases during such times."

Chapter Twenty

SHOCKS AND SURPRISES

Culture Shock Defined

"Culture shock has been described as that emotional disturbance which results from adjustment to new cultural environment. Its cause is the loss of familiar cues by which we interact in any society." So writes William A. Smalley, in his article, "Culture Shock, Language Shock, and the Shock of Self-Discovery" (FECM, Fall, '64).[1] I have not encountered demon-possession in Japan like that in predominantly animistic cultures, but I have seen examples of inappropriate behavior by Americans, including myself, due to culture shock.

The loss of familiar cues can cause a feeling of being ill at ease. In 1950's Japan American type breakfast cereals were not available. We made do with Japanese *pan* and jam, along with our fried or soft boiled eggs. It gave us a sense of relief to learn that American cereals such as puffed wheat, puffed rice, and cornflakes could be ordered from a specialty outlet for foreigners. But it was a shock to discover that cold milk was not available in the markets. Morinaga's powdered milk was recommended. When we had refrigeration we would mix a batch of powdered milk and let it cool before using. We did everything to procure the nostalgic American breakfast. We hadn't realized how dependent we were for familiar food to start off the day in the morning.

On the other hand, we found that many of the Japanese food specialties offered for dinner were enjoyable the first time we tried them. *Sukiyaki* was served us at our welcoming party. It was fascinating to see the ladies lay beef strips in a hot stir-fry pan over a *hibachi* on the table in front of us. They then mixed in various leafy greens, cut long onions, bamboo sprouts, and tofu. Liberal amounts of sweetened soy sauce added to the aroma and the distinctive Japanese flavor. All of this was only the topping to be placed on one's bowl of rice. Prior to scooping in the steamed rice the content of a raw egg was plopped into the bottom of the bowl. In seeing the look of alarm on our faces, the ladies assured us that the egg would be cooked by the time we worked down to it. We found ourselves asking for seconds even though the bowls were large.

Osashimi (raw fish) was a challenge but our Japanese friends urged us try it. When it is placed on top of *sushi* (rice rolls) and eaten with soy sauce or *wasabi* (horse- radish) it is quite palatable. It never became a favorite but I would eat it whenever it was offered by a host. I loved daikon (pickled radish) and probably ate more than was good for me. Our kids, especially considered dried octopus a treat, and we didn't mind their eating Japanese *okashi* (confectionary) for it has far less sugar than U.S. varieties. In terms of physical health, Japanese green tea and *okashi* served at traditional tea times has nutritional value. The pastor or missionary making a number of house calls feels no ill effect from drinking quantities of green tea.

In this context we should mention again that the use of human waste to fertilize the fields was widely used prior to the developed economy that enabled more use of chemical fertilizer. All fresh vegetables had to be washed thoroughly because of the presence of worm eggs. Each of us had bouts of worms. It was especially frightening to see the children pass long worms or a mass of pin worms. The worm pills seemed to take care of the problem but not without side effects. Eating salad was not as carefree as it once was; yet, we did adjust and ate well. The fear that causes some to isolate themselves into "little American communities" should not be blamed on Japanese cuisine.

Ethnocentric Pride

Some forms of inappropriate behavior have more to do with ethnocentric pride, and it is a continuing cause for maladjustment to the culture. During a busy evening hour, I was standing in line in our home town *ichiba* (market) waiting to buy meat that my wife requested. I looked up and recognized the American lady who barged in ahead of the line, demanding immediate service. I was so embarrassed that I lowered my head and tried to hide myself. I didn't want to be associated with such rude behavior. The Japanese in line didn't say anything, but the expression on their faces clearly revealed their disapproval.

More than once I have observed western tourists make a big fuss because they felt they had been short changed at a store. It was usually a case of misunderstanding because of their ignorance of the value of the yen bills or coins they were using. At the root of their instant anger is their distrust of the native people. They had not taken time to get to know them and didn't realize that most shopkeepers in Japan take pride in their honesty.

Language Shock

Language shock may be a root cause for emotional maladjustment in Japan. This may be especially so for the missionary who may have had an ability or a gift of public speaking before coming. One may have advanced degrees and considerable experience, but when you enter a foreign culture you are a baby once again as you try to express yourself. The temptation to lean on interpreters can extend the problem until one is embarrassed by a position of longevity in the land without fluency.

While in the Tokyo Language School I met a German anthropologist who had the unrealistic assignment to first learn the language and then begin teaching in a Japanese university in two years time. This might have been workable if he was studying a European dialect that consisted of a basic alphabet.

But to read Japanese even on a Junior High School level one must master 1,800 Chinese characters, many of which have over 20 strokes. This is the ground floor. To teach on a college level one should be able to read and write over 5,000 ideographs! In addition, to be able to read Japanese one must master *Hiragana* and *Katakana* syllabary, which completes the borrowed Chinese *Kanji* into meaningful Japanese sentences. Once he realized this my German friend experienced shock. His first reaction was to criticize the Japanese language. Next, he criticized the language teachers; then, in his pain, he began to reject the culture.

When we leave European based language structure and begin struggling with an Asian language such as Chinese or Japanese, we are only beginning to climb a mountain. Previous language study, couched as it is in western thought forms, may form more of a mental block than be of help. Latin based alphabets can only help as a crutch in putting the odd sounds into a visual form of Roman syllables. We are urged to leave the crutches as soon as possible.

Pronunciation comes more easily for children, as our youngsters proved by speaking Japanese with more authentic intonation than their parents. Because of the pride factor, women seem to be less inhibited than men and learn to speak more quickly. I remember how flabbergasted the inflexible American priest was in our class when the young inexperienced short term Methodist lady out-performed him. On the other hand, some with the gift of gab never master the reading and writing of the ideographs.

Language shock has been the reason for the negative attitudes of a number of missionaries I have known. They came to Japan when they were beyond the age of 30, and/or they became immersed too quickly in mission responsibilities prior to taking time to build a foundation for the language. They did a commendable work using interpreters, but they found it difficult to feel at home in the culture. At times they became bitter and blamed the culture for their discontent.

Projecting Blame

There can be a crucifying power in idealism. As a young missionary I had absorbed the classics written by Roland Allen, "Missionary Methods: St. Paul's or Ours?" and, "The Spontaneous Expansion of the Church." [2] Allen's insightful critique stated that the basic reasons for slow growth were western forms and methodology. Since the church landscape in Japan was dotted with western style church buildings, and pastors seem to fall into the pattern of their western counterpart, I assumed that much of our own problems were due to the poor foundation of our predecessors. It became easy to project the blame for our own failures onto those who went before us.

To ease the pain of continued slow growth in my own early efforts at church planting, I found myself projecting blame on my colleagues or other missionaries. It seemed clear in my mind that they were not following the indigenous New Testament ideals that Roland Allen described. I became critical of the city missionaries that didn't share the economic deprivations of our rural work. Nor did they encounter the hostile pockets of resistance that we met in the provinces. Without realizing it I was developing an adversarial approach and it was largely due to my own culture shock.

The Shock of Self-Discovery

Smalley points out that for many professionals, long habits of success have built up pride. When faced with a new culture to navigate and a new language to learn the props can be knocked out from under them. Adjusting individuals may go through a cycle of change. First, is **fascination** with the culture. The camera is kept in use taking photos of the strange and exotic. Different food is tried and curios are purchased. Then, as time passes, the newcomer experiences **disappointment**. He thinks he has been short changed in a shop. He is answered curtly when he asks a question. There are not as many smiling faces in the busy work-a-day world. Then eventually comes **disillusionment;** his efforts at speaking the language have met with failure, he becomes ill from bad food. He is sure that a trusted individual has lied to him. He feels like going home, but then in a moment of self reflection he has **a turning point**. He realizes that there are bad people and good people in every country. He recovers his sense of humor and begins to laugh at himself. This is the beginning place of **biculturalism.** William Smalley links this turning point for missionary candidates to their commitment to Christ.

> "This, after all, is the meaning of Biblical self-denial. It involves a conversion, a discovery of one's self and a change in that self. Instead of the symptoms of rejection and insecurity comes an objective knowledge of strengths and weaknesses and with the knowledge comes a relaxed acceptance of one's self, a determination to do one's best without pretense." [3]

---

[1] Smalley's article appeared originally in Practical Anthropology, 1960. Reprinted in , "Readings in Missionary Anthropology II," William Carey Library, 1984.

[2] First Editions published by World Dominion Press, 1912 and 1927.

[3] William A. Smalley, "Culture Shock, Language Shock, and the Shock of Self-Discovery." FECM, Fall, 1964.

Chapter Twenty One

READJUSTMENT TO U.S.A.

Furlough Preparations

As the end of our second five year term of service drew closer we found our selves dreaming of shopping in California's department stores for clothes that matched our sizes. We also anticipated fellowshipping in churches of several hundred members, and taking our youngsters to get reacquainted with their grand parents; their aunts and uncles and their cousins. We had a longing to see the faces of dear friends and relatives who had been prayerfully supporting our work in Japan. Included in our dreams were visits to Knott's Berry Farm and Disney Land. We had a case of what the missionaries call, "furlough fever."

Our friends in Japan were making it possible to leave the work in capable hands so that we could be at ease during our year of absence. Paul and Kathleen Pratt, veteran missionaries from Kyushu, had come to Tokyo to serve and to be with their youngsters, who were attending the Christian Academy. They agreed to live in our home and lead out in the church and home Bible classes. Since they were known by the Kumegawa church members as warm, outgoing, and talented in music, they were enthusiastically welcomed.

My trusted friend Muto Sensei, although living a busy life, agreed to proof read and pilot our quarterly magazine through the print shop. His bilingual skills made him ideal for the job. Brother Muto would find Arnfinn Andaas, the manager of New Life League's publishing, a congenial person to work with. Sudo San, who cheerfully worked in the magazine office would continue to make address changes and mail the magazines. We felt at peace as we boarded the P.& O. Lines,' Arcadia, bound for San Francisco.

Culture Shock in the U.S.A.

"Freeway shock" hit me shortly after disembarking in San Francisco. My family was urged to go on ahead with welcoming friends to a reception at the Town and Country Church in Carmichael, a suburb of Sacramento. I stayed behind to take care of custom's procedures for the luggage that a teacher at CAJ asked us to include in our extensive baggage allowance. Our friends from Carmichael left a car for me to use so I could rejoin the family. It was a former police patrol car with a hopped-up engine. Since we had not owned a car during our second five year term of service, I was more than a little shaken by the instant fast pickup of the loaner auto. The congested freeway added to the shock as I zoomed my way to Sacramento. By the grace of God I arrived safely and the warm reception of our Christian friends helped settle my nerves.

Wayne and Pauline Thomas, the ministering couple at the Town and Country Church, on behalf of the congregation, gave us a surprise reception on our first Sunday. I remember groping for words during the morning message as I mentally shifted gears from Japanese thought forms to the changing American idiom. Each of us were still making this mental adjustment when we were ushered outside of the church building after the service. There parked on the front lawn was the gift of a new Plymouth station wagon. The all white car was wrapped in gift ribbon and the tag said it was for the Hammond family! This pleasant surprise shock reduced my vocabulary to, "WOW!"

'Culture shock in reverse' is the way I tried to explain the emotional upset I experienced while beginning my graduate studies at the University of California at Berkeley. My image of America was still pretty much made up of the stuff that went into behavioral patterns prior to 1954 when I first went to Japan as a missionary. My first furlough had introduced me to some changes that can appear in campus life when I attended UCLA in 1959, but I simply was not ready to find what I did at Berkeley in the Fall semester of 1965.

Entering through the main gates I worked my way past Sproul Hall, the main administration building. Students were milling about everywhere and the first impression is simply that of size and mass –the huge size of this university campus and the masses of students who attend (27,500). From the number of beards, bare feet, and unusual wearing apparel, along with the chatter and shouting, one could well imagine himself in an Arabian bazaar.

Many of the booths represented the political spectrum –from Conservatives to Communists. Bearded nonconformists were sandwiched in between clean shaven idealists. Long locks dangling from beneath Castro caps contrasted strangely to the crew cuts of the orthodox collegiate. Bare footed coeds wearing drab sack dresses non- chalantly passed out literature while they smoked cigarettes. The guitar strumming beatniks were almost overlooked but managed to gather small crowds in several corners of the Student Union.

Various signs, placards and titles came to view as I craned my neck over the heads of the crowd in an effort to learn more about the purpose of the various booths. It was no little shock to see that Communist and Socialist literature had a prominent place on one of the card tables. Student vs. Administration policies took up the larger areas. Campus Conservatives, Fraternities, Sororities, Farm Labor groups, and even Christian Student Associations made up the rest.

With various samplings of literature in my hands I rather dazedly headed out the main gate only to be confronted by one more booth. "Sexual Freedom League" read the sign attached to this booth which was tended by a sallow-faced, sagging lipped young man. On the table were nude pictures and buttons with suggestive phrases written on them. With mixed feelings of indignation and sadness, I rapidly walked away looking for fresh air.

The Root of the Problem

There is much that is wrong at Berkeley, but to indiscriminately castigate the many fine professors and students, or to declare that Berkeley's problems are isolated from those of the rest of the nation would be grossly unfair. It has been suggested that Berkeley's bearded rebels have done society a favor in overcoming apathy to an educational problem of long standing. We are only reaping the more manifest fruits from the seeds of secular positivism and moral relativism that have been freely sown in the fertile minds of our youth for a generation.

Furthermore, the present day efforts to eradicate all evidences of religion from the public schools, carried on as they are with a puritanical zeal, issue from a different kind of religious bigotry, for the fact is that a religious vacuum does not and cannot exist in a human context. There is no such thing as a purely 'secular' society. In place of reverence for the supernatural, our schools are filled with the substitute polytheistic religions of secularism –*positivism, relativism,* and *determinism,* which are taught, at times, with a subjective bias that would put an old time shouting preacher to shame. Ernest Johnson of Colombia University made the following insightful statement:

> Secularization has been accomplished in the mistaken belief that it meant 'religious liberty.' That great ideal has been largely nullified by this negative interpretation. To the Fathers it meant liberty in religion, not immunity from it. There can be no religious liberty if the basic faith of our people is destroyed by the 'acids of modernity' in a secular society.[1]

Our Furlough Home

Martinez, California is located one hour's drive north of San Jose and about 40 minutes northeast of the University of California campus. Since my schedule included grad studies at the university and part time teaching at San Jose Bible College, Martinez was a good location for our furlough home. This was especially so since my wife and I had a close association with Jim Francis and his wife Jean, ministers of the Christian church located in Morello Hills. I had preached there in my senior year at SJBC and Jim had taken my place when we left for Japan. It was a special bonus to find a three bed- room apartment near the church location which, was given to us at a reduced rate in return for my wife's help with the managerial duties.

The church community made us feel at home right away. It was a family church which made it easy for our youngsters to find friends and fun activities. Classes for every age group were offered and open discussion was encouraged. Jim Francis spoke the Word from the heart and exhorted the flock to be doers and not just hearers. Volunteer labor by the men made it possible to make building improvements on a pay-as-you-go basis. In future years the property was expanded and a new sanctuary was constructed.

Jim and Jean faithfully served there until their retirement. They make up part of the "Builders" who give strength to the community and the nation.

At Home in the Classroom

Graduate classes took up much of my day time schedule and on weekends I was often speaking and/or reporting to churches which had supported us. Therefore, they scheduled my "Anthropology for Christian Missions" class in the evenings. One of my favorite, former professors, Emmett Butterworth, also taught at night, so his Bible course on I Corinthians was billed along with my missions course on the same brochure. The night school went well and we had full classrooms of inquisitive youth.

This was the second time that I had taught missions at my alma mater at the request of President Bill Jessup. I felt privileged and was at home in the classroom, sharing frankly with the students on my victories and failures. I openly discussed my experience of culture shock and the many mistakes I made in my attempts at cross cultural communication The book of Acts was a major source along with current mission texts that stressed the goal of planting indigenous churches. Knowing the ethnocentric pride of American youth, I stressed the great need for missionaries with servant's hearts.

---

[1] Ernest Johnson, "Religion and the Philosophy of Education," in Science, Philosophy and Religion, A   Symposium, Columbia University, 1941, p. 349.

Chapter Twenty Two

DIFFICULT REENTRY

Third Term Obstacles

"You're not taking my grandchildren to Japan again! You've already taken your turn overseas," pleaded my wife's mother, adding another familiar objection, "We have needs in this country!" This outburst occurred as the date to return to Japan for our third, five year term of service drew closer. The folks recalled the time when the news showed the rough treatment to President Eisenhower's press secretary, James C. Hagerty, by political activists in Tokyo.[1] They had mobbed his car and rocked it so violently that he had to be rescued by a U.S. military helicopter. Our State Department took it seriously, which led to the abortion of the President's proposed visit to Japan.

The intensity of the opposition of Communist sympathizers was stirred up when the U.S. entered the Vietnam War in 1965. Still fresh on the memory of the citizens of Japan was the Korean War of 1950-53, during which the American bases in Japan were involved. Their fear was that Japan, perceived as an ally of the U.S., would be drawn into another Asian war. Accommodation to Communist views would be preferable, in the minds of many in Japan, to another terrible conflict.

I recalled this kind of thinking among the leftist students at the University of California at Berkeley (UCB) who challenged three South Vietnamese students who stood their ground in front of their booth at the University. In contrast to the supposedly 10,000 student activists who were 'contending on behalf of the South Vietnamese' the three Vietnamese were united in their affirmation that pulling out the American forces would not end the war. They also upset the pet position of the leftist sympathizers by stating frankly:

> Ho Chi Minh was our leader then, (when fighting the French) a Communist but a nationalist first. That was in 1945. Now it is different: Ho is a Communist first and a nationalist second. The Viet Cong speak of 'liberation' but mean domination by Communists.

When asked, what the answer to winning the war was, one of the Vietnamese smiled at the naïve questioner and answered, "If I had an answer for that, I'd be Prime Minister now" (FECM Winter, 65-66).

Welcome Back in Kumegawa

Our Japanese church members gave us a *kangei-kai* (welcome party) shortly after our return to suburban Tokyo. The warmth of their reception made us feel at home again. When we mentioned the objections of the kids' grandmother to our return they were sympathetic. But when we spoke of the incident in which the U.S. President's press secretary's car was attacked, they couldn't recall hearing about it. They went on to reassure us that such radical demonstrations are the activities of only a few extremists.

Seemingly in agreement with our small group of believers were the warm greetings from our non-Christian neighbors. The Obaasan in the nearby confectionery stand welcomed us like we were part of the family, and assured our kids that she would continue to give them *omake* (free treats). "*Irasshai, Irasshai,*" (Welcome! Welcome!) chorused the voices of the shop keepers at the corner fruit and vegetable store near the train station. Similar warmth was expressed when we made the rounds to the various shops in Kumegawa to restock our shelves. We realized, of course, that we were returned customers, but we felt that the remembrance expressed was genuine.

Nearby Anti-U.S. Demonstration

It was natural that Steve Little, with the U.S. Navy at the nearby Tachikawa Air Base, would come to visit us. His parents had been youth sponsors at the University Christian Church in Los Angeles when I was a young man. Steve enjoyed visiting in our home and at the church service at the public hall. One photo in my possession shows Steve attempting to use *ohashi* (chop sticks) during our fellowship after church. Akada Sensei, who was gradually working into the pastor's role, was coaching him.

Steve's visit was interrupted when a radio communication from the Tachikawa Commander ordered all military personnel to

Pastor Akada is coaching Steve Little, from Al's home church, on how to use *Ohashi* (chop sticks).

return to their stations because an anti-American demonstration was imminent. To save time I drove Steve to the base hoping that he would be through the gates before trouble started. We were too late! As we approached we could see thousands of red-band wearing marchers closing ranks around the base. They were carrying signs in crude English, such as, "Yankee, go home." I parked the car some distance away, wondering what to do next.

"I'm going to give it a try!" exclaimed Steve as he got out of the car and headed toward the marchers, who were now chanting anti-American slogans as they circled around the base. I felt I should go with my guest and followed as he blended in with the marchers, imitating their cadence. As he moved with them, I felt compelled to follow. Nearby demonstrators must have thought we were sharing their cause for they looked at us approvingly. Suddenly, Steve caught the eye of a sentry inside of the base fence and began his move toward a closed gate immediately ahead. Moving quickly, Steve darted through a small opening created by the sentry, and I found myself feeling very alone in the midst of the shouting demonstrators. During a momentary distraction I slipped away and hastened back to my parked car.

The next day the news reported that violence had erupted between the police and the rioters. There were injuries on both sides and numbers who were arrested. It was difficult to estimate the extent of anti-American feelings during the mid-sixties. For the most part, it appeared that the pro-American government was in control. It was also clear that the majority of the Japanese were feeling very insecure about the war raging in Southeast Asia.

Japan's Underlying Fear

A few years earlier, Lt. Comdr Wayne Comstock, a Navy pilot, visited us with his wife, Donna. Wayne and Donna had attended San Jose Bible College at the same time as ourselves. When Wayne heard that I was making a scheduled trip, traveling the length of Japan to Tanegashima, he asked if he could go along. He hadn't yet seen much of the country and, if workable, he was hoping we could stop off at Hiroshima, the first city to experience the atom bomb. Wayne received the necessary permission for a leave of absence and I made preparations for the eight day round trip south.

Wayne was delighted to learn of the availability of Japanese *obento* (box lunch) at Japanese train stations. He found that the assortment of rice rolls, fish cake, a hardboiled egg and Japanese pickles made a tasty lunch. Using the *ohashi* (chop sticks) was a challenge and the disposable tea pot was fascinating. He kept the fragile tea pot for a souvenir, and made mental notes on the reasonable price of his meal. It was fun to serve as guide to someone who so relished first time experiences.

We reserved a room in a hotel near the Peace Museum in Hiroshima. The city had been rebuilt and to learn the story of its traumatic destruction on August 6, 1945 one needed to view the extensive display of photos and artifacts at the museum. I became aware that my friend was very sensitive to human suffering. As a Navy pilot he was introspective about the nature of his military duties. It was a pilot of a B-29 that dropped the atom bomb on this city which resulted in an estimated 92,000 killed or missing. Many others suffered from ongoing genetic problems due to the high level of residual radiation.

Lt Cmdr Wayne Comstock, a former classmate of Al's.

Large graphic photos portrayed the devastating destruction. Four and one half square miles of the city had been leveled. Only shadows of former human beings were imprinted on the ground. Ghastly burns covered the bodies of surviving victims, children as well as adults. The physical damage to buildings, steel railroad cars and tracks, and all foliage was complete. Only a steel framed dome structure at the epicenter survived as a skeleton. After viewing the effects of the atom bomb one can understand the underlying fear of the Japanese toward modern warfare.

Symbols of Peace

O*rigami*, the ancient Japanese art of paper folding is especially popular with the children. Colored paper, about six inches square, are folded into simple figures such as a balloon, crane, frog, or a Japanese helmet. The story is often told of Sadako Chan, a victim of the radiation from the atomic bomb, who prayed that she would be healed before she folded 1,000 cranes. School children rallied to the challenge to fold paper cranes, but sadly the young victim died. Yet, to this day the paper crane remains a symbol of peace. Large displays of paper crane trees are to be seen near the peace museum and at public parks during days that commemorate the atomic bombing.

My traveling companion had been shaken by two things in Hiroshima. The graphic displays in the Peace Museum were upsetting to his sensitive nature. In fact, a feeling of depression overcame both of us. We were glad, of course, that the events at the close of the war led to the surrender of Japan on August 14, 1945. There are military experts who reason that had the bomb not been dropped more people would have been killed on both sides in a prolonged conflict. Wayne was also bothered by the extra day's charge the hotel attached to our bill for returning 20 minutes after the checkout time. As a newcomer to Japan he sensed a degree of hostility coming from the hotel attendants.

Somewhat subdued, we continued on our journey to Kagoshima City where we would catch a small plane to the island. To save time I had taken the small jumper flights to and from the island a number of times. The six hour boat trip could be exhausting because of the rough crossing. So, on our 45 minute flight, when my pilot friend kept groaning repeatedly, "Oh NO!", I asked for an explanation once we had landed. His quick response was, "We flew over water with no life jackets, and over mountains and into clouds with no radio! There was no reference to compass position and we landed on a dirt runway without any radio clearance!" I realized that my sense of peace in flying had been due to my ignorance.

The bus from Noma, where the landing strip is located, took us to the port town of Nishinoomote. Pastor and Mrs. Ikeda welcomed us and served us a well prepared meal. During our visit we were shown the progress of the kindergarten and rejoiced that they now had 80 students enrolled. It was encouraging to see the uniform wearing five-year-olds begin sessions with prayer. Although it was not Sunday, we met some of the church people, who created interesting conversation by asking Wayne all about himself and his family. I could see that the spontaneous love of the Christians was succeeding in making my first time visitor feel at home among the Japanese.

Since my Navy trained pilot friend was adverse to returning by plane we took the ship. A number of the Christians came to see

Pastor & Mrs. Ikeda Work as a Team

us off. For departing gifts they placed in our hands large stalks of Tanegashima bananas. These are smaller than the size which appear in the large city markets but they are delicious. I had my doubts that the delicate fruit would make it all the way back to suburban Tokyo. Trains are crowded and there is competition for space in the baggage racks. Also, it was tempting for me to either eat from the ripened clusters or offer some of its fruit to fellow passengers.

Wayne was determined to get his stalk of bananas home. In a way, it was his symbol of peace and friendship. I observed him repeatedly jump to his feet and rescue his bananas whenever a passenger was seen thrusting his baggage anywhere near the tender fruit. And so it was, by traveling six hours by ship, two days on a train pulled by steam locomotive and with transfer to electric commuter trains, that we made it back to suburban Tokyo with one stalk of bananas in good shape.

---

[1] This June 10, 1960 incident was triggered by the renewal of the Peace Treaty, which permitted the continuance of U.S. military bases in Japan.

Chapter Twenty Three

RELIGIOUS NEIGHBORS

Invitation to a Field Trip

"Hammond, could you join Harold Sims in teaching a few students in Tokyo who have not completed their requirements for graduation?" The request came from Martin Clark, the president of the Osaka Bible Seminary. My part in this proposed extension teaching was to teach a needed Bible course; Harold would be teaching a class on World Religions. On the day that Harold Sims decided on a field trip to visit area religious sites to learn first hand what they believed, our small class agreed to join them.

Local Temples and Shrines

We first started out on foot in the Nakano area of Tokyo. We didn't have to go far to find two **Zen Buddhist temples**. Zen Buddhism emphasizes focused meditation to attain enlightenment. It is known for its cultural contribution of immaculate rock gardens and tea ceremonies. Harold later described in an FECM article how these neighborhood Rinzai and Soto sects received us courteously and answered our somewhat impertinent questions with modest and straightforward answers. "How many come to your regular worship or lecture services?" "Very few – perhaps six or eight," answered the wife of the head priest. Apparently the master of the **Rinzai temple** was away that day teaching in a Buddhist University, which might account for their economic stability.

Adjacent to the **Soto Zen temple** was a kindergarten which was their chief source of income.

Next we visited a 300 year-old **Shingon (True Word) Buddhist temple**, in which was a small image of Buddha-Tathagata, believed to have power to heal illnesses. The daughter of one of the rulers of the Tokugawa feudal period was reported to have been healed by a visit to this temple, so the gifts donated in appreciation put it on a sound basis economically. But across the way was a **Shinto shrine** where we questioned a man, who expressed regrets at the loss of government support they had enjoyed prior to the end of the war. They received practically no income from parishioners; their current income was from the weddings they held. Generally speaking, Japanese citizens look to Buddhist temples to handle funerals, and consult Shinto shrines to handle weddings.

A local branch of the popular **Tenrikyo sect** was also located within walking distance. The lady priestess treated us very cordially, stressing the beauty of all religions cooperating and being kind to each other. Tenrikyo (The Religion of Heavenly Reason) is very much a syncretistic blend of Shintoism, Buddhism, and Christianity. It was begun by Miki Nakayama, who as a young girl in 1837 A.D. began to have revelations. In a vision she was reportedly appointed as a mediatrix between the gods and men. The revelations changed her life and she began to practice charity by giving all she had to the poor. About nine years later, Miki put these revelations into writing and began propagating her beliefs. At the same time she practiced healing and a method for having painless childbirth (Thomsen, p. 34).

Tenrikyo's teaching about creation parallels the mythology found in the *Kojiki*, and the *Nihon Shoki*, the foundation documents for the Shinto religion. But when they refer to the "Parent God" who miraculously saves, they echo Christian concepts. Over time, Miki, herself, becomes divine in the thinking of her followers, and on January 26 of each year they celebrate the Ascension of the Foundress, a doctrine that is strikingly similar to Catholic doctrine about Mary (Thompsen, pp. 37, 59).

Rapid Growth of the "New Religions"

After finishing our brief visits to the local shrines in Nakano Ward, we crowded into Harold's large station wagon and went to visit the headquarters of two of the fast growing "new religions" of post-war Japan. The immense Grand Temple of the **Rissho Kosei Kai** (The Society for the Establishment of Righeousness and Friendly Intercourse) loomed into sight as we entered the Suginami Ward. This huge edifice, completed in 1964 at the cost of over ten million dollars, is said to be the largest building for religious use in Asia (Thomsen, p. 119).

The burgeoning growth of this "new religion" may be due in large part to its foundation on the traditional nationalistic faith of **Nichiren Shu.** The invocation on a posted *kakimono* (oblong wall-hanging), *Namu Myoho Renge Kyo* ("Blessed be the law of the Lotus Scripture"), is the oft repeated chant of Nichiren believers. Nichiren was the Buddhist monk, who, in the face of the threat of invasion in the thirteenth century by Mongol fleets, prayed for a *kamikaze* (divine wind) to repel them. When a typhoon sank the enemy ships, Nichiren was assured of sainthood in Japanese Buddhism. In the desperate closing days of World War II, Japanese military leaders exploited the concept of the *kamikaze* to induce young patriotic men to fly their explosives laden Zeros into approaching allied warships. They found no lack of volunteers for these *kamikaze* suicide missions. These young men were literally to become the "divine wind" that would repel the allied invaders. This patriotic idealism still runs deep in spite of an intense desire for peace in postwar Japan.

While retaining the symbols of Japanese loyalty, **Rissho Kosei Kai** adds a unique adaptation of the Japanese *hoza* (small group counseling). On four carpeted floors of the main hall thousands of parishioners gather in small groups, asking practical questions about daily life and getting helpful answers explained in Buddhist terms. The Japanese traditional reserve is overcome in the context of these friendly discussion groups held daily from nine to three p.m. Thomsen gives an example of a typical question and the response:

> Q: I always seem to have a bad cold. What can I do to get rid of it so I can do more efficient work and be more happy?
>
> A: You believe in Buddha, but you are thinking too much of yourself. If you try every day to do your utmost to bring   our religion to others, your cold will disappear. Your egoism is the cause of your sickness, and when the cause disappears, the result will also disappear. [1]

Although we were impressed by the counseling sessions we were perplexed by the casual way our guide discussed the construction costs of the giant Buddha image on the floor of the hall. While he was chatting away like a Cadillac salesman he seemed oblivious of the Japanese worshippers who were kneeling or lying prostrate on the floor.

Our last visit was to the Tokyo headquarters of the **Soka Gakkai** (Value Creation Society). This continues to be the fastest growing of the "new religions" with a membership of over ten million at the time of our visit. Similar to Rissho Kosei Kai it is founded upon the teachings of Nichiren, but it is known for its extreme intolerance of other forms of Buddhism. Their emphasis on the Lotus Scripture excludes all other Buddhist sutras. This radical form of Nichiren Shoshu got its second start in 1956 under the leadership of Josei Toda. With its emphasis on lay leadership it gained influence among the workers and trade unions.

Under an earlier leader, Makiguchi, this exclusivistic group refused to worship Amatersu-o-mikami, the Sun Goddess, during the jingoistic nationalistic period leading up to World War II. Mikiguchi and a large number of his followers were jailed for this affront to the "ancestor of the Emperor." Makiguchi died in prison, but Toda, who had been director general when Makiguchi was president, took over the leadership during the postwar period when the political atmosphere had softened. Before Toda died in 1958 he had planned for the election campaign which would put Soka Gakkai candidates into the Upper House (Thomsen, pp. 84-85). Under Daisaku Ikeda's leadership Toda's political thrust was strengthened and missionary efforts extended their faith into over 100 nations.

Taiseki-ji at the foot of Mt. Fuji is the main headquarters of the Soka Gakkai. The six-story building has a huge main hall that can accommodate six thousand people. In March 1958, at the inauguration of the Grand Kodo, more than 2,000,000 gathered. Most of them would have the deep seated conviction that the teachings of Nichiren and Soka Gakkai are the answer for the future of the Japanese people (Thompsen, p. 86).

At the office headquarters in Tokyo we were made to wait a long time before anyone came to answer our questions. Eventually two representatives came and announced curtly that they had only a short time to give us. I marveled at Harold Sim's poise and his politely phrased questions which he gave in fluent Japanese. All of us, however, were turned off at the arrogant manners and boastful responses of the Soka Gakkai officials. They asserted that their group took no offerings and yet was the fastest growing, and they never had any problems with doctrine or morals. The humility and openness we had encountered in other groups was entirely lacking.

Harold's comments printed in our quarterly magazine summed up our feelings. "This laymen's organization has nothing but scorn for all other religious groups, and nothing but organization and showmanship for religious doctrine. Their claim to be growing at the rate of 100,000 families a month is the inspiration that keeps them going. The leaders we talked to were chain smokers and gave every indication of nervous energy and extreme tension. The danger to democracy and even peace in Asia, if this movement which recently formed a political party in Japan comes to power is obvious, but I don't feel any danger religiously speaking" (FECM, Vol 5, No 4).

Reflections on Approach

Our visits to key religious sites and subsequent research raised questions in my mind about how to approach our religious neighbors. What helpful things did we learn about their motivation? What made the so-called "new religions" grow? My reflections and questions are enumerated below:

1) First, we need to understand that Japanese are motivated the same as other people. They want to prepare for and strengthen the marriage ties of their young adults. It is to be expected that they follow centuries-old traditions and make arrangements for a Shinto ceremony with its understood symbols. When their grandparents or parents die it is also customary to seek the help and consolation of the Buddhist priest. Such customs bind the family together. How can we show our appreciation for their family values, while at the same time point to the deeper foundational truth of a relationship with the Creator of all people?

2) It is a fair assumption that one of the chief reasons for the phenomenal growth of the 'new religions' is their emphasis on national identity. The Japanese people were shocked and depressed from the loss of the war. A revival of the national pride cultivated in the Nichiren-type of faith struck a common chord.

3) We therefore realize that the fast growing groups have built upon existing indigenous cultural symbols. Christianity's slow growth in Japan is said to be because it is associated with western culture and is perceived as a foreign religion. What can be done at this late date in our historical development to remove

the distinguishing marks of western identity in order to present the unadorned Gospel of Christ?

4) What can we missionaries do to avoid our non-intended emphasis on "extraction evangelism" and reach families for Christ? Does this mean, as some of our Japanese pastors imply, that we should slow down, wait and pray for the whole family, before we follow through with an individual seeker?

5) Last but foremost, I believe that the Scriptures point to a positive approach of friendship evangelism. The Apostles did not attack the opposing religions of their day but sought to build bridges of communication in order to preach Christ (Acts 17:23-30; 19:37).

Note: During the years I taught World Religions at San Jose Christian College I invited priests from the *Jodo Shinshu* (Pure Land Sect) Buddhist church in nearby Japan Town to tell us what they believe. This is one of the more popular forms of Buddhism and it has adapted itself to American culture. They refer to their temple as a church, sing hymns, and have classes and social fellowships similar to U.S. churches. Some of their teaching reflects cultural borrowing from Nestorian Christianity in the opinion of some scholars.[2] We had common ground in affirmation of moral and family values and in desires for peace in the world. However, they expressed agnostic views on the existence of God.

---

[1] Harry Thompson, "The New Religions of Japan," Charles E. Tuttle Company, Tokyo, Japan, 1963, p. 21

[2] Yoon Kwon Chae, "The First Christian Mission to China and its Influence on Oriental Civilization," CPO Box 1728, Seoul, Korea, 1997.

Chapter Twenty Four

A DIFFICULT QUESTION

Invitation to Visit Taipei

The four hour flight from Tokyo had been broken in routine only by a short stopover in Osaka before the China Airline's jet touched its wheels down at the International Airport in Taipei. Leaving the air conditioned plane, I was immediately enveloped by the hot, humid July air as I walked toward the custom's section of the air terminal. Looking about for familiar faces, I found none. I realized that this could be explained because of the hour's difference between Tokyo and Taipei.

Processing through Chinese customs reminded me of my Japan experiences –the bored look of the polite petty officials, the unintelligible rasp of blaring loud speakers, the disconcerted looks of hot, perspiring passengers, and an attempted semblance of order amidst general confusion. "That's all Sir; he'll take your bags." I saw my baggage being carried away by a uniformed porter. I hurried to catch up. Not having any Taiwan currency I tipped the porter with one of the few dollar bills that my wife had thoughtfully put in my wallet. With the look of a man who had just received a bonus he darted out of sight. Apparently I had already made somebody happy by my visit.

"Hi Al!, did you think we weren't coming?" Isabel Dittemore's familiar voice broke through my reverie as I stood gazing at the myriads of small red taxis, buses, and pedicabs that ducked in and out of the terminal's entrance way. It was good to see an old friend. We had first met Isabel when we came to Japan in the spring of 1954. Often she had mentioned her earlier work in

China, so we were not too surprised that she was drawn back to work among the Chinese she so dearly loved.

Isabel hailed a cab and gave the shirtless driver instructions in Mandarin. In thirty minutes the little Japanese Datsun made it through the turmoil of Taipei's traffic and brought us to her rented home. "Al, you know Lillian, don't you?" urged Isabel

Isabel Dittemore with Gladys Aylward In Taipei;
both had served in China.

as she introduced a small Afro-American lady with a gleaming white smile. We had met Lillian once before when she had come through Tokyo five years earlier. Harold Gallagher, minister of the Kaimuki Christian Church in Honolulu, had asked us to meet her at the airport when she came through en route to Taiwan. "Lillian Martin is a dedicated servant of God and our missionary to Formosa," Harold had written. She was going to help Gladys Aylward, the famed missionary lady of the true-life story entitled, "The Small Woman." In response to the call to help needy orphans, Lillian had quit her job, sold her home, and went to work in a Gladys Aylward orphanage for a term of service.

Lillian had now returned endeavoring to establish an orphanage work in close cooperation with the church program of Mrs. Dittemore. Being a nurse and a registered physical therapist, she was fully qualified to serve in this benevolent program. Isabel and Lillian made an impressive team as they labored together to strengthen the Christian work. Their unconscious acceptance of one another was an unspoken message of the victory of the gospel over racial differences.

The Purpose of My Visit

During the weekend I learned about their radio and orphanage work, and met many of the Chinese. I was introduced to Luke Lin, the medical student who would be my interpreter at camp. My invitation and purpose in Taiwan at this time was to help with the annual Christian service camp. The missionary ladies especially felt the need for a man around as special speaker, and to supervise the boys and to take an active part in the sports. Alan Bemo, Isabel's son-in-law, had filled the gap admirably during a year of missionary internship. But now he and his lovely wife and baby had returned to the states to finish their schooling. At first the task sounded fairly heavy. I was to be dean of men, teach classes, hold down the evening speaking spot, and participate in sports. But as it turned out, the group that gathered in the mountains was family size, and we had a relaxed and enjoyable fellowship.

The days at camp were hectic but happy. Cool mountain air was kept fresh by frequent rains. The camp site had been improvised, but we lacked for nothing. We stayed in an aging hotel, sleeping on straw mat floors similar to Japanese style. A nearby park provided a volleyball court, tennis court and swimming pool. A neighboring Lutheran church offered us the use of their building for chapel and vesper services. We ate economically planned meals in the small restaurant of the hotel. My stomach has some conservative tendencies so I was secretly relieved when Mike, the son of an American military family that was attending the camp, shared his bread and peanut butter with me.

Questions About Science and Faith

I enjoyed the fellowship of the Chinese students very much. They appreciated having the opportunity to exercise their English on someone who did not know any Mandarin. The questions of the non-Christian students were candid and revealed that they were not unlike young people around the world who are swayed by the overstated claims of scientific humanism and are given only a caricature of Christian perspectives. During my speaking sessions I approached this need and encouraged questions. For the most part this was a fruitful time however; I found a question asked by a medical student difficult to answer to their satisfaction.

"Why did God make tigers and mosquitoes?" I wondered if the student was being facetious but his facial expression was most earnest. "Don't tigers eat missionaries?" he queried as if he remembered such an account. Then looking about for support for his question, he asserted, "Mosquitoes make life miserable for everyone." A number of the students nodded assent to this last statement as they displayed the bites on their arms and legs. I elevated the question to that of all human suffering as answered in the Book of Job, and talked for some length of time but felt that my points were not connecting.

Reviewing in my mind some of the science/faith issues I encountered during my college years, I decided to share with the students some of my own personal journey of faith. This proved more effective than philosophical discussions. I related the shock I experienced when I looked up a respected friend who had mentored me in the faith only to find that he had lost his. Later, in retrospect, I realized that my friend had shored up his faith with apologetics that were anti-science in nature and filled with overstatements about what the Bible says.

From there I gave them the perspective that general revelation, which we gain from nature, and special revelation in the Bible, should have points of agreement. God has revealed his power and everlasting divinity in nature (Romans 1:20), and has shown his redemptive love in Scripture (John 3:16). Conflicts between science and Christian faith occur when science oversteps its boundaries and makes assertions of faith, or when Christians insert quasi-science conclusions into their interpretations of Scripture. I urged openness and an honest survey of options in the science/faith controversy. This kind of thinking met with the approval of the medical students.

In response to the request that I take part in sports I agreed to play tennis with one of the taller students. I felt at home when playing volleyball and usually enjoyed that group game immensely, but I had not played tennis before. After a brief lesson on holding the racquet and hitting with a follow through motion, I offered to give it a try. I sensed that my agile teacher was making it easier for me by nudging the ball in the direction of my right arm. A chorus of encouraging watchers encouraged me at the times when I returned the ball more or less acceptably over the net. For a bit I was deceived into thinking that I was a natural. Later I learned that my gentle opponent was the tennis champion at his college.

Pro-American Journalism

In reading the **China Post**, an English daily published in Taipei, I was pleasantly surprised by the sympathetic view toward American foreign policy that was revealed in most issues. In Japan we have often been disturbed by what appears to us as one-sided reporting. I have become more convinced that the claim made by the head of the Journalism Department at Sophia University in Tokyo, that Japanese journalists lean to the left, is true. Of course, I want the truth and care little for sophistry. But it appeared to me that the **China Post** was projecting a more accurate image of America than other Asian journals. As a missionary, I am most interested in this fact from the standpoint of the favorable communication atmosphere that is thereby created for the work of missionaries sent from America.

Because of the current pro-American sentiment, especially by the scattered overseas Chinese, there is an open door and an opportunity of growing dimensions for effective Christian service. I could not help but reflect as my Japan Airline's jet took me homeward to my own field of service, that we must not neglect the opportunities that providentially open to us. If we believe that Christ is the answer to the greatest need of men, and that New Testament Christianity apart from Western additives is the means, then we had better stand behind and encourage the workers that are in strategic places of service.

An Eye Opening Response

In giving my report of my week's stay in Taiwan to our church folk in Tokyo, I mentioned the difficult question of the medical student who asked, "Why did God make tigers and mosquitoes?" After giving my complex answer from the Book of Job and getting the same puzzled response, I welcomed the practical thoughts offered by the Japanese believers. They didn't seem to have confusion about why God made tigers; for they were part of God's beautiful and varied creation of animal life. If a missionary was eaten by a tiger it was his own fault for getting too close to a hungry animal.

The question about mosquitoes remained until Hideko Domen raised her hand and offered the insights of a blind person. "Don't mosquitoes live in dark, damp places?" she asked. "Yes, that's right," we affirmed. "Then, God made mosquitoes to keep us out of dark, damp places," she concluded with a smile. Heads everywhere in the room nodded, and then Hideko's contagious joy burst into laughter and spread throughout the whole group. It felt good to be home.

Chapter Twenty Five

REFLECTIONS ON METHODS

Convictions on Mission Methods

Mark Maxey's convictions about missionary methods are made clear in a book he published entitled, *History of the Philippine Mission*. Originally a B.D. thesis, it is a detailed record of the United Christian Missionary Society (UCMS) and the independent missionary work until the end of World War II. The UCMS, representing the growing liberal emphasis of the Disciples of Christ, agreed to open-membership and comity agreements. Apparently, they arbitrarily dismissed missionaries who did not agree with them, which resulted in their separation from the UCMS and the forming of independent missions. This widened the breach between liberals and conservatives in the Christian Church movement.

Writing a decade later, Woodrow Phillips, at that time head of the missions department at Ozark Bible College, redefined the approach of the growing independent missions as, "the direct support method." He affirmed that, "the local church is the responsible selecting, sending, and supporting agency in direct support missions." Professor Phillips suggested six principles that undergird the Direct Support Method:

1) **It is in accord with the missionary principles of the New Testament.** Phillips acknowledges that the new covenant scriptures contain little concerning methods in missions. He goes on to say, "What records are to be discerned describe the local assembly, under the guidance of the

Holy Spirit, selecting, sending and supporting those who went."

2) **This method is historically commended.** He pointed out that the early church succeeded in reaching the Roman world without any missionary agencies, outside of the local assemblies.

3) **It has gained pragmatic sanction.** At the time of his writing the number of missionaries of the independent movement had grown to 865. Hundreds of new churches had been started and thousands of converts had been won.

4) **It allows for full individual freedom.** Woodrow stresses that the initiative of the individual has been the key that has sparked missions. The sending church is free to correct the missionary. This permits a freedom of action that produces growth.

5) **It possesses a mobility not equaled in any other mission method.** Once a vision is caught, the missionary with the help of his supporting church can immediately enter a ripe field and follow the harvest. Decisions for expansion are not hindered by organizational machinery.

6) **The Direct Support Method of missions retains for the local church complete control of its missionary program.** Phillips affirms that "the success of the direct support method is based on the principal of integrity... Outside of the New Testament and the Christ it reveals to us, we believe there is no higher authority than the local congregation" (FECM Vol 6, No 4).

A Middle Ground Position

A number of conservative observers, while acknowledging the central role of the local church, still felt the need for a faith based mission agency. Independent missions were encountering problems which the local church could not easily manage. Mission support for a given field was usually solicited from numerous congregations. It was not always clear as to which one was the sponsoring church. Who was the missionary accountable to when reports came about misconduct or methods lacking integrity? What guidance and help could the untrained elders of a local church give to the new recruit, who was having difficulty making field choices and raising support? When a growing number had these kinds of reflections, Christian Missionary Fellowship (CMF), a faith based agency was formed among independents.

This middle ground position confronted the forty-some direct support missionaries in Japan when the Bill Walker family arrived under the auspices of the CMF. Because of close family ties, the Walkers and the Claude Likins family raised support together and arrived at the same time. Bill felt it helpful to align with the CMF; Claude came direct support. Both had solid faith and congenial personalities. Yet, for a time, tensions existed between the newcomers and the direct support old-timers. History had left a residue of suspicion and mistrust of mission agencies because of the heavy handedness of the UCMS. Could that be overcome?

The area prayer meetings of the Tokyo missionaries helped bring healing. The new missionaries were having adjustment pains. Just before coming to Japan, Claude and Evalyn Likins had lost a son in an auto accident; yet they came, feeling that the tragedy was a test of their faith. In the States Bill Walker was known as an articulate and popular speaker; now he was honestly confessing that he did not have a gift for learning the difficult Japanese language. As these and other painful adjustments were revealed the missionary community reached out to them.

Bill and his wife, Lois, made a move that helped continue the bonding between the Tokyo missionaries and their English-speaking friends. With the permission and blessing of Stan and Mabel Buttray, they began an early Sunday morning worship at the centrally located Kamiochiai church. There was healing in Bill's familiar American vernacular for tired missionaries and their families that, for the most part, had been locked into Japanese speaking communities. The children were drawn to English speaking companions of their own age. Parents shared their problems with their understanding peers. Teachers and some military personnel from the nearby military bases began coming. Japanese with English speaking ability enjoyed the fellowship. The sense of community was strengthened. Differences in mission methods were not forgotten but seen as secondary in the context of meeting pragmatic human need.

The Testimony of Christian Example

William Thompson, then the Director of CMF, visited Japan and later wrote an article for our Open Forum. In an effort to bring understanding of the background problems he pointed out that the motive behind *ecumenism* (the movement to bring the divided church into one house) was to overcome sectarianism. He went on to show that he was aware of its weaknesses in his article, "Missionary Methods in A Changing World." One paragraph especially caught my eye:

> Nevertheless, the ambivalence of ecumenism tends to threaten the evangelistic objective of Christ. Religious conviction usually arises out of the careful Christian example and doctrinal teaching found in the local congregation. It becomes easy for an undue emphasis on ecumenism to blunt this evangelistic fervor. Ecumenism as a spirit designed to eradicate sectarianism by the presentation of Christ is good. If, however, a least common denominator

philosophy replaces spiritual conviction, it will be detrimental to the life of the Christian and of the church (FECM Vol 6, No 4, p 202).

When, after exploratory surgery, it was reported that Lois Walker's condition was "medically hopeless," all the missionaries joined in prayer. Six weeks after therapy with Cobalt 60, the radiologists believed they were successful. There was relief and rejoicing in Japan. The Christian example which arises from the teaching of the local church of which Bill Thompson spoke was clearly evident in the cheerful service that Lois had given to the community. Yet for reasons that we do not understand, God eventually took Lois home, and the prayers were then directed to support her grief-stricken husband and children. The subject of mission sending methods did not seem relevant.

The Power of Self Criticism

At the invitation of a missionary acquaintance, affiliated with the Church of God in Anderson, Indiana, I attended the **Hayama Seminar**. This is an open study fellowship at a resort south of Tokyo attended annually by Japan missionaries from a cross-section of all the various Christian groups. For the most part I was impressed favorably by the spirit and content of the meetings. Respect was given to every person, and the speakers represented both sides of the issues. No one had to compromise his convictions, nor condone things with which he might disagree. It was mutually understood that the basic thing was to provide an opportunity for open discussion in the spirit of Christ that God might give us better understanding and unity.

However, I could not help but observe that some who presented study papers and took part in the discussions revealed attitudes that were self-vindicating with regard to their particular group or position. Others revealed their ability to be candidly self-critical. Those who endeavored to justify their group position were not exclusive in their thinking, and they did give us information to correct possible misconceptions. But my personal impression was that their contribution was limited in value because of its nature as an apologetic for a particular distinctive in Christendom.

On the other hand, I was moved and challenged by those participants, who revealed insights about newly discovered truths that cost them something – they were not afraid of being frankly critical of their own group's shortcomings. The former type of speaker, it seems to me, tended to justify his particularism by appealing unconsciously to the relative nature of truth. The latter, however, appeared to be more aware of the source of spiritual authority and of the need for submission to biblical corrective. **Their position reflected the truth that Kingdom boundaries transcend denominational walls.**

Correctives that are projected from the 'outside' are seldom heeded or appreciated. We are reminded of various mission friends, who have made tours of the mission fields in Asia and then later passed on their criticisms to others. These half-digested perspectives usually contain enough truth to make the critic feel like an authority, but they often also contain generalizations that do great injustice to the work and the laborers.

An accurate appraisal of the work on any given field must necessarily be made by one who has shared the daily mission stress for a good number of years. This is to say that criticism is most effective in its influence for good when it comes from the inside. **Constructive group self-criticism is the great need of the hour**. It can function to eliminate the self-appointed 'expert' and it alone can warm hearts and win friends from the other side of man-made fences (FECM Vol 8, No 1).

As I apply this principal of constructive self-criticism to our Direct Support Missions, I first feel compelled to honor those persons who have worked to make it effective. The volunteer forwarding secretaries have been the key individuals who have given integrity to the financial receipting and reporting necessary to any enterprise. Doris Isbell faithfully served our needs, although she was busy as a secretary for the Bible College at that time.

Next on my list would be Harrold McFarland and those who followed him, who established Mission Services, and published Horizons magazine. Fresh in my memory is the way they made our needs known while in Japan, especially when they publicized the emergency conditions that occurred following a typhoon. We never felt alone.

One constructive criticism is that for a time we confused the means for sending missionaries with the doctrinal issues involved in the liberal/fundamentalist controversies of the 1920's and '30s. Some linked mission agencies themselves with apostasy. A study of mission history should put this notion to rest. Paul's declaration in I Corinthians 9:22, "I have become all things to all men, that I may by **all means** save some," affirms the principle of freedom of method.

Exercising this freedom of method, **Team Expansion**, an innovative mission organization, was born in 1978 after a three year period of prayer. Horizons magazine reports that they have become the largest missionary sending agency in the Christian Churches.[1] Their community approach and cultured enthusiasm for mission needs worldwide has caught on with increasing numbers of Christian youth. We rejoice that they have recruited missionaries for Japan, and the ones we know have an infectious enthusiasm that gives hope for the future.

---

[1] Horizons, December 2006, pp. 4-15.

Chapter Twenty Six

CROSS CULTURAL MARRIAGE

Attractive Japanese Women

A consensus of observant American men is that women in Japan are petite, pretty and proper. Only some of them are knockout beauties, but most of them are trim, well dressed, and agile. The ladies joke about their legs as being shaped like turnips (*daikon ashi*), that is, short and stocky. But their charming smiles and twinkling eyes have unsettled many a young man's heart. A US navy man from a nearby base, Tom Smith,[1] met one of our young ladies when he visited our Christian Camp and was smitten.

"Is it O.K. to date a Japanese gal?" he asked. "Only recently has Japanese culture tolerated the concept of dating," I replied. "Remember, that the traditional custom has been to closely moderate boy/girl relationships, and marriages are still to a considerable degree arranged by the families." "Oh, I am not talking about marriage!" Tom quickly corrected his intentions. "I mean is it O.K. to have a casual relationship like going to the movies?" "If from the start you make it clear that you are only establishing a friendly relationship, and keep everything in the open, it may be O.K.," I responded. Tom was a Christian and I felt his basic honesty would restrain inappropriate behavior.

From Friendship to Courtship

Kiyoko and I are thinking about marriage and wanted your advice." Tom's comment took me off guard. I suppose it was my preoccupation with the mission work that had blinded me to the cues that indicated cupid had been at work. Tom and

Kiyoko had been attending an English speaking church together. Also, Tom had frequented our home and had long talks with Eleanor about domestic roles. I believe that she knew before I did that marriage was on Tom's mind, but both of us felt that he needed to have clarification about what that meant.

"G.I.'s think that marrying a Japanese gal is going to give them a built-in servant, someone who brings their slippers to them every morning. That there will be a no-hassle arrangement in which the domesticated Asian wife caters to every whim of the dominant American male. This is a myth!" I stressed. "Kiyoko's father is the Director of a large business and he expects that his daughter will finish her college education. Also, any possible suitors would expect to be college graduates. Tom, you are dating a gal in an upper class family." My words shocked Tom, but didn't deter him from the goal of matrimony. He began to think about a college education.

"We talked to Kiyoko's Dad, and what you said about college was true. So we promised that Kiyoko would finish college and that I would also enroll in a college at the first opportunity." His words were impressively sincere, but I felt compelled to go on and describe the cultural differences between Japan and America. I asked if he would study their culture and learn of Kiyoko's expectations from marriage. He affirmed that he would do so. Kiyoko also felt that they had the green light from her parents.

Fear of Formal Ceremony

One reason that mission service appealed to me over church ministry in the states was that I imagined I would not be involved with marrying and burying. I felt more at home with the informal settings of teaching or evangelism and tensed up with formalities that demanded proper dress clothes with ties. Japanese ceremonies are even more formal and exacting as to what is expected of the minister during marriages or funerals.

Okabe Sensei helped me put together the message for my first Japanese Christian wedding held in the rural town of Kushira.

My use of Japanese was quite limited at that time, and Okabe's insistence on my using very formal Japanese wording in the ceremony only increased the stress. I studied hard and practiced extensively and somehow survived without any obvious blunders. I appreciated the longsuffering of the Japanese church members and the happy smiles of the couple who tied the knot.

At a later time, I was asked to use both English and Japanese during a ceremony for a Japanese Christian woman and a Swiss man, whose friends could understand the English but not the Japanese. My Japanese had improved by that time but I still felt stress during the wedding feast when they served *sake* for the toast to the new couple. My wife and I do not drink wine of any kind, not because we thought the Bible taught absolute abstinence, but because we had scruples about causing anyone to stumble. When the toastmaster asked everyone to pick up their wine glasses and toast the couple, I interpreted this into English, but we both picked up our tea cups. This caused the M.C. to repeat the request and to describe the Sake glass as containing the clear liquid. We held tightly to our tea cups and faithfully interpreted his request into English. The Japanese probably excused our actions on the basis of the foreigner's ignorance of custom.

The pastor in attendance spoke up to ease our embarrassment. "Reverend and Mrs. Hammond have taken a Nazirite vow," he explained, "we almost made them break their vows." "Oh, we are so sorry," exclaimed the gathered guests, as they bowed from their seated positions. With relief we telegraphed a "No harm done" expression on our faces and indicated we were ready to begin participating in the banquet set before us.

When we reflected on our role at the wedding we wondered if we had done the right thing. We could have raised our wine glasses and only pretend to sip the contents. However, a visit to my English-Bible class by several of the young men wedding guests made me think our actions served a purpose. Reminding me of our actions at the feast a spokesman for the three who attended my class, said, "We appreciated your convictions. In Japan we are pressured into drinking too much sake to please our employers and to close business deals. It was refreshing to see someone just say, 'No.'"

Traditional Japanese Weddings

The Japanese traditional wedding is attended only by family and friends. There has been little change in the wedding attire over the years. The bride wears a pure white gown (*shiro maku*) and has a large bonnet on her head covering a traditional hair style dressed with combs and ornaments. (A humorous reminder shared by Japanese friends was that the large hat served the purpose of covering the bride's horns). A Shinto priest officiates at the brief ceremony and solemnizes the vows. The assent of bride and groom is affirmed by the sharing of three glasses of Sake. Following the short ceremony the bridal couple proceeds to greet the guests at a lengthy reception party where exquisite food is served. The bride may change from the very expensive archaic wedding dress to a colorful kimono or perhaps a modern western dress. The brides are prepared to change clothes at least three times during their wedding day.[2]

During the post war period there has been a growing adaptation of western wedding practices. Movies and Television have romanticized the marriage ceremonies so it is not surprising to see the practices of the Japanese couple closing the ceremony with a kiss, running through a shower of rice en route to the reception party, and cutting and sharing portions of the wedding cake. The bride may also throw a flower bouquet over her shoulder at the group of unmarried ladies anticipating the early marriage of the one who catches it. So popular are these romantic images that a plethora of wedding chapels have been built throughout Japan that offer western style ceremonies.

Increase In Cross Culural Weddings

Marriage between Japanese and foreigners was rather rare in the 1960's but by the year 2001 the Japan Times reported 39,700 international marriages.[3] American GI's marrying Japanese women was the more common statistic in the early period. But in recent time the higher percentage of these marriages are between Japanese men and women from other Asian countries. A major reason for this may be that many Japanese women find it more attractive to work and earn money for their own enjoyment rather than become restricted domestic persons.

When commoners marry royalty there is not always a storybook ending. Young people were saddened by the reported loss of freedom and self-expression experienced by Michiko Shoda after she married Japan's crown prince in 1959. Similar isolation is being experienced by the present crown princess, Masako. A recent novel intimates a parallel between Princess Diana's problems in Britain and those of the imperial wives in Japan.[4]

I considered the request by Tom and Kiyoko in the mid 1960's for me to perform their wedding ceremony to be an honor. I overcame my apprehensions and prepared for a bilingual Christian ceremony. I felt more assured that their marriage would last because both were believers and their parents had given their blessings.

They did keep their word and Tom eventually finished college. They moved to California and were blessed with four children. Tom and Kiyoko both worked to provide for them, enduring long commutes. I was saddened to hear in recent correspondence that there had been a breakup. American culture is not currently known for being supportive of stable marriage patterns. Thankfully, Kiyoko writes that the youngsters are doing well.

---

[1] Pseudonyms are used to protect the privacy of the couple discussed.

[2] Japan Traditional Weddings, http://www.japan-guide.com/e/e2061,html

[3] The Japan Times, February 8, 2004.

[4] Book Review: "The Commoner," by Charles Mathews, San Jose Mercury News, February 10, 2008.

Chapter Twenty Seven

INNOVATIVE WOMEN

Lessons from the YMCA

With my encouragement, Shigeru Akada, a graduate of Osaka Bible Seminary, was gradually doing more of the preaching in our suburban Tokyo church. Since he was Tokyo-born, his speech and demeanor fit in well with our members. This opened up more time on my schedule, so when Muto Sensei contacted me about the need for a chaplain at the Tokyo YMCA I thought I would inquire further. I learned that they simply wanted short devotions in English brought during their chapel times, and a series of messages during their summer camp. They expected, of course, that I would interact with the students as they tried to use their conversational English. Since the largest program at Tokyo's YMCA was the English school, many of the students were non-Christians with business careers in mind, and the greater number appeared to be women. I considered the position an opportunity for outreach.

Most of the students had been exposed to years of English grammar study and could read at a high school level. However, they lacked opportunity for hearing and speaking English. Since no chairs were provided during the chapel period, large numbers stood about in small clusters in the spacious hall as they faced forward. I stood on a platform equipped with a speaker's stand. To give them a visual focus I hung large sheets of white paper from the pulpit upon which I wrote key English words in large black letters related to my short biblical messages.

During most chapel sessions the expression on the faces of both male and female students appeared strained as they tried to grasp the meaning of the spoken English. A few nodded their understanding, and a time or two my humor appeared to connect with larger numbers. I looked forward to the summer camp when there would be more time to get feedback and to clarify the Christian ideals I was trying to present. Since the camp would be attended mostly by girls, I asked permission to bring my daughters along. I felt this would afford an opportunity to bond more closely with Sharon and Mary, and the contribution of two bilingual American youngsters would add interest to the camp.

On a bright summer day my girls piled into our Nissan Cedric chatting with excitement as we drove several hours to the cool higher elevation of the YMCA camp. I was impressed with the well constructed facilities and the colorfully painted totem poles on the grounds. The appearance of out-houses gave the otherwise fairly modern structures a rustic setting. I was awed by the gathering of some 150-200 active young adults, most of who were women, but reassured by the efficient organization that kept the schedule moving.

The relaxed camp atmosphere permitted better communication. Thanks to my daughters' companionship, rather than being portrayed as a demanding teacher I was perceived as a doting father. In the daily outdoor chapel sessions I was permitted to use a bilingual approach, clarifying my English with Japanese equivalents. Scheduled outside barbecues in small groups settings gave additional opportunities for informal conversation. I learned that they had some good cooks in the making.

Somewhat like our annual Motosu Christian camp they had evening skits and talent shows. We learned something of Japanese culture and they were introduced to the antics of my pre-teen and teen-aged daughters. Appearing with make-up and make shift costuming they put on a mini-vaudeville show. I remember thinking that I wished their mother had been there – either to talk them out of it, or to reassure me that they were quite normal. The campers seemed to enjoy the innovative performance, although a few of them now looked at me with raised eyebrows. It was good for me to get to know my two giggly, fun loving girls at this stage of their lives, and I had the privilege of seeing them grow into beautiful mature ladies.

A Dedicated Sumo Fan

Andrew and Betty Patton are gracious people. They let me use an upstairs room of the Higashi Nakano Church for the mailing office of my magazine, and they helped with the printing of the English edition of the Pastoral Song that Muto Sensei and I were translating from Stephen Iijima's Japanese original. Andrew had been the president of the Tokyo Bible College. In later years Andy and Betty were in charge of the Shinshu Bible Camp which hosted large numbers of youth. Betty became known as an excellent cook. But her more broadly proclaimed reputation came from her intense interest in Japanese Sumo wrestling.

On one of my visits to the Patton's home behind the Higashi Nakano Church I came upon an impressive scene. The TV in their front room was loudly blaring out the news that one of the smallest wrestlers, Wakanohana, had won the Japan national tournament! Along with Andy and Betty a group of Japanese men onlookers appeared elated with the news. Betty was the focus of attention as the men looked at her with admiration. "Just like you said," exclaimed one of the onlookers, "the big contenders were no match for the tricky skill of Wakanohana." It was explained to me that Mrs. Patton had become so familiar with Japanese Sumo that she developed an ability to predict the winners.

I had not come to a place of appreciation for the sport of sumo wrestling. My background had given me the image of athletes that were disciplined and lean. Since being pushed out of the ring was a loss, professional sumo wrestlers devoured huge quantities of rice and beer in order to put on weight. As a rule, the heavier men were more difficult to shove. The image of the huge squatting sumo wrestler conflicted with my notion of the relationship of sports to health. Over time I came to understand that sumo was a clean sport and that tremendous skill and discipline were involved. More importantly, I realized that Betty Patton had discovered a meaningful point of contact in communicating with Japanese men.

Devotions With Depth

Tribal missionaries, CW and Lois Callaway, impressed me with their humility and long years of service. Since Lois had a gift for expressive writing I asked her to be the Devotional Editor

CW & Lois Callaway, seated behind young boy, were visiting Japan. Lois served as Devotional Editor for many years.

for our quarterly journal and requested a background sketch of their fields of service. She responded with the following note:

> We intended at first to go to Burma to work among the Rawang tribe that Robert Morse is now laboring among... The story of how the Lord used our time in Burma is a story in itself. Then, when refused a permanent visa for Burma we went on to China for one year of hard study of Chinese. The next two years our Chinese rusted while we studied the southern Thai, but then we began contacting the Yao tribal people who were our goal for evangelism and found they spoke Chinese. We then proceeded

to the mountains where we lived in a Yao tribal village for 7 years. During that time we learned Yao the hard way – just by listening to them...Now we are engaged in language analysis and in the initial stages of Bible translation and a literacy program. Talk about needing the gift of tongues!

Because of their patient adjustments to upsetting field changes during turbulent years in Asia, the Callaways made good role models for future missionaries. Lois became an innovative devotional editor for the magazine. She solicited devotional material from most of the fields of Asia. A number of the contributors were national leaders. All of this was done in the midst of busy schedules of tribal evangelism and translation work. Her emphasis on prayer helped set the tone for our attitude as we wrestled with controversial issues. An example of this is seen in an article by Yoon Kwon Chae, "The Dawn Prayer Meeting," the basis for church growth in Korea.

> For most Korean Christians, the church service starts at four o'clock in the morning every day... At the church, under the dim kerosene lights, the kneeling figures multiply —kneeling and praying with their heads almost touching the freezing floor. As the prayers increase, the voices heat the chilly air and even some sobbing can be heard. Then someone starts to sing. The rest join him. Once the song service starts, it hardly knows when to stop, until someone stands up and starts to read Scriptures. Thus starts the dawn prayer meeting.[1]

Traveling Secretary

Life had not been easy for Doris Isbell. Her husband had been killed in an auto accident when they were starting a church in Martinez, California. We knew her as one of the key secretaries at San Jose Bible College. She had a remarkable memory for names and in later years edited the Alumni news for the college. We benefited by her volunteer service as our forwarding secretary during our years in Japan. We were delighted to hear that friends had made it possible for her to make an Asian tour that included Japan, Korea, Okinawa, Formosa, Philippines, Hawaii, and Alaska.

The fact that we had initially begun our life in the ministry at the Martinez church which she and her husband had begun gave us a close relationship with Dot. Eleanor and I was only one couple who had served as ministers there. A number of students had done their best to continue the work. The maturity of Mr. and Mrs. Art Gott brought the church plant further along and they passed the ball on to us. Jim and Jean Francis assumed the leadership for the long haul after our decision to go to Japan. Dot had been the prayer warrior that had helped forge the links of the team that gave continuity and led to the ultimate establishment of a stable, growing congregation.

Since this was the chance of a lifetime, Dot Isbell made the most of her visit in Japan and other Asian countries. Her intent was to make available an updated collection of colored slides available to Bible college students and the members of U.S. supporting churches. We made sure that she met our friends and fellow missionaries in Tokyo by sponsoring a rally in the Onta public hall. I held down the home fires while Eleanor guided her to points of interest in the area. With our encouragement, Dot formed an alliance with single missionary, Exie Fultz, and traveled all the way to Kyushu and the island of Tanegashima!

Pastor Ikeda complied with the adventuresome ladies' request and guided them to the thatched roof mountain top home of Brother Sakae. Since the memorial service for his wife, Sakae San's home had become a preaching point. When Harold Sims had visited the island at the request of Pastor Ikeda and myself there were six confessions of faith during the various meetings. It was significant that two of the baptisms took place in this isolated village. An old timer said, "This is probably the first time this village has witnessed a Christian baptism since the creation of the world!"

What thrilled the ladies was the spiritual richness of Brother Sakae's testimony in the midst of what could be considered poverty. The small wooden home with the thatched roof had only one room. The dirt floor kitchen was not partitioned but merely a step down from the straw mat area. Utensils were sparse and cooking was done over a wood fire. The toilet was simply a cavity covered with two parallel planks and located about twenty feet from the farm house. Mr. Sakae's clothing was clean but quite threadbare. His hands were tough and calloused from hard toil. Yet they heard no complaints. His testimony was one of gratitude for the goodness of God. Dot and Exie realized that they were privileged to be there. Later, they spoke of this visit as one of the high points of their travels.

A Welcome Stop

"Please, Mrs. Hammond, talk to the authorities and explain to them how far we must walk to the train station. It takes half an hour and if I have shopping packages it takes me longer." "Do you think they would listen to me, an American? Wouldn't it be better for a Japanese citizen to make the request for a bus stop?" queried my wife of our new neighbor. "No, Mrs. Hammond, they would respect you more. You have been here a number of years, and you have children that go to school every day. If you make the request they will listen."

Newer houses were now lined up in a row on the land that Masuda San had sold. One of the reasons the land was cheaper was its considerable distance from the train station and bus stops. We were the first to build on this former wheat field. Now that there were a growing number of homes, our persistent neighbor felt there should be some push to put in a local bus stop. My wife agreed to take on the project.

With Sudo San's help with the Japanese wording, Eleanor made up a petition that described the need of the growing community in Onta. After getting my signature and that of our near neighbors, the Omino family, she passed the petition on. In a short time members of our block penned their names on the document and my wife began an extensive process that began with a visit to the city office. Bureaucratic processes move slowly, but eventually an Onta bus stop sign was installed right beside the Obaasan's confectionery store at the entrance of our tract. For months we were greeted at the bus stop with beaming smiles and expressions of appreciation.

---

[1] FECM Vol. 3, No. 2, Summer 1963, p. 64

Chapter Twenty Eight

URBAN EVANGELISM

The Billy Graham Crusade

From many standpoints the 1967 Billy Graham Crusade in Tokyo was an outstanding success. Our Tokyo churches gave almost full cooperation in these joint efforts. Perhaps one of the strongest points of the crusade was the unity it created between all of the diverse groups. Because of the careful handling by the invitation committee and their assurance of doctrinal integrity the Billy Graham Crusade had the backing of the Bible-believing churches in Tokyo.

During the ten days of the crusade, the Budokan with a capacity of 15,000 was filled to overflowing nightly. On the last day of the meetings, the Korakuen baseball stadium with a capacity of 36,000 was filled to standing room only. The total number of inquirers for the 10-day meetings was 15,854 with 191,750 persons hearing the messages. This demonstrated what two years of preparation and widespread cooperation could do.

Our Tokyo churches all benefited to some degree, but the hesitancy of many of those who had made decisions during the large meetings to identify with a local church indicates that mass evangelism while being one important method is not a panacea. The patient sowing and watering on the local level is all important to the success of a harvest time. Of the eight contacts that our door-to-door-campaign in Higashimurayama produced in connection with the crusade, three came either to our classes or a special service; the others failed to respond. Our churches in central Tokyo that have attractive buildings in more strategic locations did a little better, but the number who followed through with baptism was disappointing.

One mature man who had been on my heart and prayer list for seven years attended the crusade with me and sweated it out but still could not overcome either his pride or confusion in order to make a decision. The feeling of disappointment in such occasions is difficult to avoid; yet we recall the testimonies of some of the brightest Japanese Christians that they had taken a similarly long period of seeking before Christ dawned on their hearts. We rejoiced that many from our current classes, and others who had been contacts through the years, did attend these meetings.

On the positive side, we have a heartening memory of the buoyant fellowship, the uplifting music, the impressive scene in the seating section of deaf persons who were hearing the message through animated signing, and the way in which Billy Graham's humor drew initial laughter from English speakers prior to interpretation. We felt pride to see our son Tim, along with others from the CAJ choir, join the large Crusade choir on the platform. And we felt the reinforcement of the larger community of Christians for the work we were doing in Japan.

Seminary Team Meetings

We followed up after the Graham crusade with evangelistic meetings that were conducted by team members from the Osaka Seminary. Our hard work in the local area resulted in good attendance in the public hall, an apartment tract meeting room, and our home classroom. We heard the team again at Pastor Itagaki's church in Nakano, forty minutes away. Many heard the gospel and a good number of these contacts had also attended the Billy Graham Crusade, but there were no immediate decisions in spite of the dynamic preaching. Yet, good seed had been sown and we believed that God's word would not return void.

In a previous year we had a similar size team come from the college; one teacher and two female students. We appreciated their coming as two key converts resulted from their special meetings – Mrs. Maema, a mature widow with grown children, and Miss Koyama, a kindergarten teacher and close neighbor. Since that time Mrs. Maema's daughter attended services and summer camp, and one son had come on special occasions. Mrs. Maema had spent a long time in thought and prayer before becoming a Christian and was one of the most active in church.

One evening after one of the special sessions was over the two female college students got into a rather prolonged argument. Since my wife and I were busy saying farewell to the guests we couldn't catch the nature of their intense disagreement. It must have been a heavy theological issue, we thought. Later I asked the professor, "What was that all about?" He responded sheepishly, "One of them is from Hokkaido in the far north, and the other is from Kyushu in the south. They were arguing about which region had the best watermelons." The humor of the situation caused us to have a good laugh, breaking the tension. It reminded us of the cultural favoritism in the U.S. displayed when comparing Florida oranges to Californian. Since God is so patient with us we must learn to be patient with one another.

Other Cooperative Crusades

In 1968 we shared in two other smaller crusades with good results. Joe Garman, a young graduate of Ozark Bible College, offered his services to a number of countries in the Far East. Jane Kinnet Hill, who was from my home church, and an experienced missionary from Korea, assured me that this young man was a gifted evangelist for 2,000 had come to Christ under his preaching in Korea! With that assurance we helped sponsor Joe in Japan. As a result there were 6 decisions in Kagoshima, 8 in Shikoku, and 16 in Tokyo. Stephen Iijima, who served as Joe's interpreter, was impressed by the complete sincerity of the young evangelist.

In the fall we cooperated with the nationally known Koji Honda Crusades. I served on the planning committee for the West Tokyo Crusade which was held in a large hall in Koganei, 30 minutes south of us. I have never known a time when I enjoyed Japanese preaching more. Honda Sensei had a wonderful sense of humor that is balanced with appropriate expressions of the gospel. Five from our area made decisions; three of them were connected with our Kumegawa meetings. All of those who attended the crusades were strengthened in faith and given a larger vision.

Open Doors Closed Hearts

Phil Foxwell, whom I knew as a seminary teacher that used his knowledge of magic to attract youth, called me on the phone. "Al, I am leaving on furlough, could you take my class at the Bridgestone Tire Company? It was begun by Carrico, who plays the guitar well, and I took over when he left. The location is near your place and it is an opportunity for sharing the gospel in a secular company." I responded, "I can't play the guitar nor can I perform magic tricks, but I can teach the Bible and answer questions." "Good enough. Just go slow and there may be responses in time," Phil reassured me.

Mr. Ishibashi (literally "stone bridge") founded this large internationally known tire company and named it, Bridgestone, which was a simple reversal of the two Chinese characters in his name. He permitted his workers to use recreational rooms for meetings of their choosing. A dozen or so young men had initiated a meeting with Carrico to strum his guitar and teach them choruses. Later they were receptive of Phil Foxwell, who had intriguing slight of hand gifts. I wondered if my pragmatic Bible teaching approach would be acceptable.

I found that the young men at the Bridgestone Tire Company were a friendly bunch and they helped me through a few of the choruses they had been learning. One of them had a guitar which gave us support to keep us somewhat on key. Our initial times of getting acquainted went well. They were filled with curiosity about America and my personal life. I learned that some of them were married and all had aspirations for the future. They were proud of their country and spoke well of their company. I enjoyed the interaction with this congenial group of young men.

Over time, however, it became noticeable that simple Bible lessons triggered defensive reactions. I began to include remarks that demonstrated my appreciation for Japanese culture, and I slowed down the rate with which I introduced new truths. I became aware that they equated Christianity with America, and Japan's journalistic posture at that time was denigrating the U.S. I was learning that the young men at Bridgestone were conditioned to an unquestioned acceptance of Japanese cultural superiority. Their intense loyalty to their own culture lacked the objectivity that I had experienced with self-reflecting students in our home classroom.

The Bridgestone group did accept our invitation to attend youth rallies held in the Onta public hall. They appeared to enjoy the game time which was designed to help teach English. On one occasion a ventriloquist entertained us and did a good job of making his dummy respond as if alive. This was highly enjoyed by everyone. A Japanese minister would put a capstone on the meeting by bringing a message that related well with youth. Because of this kind of exposure, I assumed that our visitors from the tire company were moving closer to an understanding of the Christian faith. But I was wrong. At a closing meeting at their company they wanted me to know that they had talked it over and decided they were content with their Japanese traditions. Once again I experienced the pain of rejection, and asked the Lord to give me patience and insights as how to better present the beauty of Christ.

Evangelism Through Writing

In 1968 the Japanese bestselling novel, "Shiokari Pass," written by the well-known author, Ayako Miura, captivated the public. It is written with a beauty and sensitivity that is characteristically Japanese. Based on a true story of the life of Masao Nagano, an unpretentious person who lived simply and frugally in order to support his mother and give to people in need. He rose to be a high-ranking railroad official. When awarded an Imperial Grant for his services to the state, he gave it all to found a Young Railway men's Christian Association.

It is a love story that tells of the affection of Nobuo and Fujiko when they first met as children. Their love matures and endures through the years, as they go through sickness, separation, and hardships. The choices they make reveal the *agape* love of the Christian Bible. Miura's novel does much to dispel the deep seated prejudice against Christianity. She writes with clarity and boldness of the name calling and unjustified antagonism against those who follow Jesus. By the time the reader gets to the conclusion he is in love with the hero, who gives his life to save others at the Shiokari Pass.

The English edition came out in1974, [1] and since then the story has been put into film. I confess that although I heard of this moving novel, I did not read it until I got hold of the English edition. The power of this true Christian story expressed so well in creative writing is an effective means for penetrating Japanese consciousness with the beauty of the gospel and the love of Jesus.

---

[1] Translated by Bill and Sheila Fearnehough & published by Overseas Missionary Fellowship, 1974.

Chapter Twenty Nine

A TIME OF CHANGES

A Change in Plans

With great anticipation we awaited the arrival in 1968 of Wayfull and Helen Jew, graduates of San Jose Bible College, who were to become our coworkers. My ties to this

Wayfull & Helen Jew anticipated working with us, but since he was Chinese, local pastors recommended that they serve in China, where they have been 40 years.

talented Asian-American couple went back to my undergraduate days at SJBC. Willy Jew, the Chinese-American older brother of Wayfull became a close friend when I was working part-time at the West Coast Carburetor company to help pay for my school tuition. Willy had become a Christian when in a T.B. sanitorium because of the faithful visits of Audrey West, my English teacher at the college.

Audrey was more than an English teacher. It was at her early Morning Prayer meetings that I was first challenged for missions. Audrey, herself, decided to go to Japan to serve in 1953. A year later she and her husband, Bob, met Eleanor, baby Tim and me upon our arrival in Yokohama in April of 1954. During her long Japan service Audrey lost her husband, but as I write these words in the year of 2008, she is still faithfully serving at the age of 99 in the mountains of Okayama!

Wayfull's wife, Helen, is a Japanese American, born and raised in California and still conversant in Japanese. We saw this as a great advantage for service in Japan. Wayfull and Helen had sat in the missions' class which I taught on furlough. We felt that they were ideal for service in Japan. But to our chagrin, our pastor friends voiced reservations. "They are an outstanding couple," they agreed, "but in Asia the husband must be looked to as the leader. Since Wayfull is Chinese, it may be best for them to go to a country where they speak Chinese." We were not prepared to hear that, but after a time of thoughtful reflection, we realized the truth in what they said. Following a short but sweet time of fellowship Wayfull and Helen left to visit Audrey West in Okayama. We eventually heard of their final decision to serve in Hong Kong.

A Change in Magazine Format

For eight years **Far East Christian Missionary** had been on the masthead of our quarterly magazine. God had blessed the project with access into most of the Far East countries where we had missionaries. Increasingly the grapevine had carried the excitement of our open forum to fields outside of Asia. After polling our field editors and soliciting feedback from readers we decided to change the name of the journal to **Christian Mission Today**. An explanatory paragraph was included at the top of the inside cover:

CHRISTIAN MISSION TODAY is an independent, non-profit, religious publication established in 1961 under its former name, *Far East Christian Missionary*. It serves as an open forum of missionary thought in which all Christian leaders involved in applying the principles of New Testament Christianity in today's mission efforts are invited to share their convictions. Opinions contained in the articles are published to stimulate thought and do not necessarily reflect the attitude of the publisher.

In the last issue with the name, Far East Christian Missionary, (Vol 8, No 4), Lois Callaway in Thailand was listed as Devotional Editor. Betty McElroy in the Philippines was Editor of Our Missionary Women. Asian field editors were listed alphabetically by countries: Hawaii, Glen Powell; India, Tom Rash; Japan, Al Hammond; Korea, Dick Lash; Pakistan, Lee Turner; Philippines, Barton McElroy; Ryukyu Islands, Claire Boulton; Thailand, Mel Byers. Two important names were omitted: Robert Morse of Burma was cut off from outside communication by civil war, later described by his wife in Christian Mission Today (Vol. 11, No 4), and Harold Taylor of Korea had retired. All of these served well and made FECM a mission journal that was welcomed by national leaders and missionaries alike.

To increase our circulation and influence we broadened the area of outreach. Volunteer field editors were added from countries outside of Asia: Richard Hostetter, Ghana; John Kernan, South Africa; Douglas Priest, Ethiopia; Don Stoll, Rhodesia; Harry Scates, Brazil; Bertrand Smith, Chile; Dr.Gerald Bowlin and William Morgan, Mexico; Vic Reid, West Indies; Edward Fauz, Germany; Roy Goldsberry, Italy; Dr. J.H. Jauncey, Australia; Marguerite Huckins, a former editor of the Women's Department, Alaska; and Glen Powell, still retained for multicultural Hawaii.

Financial pressures were enforcing our decisions. Printing costs had risen and, more threatening, the special rates for printed matter mailing were eliminated. Japan's growing rate of inflation added to the problem. As we encountered heavy decisions we began to request the help of national advisors and added their names in the journal's information box: Diego Romulo of the Philippines, Stephen Iijima in Japan, and Nicholas Quemesha for Africa. As we received recommendations from the fields we planned to add more names to the list.

Changes in Family Needs

Billy, who was born in Tokyo, was now old enough to enter the first grade at the Christian Academy in Japan. It brought a tug on our hearts to see him go off to school with his brothers and sisters. Yet we felt thankful that he could have the experience of broader social contacts in a Christian environment. He retained his Japanese friends in the home neighborhood and continued to develop bicultural skills. The only negative experience he had in the commute to and from school was when he struck off on his own on the train and missed his stop. He kept his cool as he waited for instructions and made it safely home.

Rising tuition costs for our five in a private school were adding to our financial pressures. As every parent is aware, additional costs for the individual needs of growing children add to the bill. On the one hand, I was glad that Tim had joined the wrestling team for which expensive sports gear was not required. Yet, Eleanor felt agony when watching the matches in which they seem to tie one another into figure eights. Sharon was learning the violin and increasing proficiency would require that she have her own instrument. One CAJ bill I didn't mind paying that added nostalgic sweetness to our lives was for the special order cinnamon rolls that one enterprising teacher made available periodically.

We searched for a part-time job to supplement our income. Since I had a graduate degree in Asian Studies and was experienced in Japanese culture I applied for a position to teach Japanese Language and Cultural History with the University of Maryland extension program taught at our military bases. After extensive screening they gave me a permit and asked for a syllabus for the course described in their catalog. I prepared the syllabus carefully and included extensive bibliography. This may have been a mistake. Those GI's interested in studying Japanese language and culture did not want a college level course, but preferred a simplified study in which they could learn to say, "Where is the men's restroom?" or "You are very pretty."

At my wife's suggestion I applied for a teaching job at CAJ in exchange for a reduced tuition for our children, but they already had a missionary who was teaching Japanese language and culture. So I tried again and applied for a teaching post at the American School in Japan and was informed that I did not have the necessary credential for the position that was open. I learned that it was not easy to find jobs that would supplement our income. The financial pressures remained.

Changes in Leadership Needs

"Sensei, If we only had fifty *tsubo* (a *tsubo* is six feet square) of land there would be a future for the church,." pleaded Akada San. I realized that our young associate was getting restless as questions were raised in his mind about his future. Japanese relate the ownership of land and a building to the permanence of the church's future. Fifty times 36 square feet of area is not very large (1800 square feet). but on a Japanese scale it would be adequate for a church that could seat a hundred.

It was amazing that in 1960 we had bought one hundred *tsubo* of land for only $2000 and built the mission home and classroom for $4000 using the free materials from a closed base housing duplex. Since that time the price of land in Japan had catapulted so high that the majority could not even dream of owning a home. Churches that were begun in homes or rented buildings were blocked from expansion. Akada San was asking for land that was half the size of the mission property. I understood the need but did not know how to respond.

A Change in Fields

Dr. J.H. Jauncey's book, *Science Returns to God,*[1] attracted me. His positive approach to science/faith issues was appealing. The fact that he had doctorates in both science and theology gave him credibility. I learned that he was the principal at Kenmore Christian College in Brisbane, Australia. I wrote to him asking if they could use me there as a teacher. My brainstorming about the financial problems had made me wonder if we could rotate out of Japan for the peak years of high tuition and benefit from the free public education in Australia.

Dr. Jauncey was a regular reader of FECM and acquainted with my editorial views. He wrote in a very cordial manner that they would be delighted to have me come and join them in Kenmore Christian College. The problem was that they had not grown to the place where they could pay a sufficient salary. He suggested that I write to the University of Queensland which was near their location, and he gave me the necessary addresses. He felt that if I could teach part time in both colleges it would be a workable situation.

The Registrar of the University of Queensland responded to my inquiry that Professor Joyce I. Ackroyd, Chair of the Department of Asian Studies, was on a study leave in Japan and they would contact her. She was staying at the International House in Roppongi, Tokyo. After making contact by mail an appointment time was set up for an interview. Eleanor joined me as we went to Roppongi and spent several hours in discussing the position of teaching Japanese Language and Culture that was open at the University of Queensland.

Professor Ackroyd gave me the green light for the position in Queensland and even included motherly advice in how to live in "the land down under." Eleanor and I were both excited to find this resolution to our financial woes. I wrote to the Board of Elders at the University Christian Church in Los Angeles explaining our proposed change of fields. The letter mentioned that although I would have a modest salary and the school tuition would be minimized, I would need travel funds to Australia.

What I had not realized was that Eldred Illingsworth, chairman of the church board, was also serving on the board of San Jose Bible College. He was aware that Woodrow Phillips, the new college president, was looking for someone to chair a proposed mission department. Anticipating a trip to Brisbane and a new job, I was shocked to get a phone call from San Jose, California, made during a board meeting at SJBC. Ralph Maier, a former roommate and now chairman of the board was calling: "Al, we heard about your proposal to go to Australia to teach in Queensland, but we need you here!" President Phillips chimed in, "Yes, we need you, Al; our location on the West Coast makes it strategic for a mission department. You can multiply the results of your ministry by training future missionaries." Momentarily overwhelmed, I simply answered, "I appreciate your call. We will pray about it and get back to you."

---

[1] J.H. Jauncey, "Science Returns to God," Zondervan, 1966.

Chapter Thirty

IN THE VALLEY OF DECISION

Difficulties in Change

As a family we were having second thoughts about moving to Australia or to California. In our Kumegawa home Eleanor enjoyed both her family security, and her opportunities for teaching and serving. She was now respected by the neighbors and well accepted by the various shopkeepers in town. Our five active youngsters felt comfortable with school at CAJ. Tim looked forward to graduating with his friends in less than two years. Sharon had graduated from the junior high level and enjoyed high school work. Mary, Jim, and Bill felt close to neighborhood friends as well as school chums. They would miss our dog, cat, and canary. Why was Dad talking of moving?

With new doors opening for service I was also having reservations about any hasty move. Dr. Don Hoke, President of Tokyo Christian College, had been asked by Moody Press to edit a new book on the Church in Asia.[1] He singled me out to write the Japan chapter and assured me that because he had been serving in Japan for twenty years I could expect a critical review. The assignment included a survey to update statistics from all the evangelical churches. A representative of the Hayama Seminar requested that I bring one of the annual studies on the indigenous church. As was their custom, another missionary was chosen to critique my paper. I felt both privileged and pressured by these writing assignments.

The open doors at both Kenmore Christian College and the University of Queensland challenged me. The prospect of free tuition in Australia's school system was appealing. Yet, the statements of two highly respected individuals caused me to wonder if it was the will of God to respond to the request to head up missions at my alma mater in California. Woodrow Phillips had stressed, "You can multiply the results of your ministry by training future missionaries." Robert Bolling, the Missions Chairman at University Christian Church, my sponsoring congregation, wrote, "It may well be that the events which seem to be falling into place in the Australian area are indeed significant for your future. I personally will be sorry that the dedication and talent which you have would not be directed to work in one of our California schools."[2]

Resolving Conflicts

An internal conflict had to do with the personal acknowledgement that my views on education had changed since graduating from San Jose Bible College in 1952. I still felt that an undergirding of the Word of God was essential and should be central in the training of future ministers. However, I also believed that exposure to broader areas of the humanities and social sciences were necessary for effective cross cultural communication in today's world. I wondered if the views of SJBC had also changed over the past seventeen years, or if they were committed to a more restricted focus on Bible and pastoral tools.

To make an open declaration of my modified views I penned an article for Christian Standard Magazine entitled, "From Bible College to Berkeley." I wrote candidly about the strengths and weaknesses of both approaches to education. At the same time I exchanged letters with Bob Sargent, the Academic Dean at SJBC, and shared my views. In the event that the college wanted to retain an unchanged Bible College focus on ministerial subjects, I recommended Mel Byers as a better choice since Mel's spiritual demeanor and unrestrained idealism attracted youth.

Edwin Hayden, Editor of Christian Standard, gave me feedback on my article; "From Bible College to Berkeley," that made me realize that a conservative sector of our movement still held to the single focus concept for leadership training. He wrote,

> It has been some time…since an article has stirred up the readers as did yours on 'Bible College to Berkeley.' A number of our folk have so departed from the educational concepts held by Alexander Campbell, for instance, that they regard as heretical any suggestion for the kind of educational program on which he insisted! Some who might have been able to forgive the heresy of your educational philosophy were very sure that your complimentary reference to Martin Luther King indicated that you had received disproportionate amount of your thinking from Berkeley.[3]

Responses from Bob Sargent, however, assured me that while they wanted to keep the Bible in the center of their curriculum, they were in the process of broadening their general education courses. He felt that we were in essential agreement.

Possible Financial Solutions

Dozens of letters were sent out exploring the possibility of the local churches enlarging their budgets for our mission. One response let me know that the greater portion of the $18,000 they had raised from a Faith Promise rally was allocated for a new missionary family bound for Africa. The pastor of a rural congregation was sorry to report that the poor potato crop that year resulted in a decrease in their giving. A few churches assured us of a portion of the travel funds needed if we decided to return to the States. Most of them promised to maintain the budget amount to which they had agreed and reassured us of their love and prayers.

In the process of brainstorming about how to pay the bills we came up with the following reasoning: (1) If we could live elsewhere we could turn the mission home over to the church which would answer their need for land and building. (2) If we left the country we could offer our Nissan Cedric station wagon to pay for the past, and perhaps a future, print bill. (3) Since our rural work on Tanegashima had reached self support through a sister church arrangement, we could suggest the same method for the Kumegawa work. Eventually we committed it to God in prayer; gave a tentative yes to the SJBC position and asked Bob Sargent for a job description.

Implementing Our Decision

As we thought of turning the mission home over to the church we realized that we should take care in the transaction to prevent misunderstanding or create an attitude of dependence. For eight years Akira Takekawa had been with us and weathered the difficult times. He had volunteered to teach Sunday School and could be counted on to give a cheerful welcome to the students who came. I considered him a functioning elder and appreciated his sage advice. His wife, Haruko, was a big help to my wife in her work with the women. I realized that they were looking for a better place to live. A plan came to my mind to include them in the housing transaction.

We contacted Pastor Stephen Iijima at the Minato Church and asked if they could take the younger church in Kumegawa under their wing and help them establish a *shukyo hojin* (religious incorporation) for the front 50 tsubo of the mission property. After talking it over, we planned on selling the back half of the property to Takekawa San at a reasonable price. This would provide a home for the Takekawas and the funds from the sale could be used to erect a second story parsonage on the front section. At the same time, the remodeling could be done to give a church appearance to the front and double the size of the interior classroom. Akada San would have his requested 50 tsubo and a church structure as well.

At an agreed time Akada Sensei, Takekawa San, and I met with Iijima Sensei and his elders at the Minato Church site in the Minato ward. Misunderstandings were clarified and the agreement was made that their established congregation would oversee the younger Kumegawa church until it had the internal strength to stand alone.

After the surveryor had evenly divided the property I turned the deed for the front parcel over to the Minato Church.

Next on the list of problems that needed a solution was the continuation of Christian Mission Today. When I learned that Don Burney had a print ministry in Shikoku, I explored the possibility that he might become the Publication Manager and take on the job of printing and mailing CMT. I would continue with the editing and solicitation of articles from the missionary community. But after careful consideration Don replied that he had too much on his regular schedule to take on an extra project.

Next I contacted Robert Warrick, who was connected with the Christian Academy, which was fairly close to New Life League where the magazine was published. He agreed to accept the role of Publication Manager and pilot the quarterly through NLL. Since Arnfinn Andaas was still in charge of production at the printing establishment and was familiar with our expectations, I felt that this was the best arrangement.

Farewells and Requests to Return

After staying ten years in our Tokyo home it took a great deal of preparation before we could leave. After emptying the attic and the closets into the classroom, we began sorting what we could give away, take with us, or throw away. The man who collected paper waste made a haul when he stopped by. Acquaintances were delighted with keepsakes that they could take. The "take with us" list began to grow as friends brought farewell gifts of beautiful Japanese dolls, ornate pottery, decorated umbrellas, and colorful *Ohashi* (chop sticks). Jim was pleased when a buddy gave him his prize collection of beautiful mounted butterflies.

Funds had come in and we had passage booked on the President Wilson, leaving Yokohama on May 29, 1970, bound for Los Angeles. Omino San, our next- door neighbor used his truck to take our heavier baggage to the pier. Friends made sure that we were driven there, but most of them traveled by train, arriving early. Unlike departure by plane, ships allow more time for farewells. After finding our stateroom, we went to the passenger's lounge where we had time to quietly rest. A few of our church members found us and we began to converse. The others were waiting on the pier to take part in the traditional farewell in which paper tape streamers are held which were unraveled from departing friends from their position by the rail on deck as the ship separates from the pier. Sudo San, the aging senior who had worked in our mailing office, pleaded, "Hamondo Sensei, Please return to Japan." Seki San, Maema San, the Takekawas and others made the same request.

While sitting in the ship's lounge, I remember looking about at the faces of our children, who had their future before them. Four years from that departing day I was to return with Tim and Sharon, who helped me guide a group of SJBC students. In later years, Tim was to return as a short term missionary, serving for one year in rural Wakayama and later as a business man and guide. Sharon and her husband with their two small boys, Daniel and David, came for three years to serve with the Language Institute For Evangelism in Japan (LIFE). Mary visited on her way back from China, fearful that she had forgotten her Japanese, but thrilled when it came gushing out as she visited with a childhood friend on the veranda of Masuda San's home. Jim and Bill, although much traveled, have not yet returned, but retained their taste buds for *sushi* and *oyakodomburi* (chicken and egg over rice).

Over the years I returned many times to update my knowledge on the well being of the Christian community and to introduce prospective mission students to the trials and joys of mission service. The amazing, yet disconcerting changes that took place are the subject matter of the next chapters.

---

[1] Donald Hoke, Ed., "The Church in Asia," Moody Press, 1975.

[2] Letter from Robert D. Bolling, January 29, 1969.

[3] Letter from Edwin Hayden, October 2, 1969.

Chapter Thirty One

RAISING MISSION VISION ON CAMPUS

Classroom Challenges

Once the reassuring rounds of visits had been made to our widespread family members and we were settled in rented housing in San Jose, I approached SJBC's academic dean about the basic thrust of my job. He stated that my primary purpose should be to raise mission vision on campus beginning with the classroom. During the fall semester I was assigned to teach the book of Acts and the Corinthian Epistles on a missions track, as well as Survey of Missions. Teaching Acts gave opportunities for applications to modern missions. The Corinthian Epistles are filled with examples of cross cultural problems in an urban setting. Survey of Missions focused on God's providential care for the church through the ages.

Arthur Glasser, Key Speaker

I realized how easy it had been when I taught only one course on furloughs. Then I could give spontaneous illustrations without worrying about redundancy. Now, I had to be careful that I kept

199

within the boundaries of each course and did not repeat the same stories from my pool of experiences. During the spring semester I agreed to teach Anthropology for Missions, Theory of Missions, and Journalism for Missions. Constructing specific course plans for each of these areas took long hours of time. I learned that teachers are like farmers; their work is never done.

A Special Emphasis Week

Feeling that the students needed a special mission challenge at least once a year I proposed a Week of Missions for May 16-21, 1971. President Phillips agreed that contacting key speakers from Fuller Theological Seminary's School of World Missions would be a strategic move. Since I had previous correspondence with Donald McGavran and Arthur Glasser in connection with my missionary journal, I invited them to come and speak for us in chapel and mission classes.

Dr. McGavran, the Director of the School of World Mission, had served for 30 years in India in institutional missions with the Disciples of Christ. Although he had received a liberal education at Yale Divinity School, Union Theological Seminary, and Columbia University, he had a turning point in his studies in which he affirmed the integrity of Scripture. Dissatisfied with the meager results of institutional missions, he wrote, *The Bridges of God*, [1] which became the first of his many strategic publications on church growth. He documented the spontaneous growth of "people's movements" which contrasted to the slow mission-station approach.

Dr. Glasser served in China with the China Inland Mission until that field was closed by the communists. He graduated from Cornell University and Faith Seminary, which was ultra separatist at the time. Glasser continued to embrace the importance of biblical authority, but through his wrestling with Scripture in ongoing graduate studies he went beyond separatism to acquire genuine longing for evangelical unity.

After the closing of China, Glasser became the North American Director of the China Inland Mission, renamed the Overseas Missionary Fellowship (OMF). I became acquainted with Glasser's challenging theological thought from reading his editorials in OMF's journal, **East Asia Millions**. McGavran was a creative church growth pragmatist; Glasser was an in-depth theologian.[2] Both of these men were prolific writers with many cutting edge books and articles to their credit. We were privileged to have them at this formative stage of our mission department.

It was also timely and an inspiration to have Pastor Edward Butler complete the trio of speakers to cover the Monday, Wednesday and Friday chapel periods. Rev. Butler was an outstanding pastor of a growing black American congregation in nearby East Palo Alto. He was much in demand as a speaker on racial relations from a Christian perspective. He gave us powerful insights that promoted understanding of race relations. We were made aware that we had a mission field at our doorstep.

The special speakers did an excellent job in chapel on week days developing our theme, "Facing Facts in Modern Missions." On Friday night we had our first Mission Fair, which included display booths for various missions, indigenous foods, international dress, music and cultural exhibitions. The students fully participated in this colorful event which was sparked by the mission club. Over time this annual closing event of the Week of Missions was referred to as the International Banquet.

Summer Mission Experience

Dean Cary, a former missionary to Mexico, through the influence of President Phillips became the Public Relations Director of the college. He came up with a plan to give practical training to mission-minded students during the summer. The program was called, "Summer World Institute of Missions," (SWIM). I recognized the need to close the gap between classroom theory and field experience and gladly participated in leading two car loads of students to Mexico City.

My junior high school Spanish was woefully inadequate so I asked Herman Lopez, a Mexican-American student at the college, to be our interpreter. Herman was born in the U.S. and had never been to Mexico so he was looking forward to the experience with anticipation and some anxiety. Faye Daniels, our African-American librarian, wanted to go also to see if she could adapt to mission life. Her cheerful disposition and ready humor was built-in therapy for the rest of us. Sue Peck, a tall, lanky gal, who was dubbed "Soupy," by her friends, was adventuresome and eager to learn. As one who had been in South America and knew some Spanish, Fred Gallaher, was a good man to have along. Don and Karen Arneson, a married couple, drove the other car. They were asking the question as to whether missions were for them. Finally, but not least, I brought along my high school aged daughters, Sharon and Mary, who bonded easily with those of different cultural backgrounds.

If you are thinking of comfort in traveling, driving to Mexico City is not the way to go. There is enchanting beauty in the desert like scenery in northern Mexico but the roads in 1972 were badly in need of repair and the restrooms in the gas stations were not customer friendly. Our first real rest stop was at the orphanage in San Luis Potosi. When we arrived late at night we aroused the dogs, who set up a racket that woke Ted Murray, the bleary-eyed director of the orphanage. Looking at his watch he blurted, "You were due to arrive four hours ago," yet he assured us we were welcome and guided the gals and the guys to separated parts of the orphanage to prepared beds.

Herman Lopez and I shared one small room and were so tired when we finally got to sleep that we would have slept until noon. However, we both woke early when little hands explored our faces and our baggage as the orphans eagerly urged us to get up to play. We found ourselves captivated by their engaging smiles and innocent queries and did our best to humor them while we readied ourselves for the day. Breakfast of bacon and eggs with toast and jam was served in a spacious dining hall in family style with Ted and his helpers overseeing the needs of his guests and the hungry youngsters. While we ate, Ted explained the orphanage operation, how they grew some of their food and raised their own pigs and chickens to keep costs down. Although the Murrays seemed a little frazzled by their responsibilities, they appeared to be at home in the work.

Eager for affection the children bonded with our team as they played games with them throughout the day. We felt their love and did our best to respond to them.

Departure time was both difficult and touching. Waving our goodbyes we started out for the long drive to Mexico City. Dean Cary had advised me, "When you drive in Mexico City, think of water; go with the flow." We finally arrived in the capitol and understood what he meant. No one observed lanes; drivers simply darted into any space that opened a fraction. Miraculously we arrived at our destination safely, the home of Gil and Marie Contreras.

Gil and Marie were graduates of San Jose Bible College. I had known his wife as Mary, a zealous student who joined us in street meetings in a declining area of San Jose, California. Mary had persuaded Catholic-raised Gil of the New Testament position on the church. After finishing his work at San Jose State University, Gil studied at SJBC and developed into one of the most successful church planters in Mexico. Under the influence of Gil and other dedicated Mexican church leaders Herman Lopez was changing from a self-conscious minority-member to a bold Christian leader. I wondered if intimidation by the Anglo majority had weakened his sense of identity. It was reassuring to see him gain confidence in himself.

Cultural Exposure

The central base of the SWIM program was in a rented seminary building where we had room and board along with morning messages by area leaders. My daughters were attracted to Consuelo, the matronly cook who showed affection to them. They laughed at my tendency to call her, "Consuelo San," because of my unconscious inclination to use Japanese expressions. We fared well eating her tortillas and beans with an occasional enchilada. The morning messages by experienced leaders filled us spiritually, creating a desire to be of greater service.

It was a delight to meet Harrold and Adele McFarland, founders of Mission Services, who were visiting that summer. **Horizons** magazine, edited by Harrold, had helped considerably to make our needs known when a typhoon had done extensive damage to the mission in Japan. Students from other colleges were also part of the program which included afternoon cultural trips to such places as the Museum of Anthropology, and the ancient religious site of *Teotihuacan* where you find the huge pyramids of the sun and the moon. These were reminders of Mexico's earlier glory architecturally. At one time the population of this religious city rose as high as one hundred thousand, but the gory human sacrifice practiced on the top of the pyramids to appease ancient gods was probably the reason for its decline.

Prior to another of our cultural outings Mary stayed in her room to get some needed rest. A roommate had turned the gas heater on to warm the room before she left, but although the gas came on, it did not ignite! When we returned it was soon discovered that Mary had been overcome by the toxic fumes. Fred Gallaher, who had some training in emergency first aid, realized she needed to get some oxygen. It was late at night as Sharon, Fred and I headed toward a hospital with my very groggy daughter. They did not have a supply of oxygen at the first clinic, nor at the second! With a third try we found a hospital with an oxygen bottle and Mary revived. We were very thankful as Mary soon became her cheery self. Since this was the very beginning of many short term training trips, especially to Asia, I breathed a prayer that we would never lose a student.

The pleasant closing to our cultural ventures was visiting the *Ballet Folk-lorico* in an antiquated opera house that had very high, steep inclining balconies giving us a bird's eye view of the colorful pageantry on stage. We returned to the seminary for the last night, said our goodbyes the next day and began the long drive back to the USA. Faye Daniels announced that she now knew that the

Lord did not want her to be a missionary. This too, is an acceptable result of the summer training program. The Lord wants us to find our niche in the kingdom and serve with joy.

---

[1] Donald McGavran, "The Bridges of God," New York, Friendship Press, 1955.

[2] Paul Pierson's evaluation of Arthur Glasser is made in the Introduction of, "The Good News of the Kingdom," Edited by Van Engen, Gilliland, and Pierson, (New York: Orbis Bookd, 1993).

Chapter Thirty Two

RETURN VISIT TO EAST ASIA

Invitation to Explo 74

Campus Crusade, an evangelical parachurch organization begun by Bill Bright on the campus of UCLA in 1951, impressed me when I was a college student. Perhaps I was previously helped more by the literature of Intervarsity Fellowship because I was first introduced to their Christian outreach to college students. But the uplifting performance of the Campus Crusade team in front of Sproul Hall at UC Berkeley was a model of what a positive approach can do. Attractive co-eds sang inspirational praise choruses, followed by encouraging testimonies from brawny Christian football players. Rather than provoke the large gathering before them, they gave humble, effective testimony as to what Christ had done for their lives.

When I learned that Lowell Applebury was affiliated with Campus Crusade I was drawn to him for several reasons. Lowell was the son of one of our former Greek professors and was being hired as part of SJBC's administrative staff. So when he invited me to Explo 74, the Campus Crusade plan to initiate a massive Asian Christian gathering in Seoul, Korea, I was immediately interested. He was receptive to my idea of tying together a visit to Japan and Korea and encouraged me to recruit a team of mission-minded students for the summer trip. Lowell would make sure that we had front row seats at the meeting site in Seoul.

Recruiting A Team

Youth attract other youth and good music communicates when words fail, so thinking I quietly went to work to handpick a team of mission-minded students who were gifted in vocal or instrumental music. I sought out Danny Hedges and Jim Yost because both were experienced in youth ministry and played guitars. Dave Roundy was a quiet student, but could use the bow on his violin to play either outstanding classical music or country hoedowns. Nariany Sikyang, a cute Micronesian student, could enchant us with her ukulele. Gail Proksch could thrill an audience with her beautiful vocal range. Marcia Bell, Ginger Walhood, Richard and Judy Carl were great supporting vocalists. Pat Baker chose to use his semi-professional skill of photography to encourage the team. I also recruited my own college age youngsters, Tim and Sharon Hammond, who could serve as guides and interpreters in Japan. Unlike their Dad, they could both sing well.

By way of preparation we took the students to San Francisco in order to obtain their visas from the Japanese Consulate, and to visit the Japanese Cultural Center. In this way they would have a little exposure to Japanese formalities, and have a chance at noon time to practice the use of *ohashi* (chop sticks) at one of the restaurants in the center. They could also pick up handy language and travel guides at the Kinokuniya book store. It was reassuring to see how a team spirit was developing. There was a healthy respect for each other, and spontaneous expressions of joy and excitement.

Reception in Seoul

Our charter flight took us to Anchorage, Alaska, and then on to Tokyo. Our legs were cramped because of the compacted seat arrangement, so it was a relief to spend a night at a youth hostel in Tokyo before going on to Seoul, Korea. On August 14 we arrived in Seoul and were greeted by a group of orphans, who were holding a large sign welcoming us to Korea.

My friend, Dr. Yoon Kwon Chae, had written that he would be in the States that summer, but he had made preparations for us to stay at the orphanage which was at that time located not far from the site where Explo 74 would be conducted.

Knowing that our custom was sleeping on beds and not on the floor as did the Koreans, and lacking western style beds, they folded bedding on top of tables. We managed to adjust to the extra height and slept reasonably well. Food was brought to us that was tasty and nourishing. In every way the leaders of the orphanage did their best to make our stay a pleasant one. Since Lowell Applebury had affiliation with Campus Crusade he gathered all the information necessary and guided us to the location where the mass meetings were held.

Since over one million people were walking through the streets toward the abandoned airport on the Han River, there were many policemen on duty. However, unlike noisy political demonstrations, this was a quiet procession of Christians with good will showing on their faces. The duty officers appeared to be relaxed and were predisposed to be helpful. We noted that most of the people were carrying cushions and we were to learn why upon arrival for there were no chairs. Everyone sat on the ground facing a platform from which the speakers were to give their messages. Special compact radio sets were made available to us so that we could turn to a channel that gave an English translation. Speakers from many different Asian countries were on the program. As we looked around we became aware that we were sitting in a sea of people, the largest gathering that we had every seen. It was reported that 1.5 million people attended these special meetings. Truly this would give an answer as to what Christian missions had been doing in Asia in the last century.

At the very time of the opening of the crusade there was a tragic incident in which a Korean student, who had been raised in Japan, attempted unsuccessfully to assassinate President Park. His shot, although missing his intended victim, fatally injured his wife. Because this deranged Korean youth was from Japan it aroused painful memories of an earlier day when their queen had been killed by Japanese invaders. The peaceful atmosphere changed to one of tension and distrust.

Akira Hatori, a well respected Japanese radio and television evangelist, was one of the scheduled speakers. He was fully aware of the tense relations between Korea and Japan. His country had occupied Korea for forty years and had forced the Koreans to learn the Japanese language. During his opening remarks he apologized for the former belligerency of his nation, and stressed that he was speaking on behalf of the kingdom of God in which all members were brothers. As he stressed the good news of the peace and joy of the gospel, an audible rumble of "Amens" rolled through the vast audience.

Stopovers Enroute to Japan

Our Korean hosts saw us off on the bus bound for Taejon. They made sure the driver knew where we should get off. We had been pampered during our short three day stay at the orphanage in the capitol. This preferential treatment may have been because of our close connection with Dr. Yoon Kwon Chae, the director of the Korean Mission in Seoul. We arrived in Taejon on Saturday evening and were received as fellow workers and given assignments for Sunday, the next day. Our dinner was basic Korean fare and we were given bedding to sleep on the floor.

On Sunday, my son, Tim, and I were given directions to a large Presbyterian church in the city. I was impressed by the effort of the Korean Christian Church leaders to keep contact with other communions. Tim had both training and experience in vocal music and he was expected to sing a solo prior to my message. A staff person in the congregation had the ability to interpret my English, but I was encouraged to speak in Japanese since, I was told, most of the adults could understand. Tim's beautiful solo connected with the worshippers as his testimony. My Japanese caused the nodding of heads from the older members, but produced puzzled expressions on the younger faces. One of their pastors must have explained my intended meaning, for after his follow-up more heads nodded.

Upon hearing fragmented reports from the other team members I felt that their youthful efforts had sparked some spiritual freshness, but the shortness of time prevented the building of relationships. From Taejon we continued our journey to Pusan, the port city where we were to board the overnight ferry to Shimonoseki, Japan. I was getting excited for it had been four years since our departure from Japan. I was looking forward to seeing old friends, and gave the impression to our team members that the best was yet to come.

Back Home in Japan

After clearing customs the team split up. According to plan, Tim was to guide a north bound team including Lowell Applebury and a few others to Okayama and beyond. I led a south bound team to Kagoshima prefecture where we had begun our missionary work. Applebury was eager to visit Audrey West in the mountains of Okayama for he had known her from college days. We later learned that Lowell had become sick during his stay, but had witnessed to the doctor who attended him. Audrey was overjoyed that as a result of this encounter the doctor, whom she knew personally, became a Christian. Lowell had harvested seed that she had sown.

Walter Maxey, the son of Mark and Pauline, had been raised in Kanoya, but received his college education in America. He returned to Japan in 1971 and after taking an intensive refresher course in the Japanese language at the International University in Tokyo he returned to Kagoshima with his wife, Mary. Walter was a good organizer and arranged to have team members share in the rural churches in the Satsuma Peninsula while I was free to cross the bay to the Osumi side and speak in the Kanoya church and the leper colony. Yoshii Sensei was my gracious host.

While we were in Korea, Sharon offered to serve as guide in Tokyo for Gail Proksch, Nariany Sikyang and Pat Baker, who

211

either did not have Korean visas or the extra funds to go to Korea. Paul and Kathleen Pratt graciously extended hospitality and encouraged them to share in their congregation in Isehara in southern Tokyo. After we returned from Korea, Sharon reconnected with our group in Kagoshima in time to travel with me to our family's earlier home on Tanegashima. After nostalgic visits with Pastor and Mrs. Ikeda and the mountain home of Mr.Sakae, we hurried to catch the plane at Noma to get off the island before an approaching typhoon.

A Grumpy Hostel Manager

"You can't stay here; those are not Japanese Youth Hostel membership cards." The belligerent attitude of the manager upset me. I had promised our group that they would receive warm hospitality in Japanese Inns. In our correspondence I had been assured of reservations on the basis of the International permits we carried. We were hot and tired from long hours on the train. The fellows were unshaven and none of us looked our best. As he glowered at us I wondered if he associated us with California hippies. Knowing how difficult it would be to find somewhere else to stay in Kyoto, a cultural center, I made a suggestion. "Our group is tired and need rest we can pay extra if you can make room for us." Apparently surprised at my soft approach, he curtly agreed and had an attendant show us our bunk rooms.

"You remember what you told us, Mr. Hammond." Danny Hedges saw me sitting on my bunk bed with a very despondent look. "No, what did I tell you?" I asked. "You said that this kind of rude treatment is an opportunity to do something positive to turn it around." I forgot that I had said that, but it sounded like a Christian response. Getting our heads together we came up with a plan.

Confronting the manager I made an offer. "Sir, you may have noticed the musical instrument cases that our youth are carrying. This evening we are willing to put on a musical performance, without charge, for all the young people in the hostel." (I didn't tell him that we never did charge). Perhaps because we looked better after a shower and a change of clothes the manager grumpily accepted my offer. "*Yoroshii,*" (Good/O.K.) was his short response. He went on to sternly caution us to observe the 11 p.m. curfew.

After dinner the hostel youth began filling the dining hall which doubled as an auditorium. They watched with keen interest as Dave Roundy warmed up his violin and Jim and Dan adjusted the strings on their guitars. Since all the team members had sung together in Korea and Kagoshima, they were ready to go. I had asked Sharon to interpret for the group and she was game to do so but a little nervous. It had been four years since we had spoken Japanese on a daily basis. That evening I was proud of all of them. Their singing and instrumental accompaniment was lively and inspirational and their testimonies rang true. They were given rapt attention and an enthusiastic ovation. Most amazing was the positive response of the hostel manager, who had refreshments served and permitted them to go beyond the curfew as the youth visited around the tables.

Chapter Thirty Three

JAPAN VISIT AFTER INTERLUDE

A Period of Despondency

My training was in the old school of mission thought. An individual made a long-term commitment based on a call from God. He or she chose the field of service that best matched their gifts, but "shopping around" by repeated short term missions was not encouraged. After the soul stirring experience of Explo 74 I anticipated early decisions for missions from a good number of the 14 member team that had traveled with me to Korea and Japan. But the world was changing and youth culture was changing with it. Because my adjustment to the changes was late coming, I entered a period of disappointment and despondency.

"Mr. Hammond, Lone Hill is without a pastor and they are looking for a senior minister and I recommended you." Danny Hedges served as youth minister at the nondenominational church that was named after the section of Los Gatos that was distinguished by a single hill. Since I was feeling a sense of dryness in my classroom presentation, my ears perked up. I probably could preach part time and keep my mission classes going at the college, I mused to myself. "Thank you, Danny, tell the church elders that I will consider it."

Including one's family in your ministry brings growth that would not be produced by a single individual. The Lone Hill congregation had an organ and its music was still preferred by the older members. My wife had been trained to play this traditional instrument. At the same time the church was concerned that there be a growing youth program. Eldest son Tim was working on his M.A. degree in vocal music at San Jose State University and looking for a chance to practice his choral directing skills. Sharon, Mary, Jim and Bill were eager to volunteer as enthusiastic vocalists in his choir. Within a relatively short time the "New Dawn" choir was born and attracted youth from the area. My family opened the door for ministry at Lone Hill Church.

Return to Missions Emphasis

My enthusiasm for mission trips had returned during the five year interlude between 1974 and 1979. The lesson learned was that a vision for missions must be "caught" and not just "taught." Also, I needed to learn patience to wait on God's preparation of seed that had been sown. Decisions for missions were eventually made by a number of those who experienced Explo 74. After finishing his grad studies at Fuller's School of Missions, Jim and his wife, Joan, went to serve in Irian Jaya. Gail Proksch and her new husband, volunteered to serve with Wycliffe Bible Translators. Nariany Sikyang returned to Palau, and after becoming an influential leader in a Micronesian college sent a number of students to SJBC. Richard and Judy Carl began service in the Fijian Islands. Dan Hedges gave his name to Ginger Walhood in marriage and went on to get a doctorate. He became a key recruiter for Korean graduate students to a Christian university. The others continued to have an interest in world wide missions and retained their ability to communicate cross culturally.

After serving three years with Lone Hill, the church was ready for a full time minister, and I had discovered that wearing two hats was a recipe for burn out. I returned to full time teaching at SJBC and began recruiting for a Japan tour for the summer of 1979. George Gardner, John Heberling, Mike Huskey, Kathy Kurtz, Casey Larsen, and Sheila Marques were the respondents. To prepare us (including myself) I received permission from the dean to begin a class in Japanese culture and language. This gave me the opportunity to brush up on the language and it produced performance from some of the students that I could not have anticipated.

Breathless / Bathless Arrival

By the time we landed in Tokyo, made it through customs and traveled to the Ichigaya Youth Hostel, there was barely enough time to make it to the Kamiochiai Church. We were scheduled to take part in an area wide church rally and I was to be one of the speakers. Delays in processing at the hostel did not allow us time to take showers before we had to rush by local trains to our destination. My hearing and memory were strained as I listened to hear the call of our station. This was our first Sunday back in Japan, and in the sultry August weather we were concerned about our social acceptability. We arrived breathless and bathless.

Our self-consciousness was accentuated when they led us to front pews upon entering the crowded assembly. The familiar faces of old friends and the friendly sound of the exchange of greetings helped me to relax. I gave our students a look of reassurance as I reached for a song book. After brief words of welcome we were led in singing some of the popular hymns. I watched to see if my students remembered how to read the simplified Japanese syllabary that gave cues to pronunciation. One or two were singing confidently; the rest looked lost.

My adrenalin began to flow when I heard Sato Sensei announce that I would introduce my guests from San Jose Bible College, and explain our itinerary for the summer. Feeling my own self-consciousness, and sensing the tension reflected by my students, I cracked a joke. The news had recently announced that a student who was traveling with a group similar to ours was bitten by a shark in the Philippines. After frankly acknowledging that we did not have time to take showers before we rushed to this meeting, I stated my belief that our B.O. would ward off any shark attacks. The laughter that was released broke the tension. We felt accepted, bathless or not.

Cultural Adventures

After necessary money exchange and train pass confirmation we had time on Monday to visit Tokyo Tower and the roof garden of the Takashimaya department store. Cameras were clicking as we tried to capture our birds eye view of this city of ten million people from the top elevation of the world's tallest tower. Tall office buildings dotted the landscape; religious temples and shrines were also visible. Contrasting this structural perspective from above was the family-like atmosphere of the playground and food booths we visited on the spacious roofs of the department stores. Business moguls had wisely designed these miniature Disneyland play areas for husbands and their children while their wives were spending their money on the merchandise in the floors below.

Riding the Shinkansen (Bullet Train) to Osaka was an adventure in itself. This marvel of railroad engineering began in 1964 and gradually extended to all the major trunk lines in Japan. I remembered all too well my journeys on the older coal burning steam trains and thoroughly enjoyed the modern improvement. Martin Clark, President of the Osaka Bible Seminary, and his wife, Evalyn, were most cordial to us during our visit in the city of Osaka, which was now only three hours away from Tokyo on the new train. The Clarks opened their home and the seminary dorms to us during our short stay.

It was during a bus ride in this busy commercial city that I learned how Mike Huskey and Casey Larsen would exercise their use of the Japanese language. The presence of half a dozen American students did not go unnoticed on the crowded bus, especially when Mike and Casey began insulting one another in Japanese. "Your nose is too long," declared Mike, as he pointed to Casey's nose. "You are fat!" countered Casey as he pushed on Mike's paunch with his finger. When their antics produced spontaneous laughter from the passengers, it egged them on to further exaggerate the insults, tagging each other with animal names. "You are a monkey." "You are an elephant." The insults continued in mock seriousness.

A Japanese lady passenger thrust a 1000 yen note in Mike's shirt pocket just before she got off the bus. "*Domo arigato gozaimasu*" (Thank you very much) she declared as she covered her mouth but continued to laugh. Up until this point I was trying to hide, but I began to realize that the fun performance of these young guys had unknowingly triggered the Japanese funny bone. A people of great reserve, they enjoy their professional comedians who do what they would never think of doing in public – they insult each other. Mike and Casey were doing this and expressing their insults with the added humor of foreign accents spoken in childlike Japanese. Jokingly, I told the fellows later, "Keep this up and I get half of the profits."

Martin drove us in a van to Osaka's seaport where we boarded a ship that would traverse the inland sea en route to Beppu, Kyushu. From there we would board the train and travel to Kanoya, where a youth rally was scheduled. When I heard of the sheer beauty of travel on the Inland Sea I took pains to include this adventure in our travel plans. I didn't realize that most of the journey would be at night when there was little visibility. Since we were tired, it was reassuring to be shown a place to lie down amidst a room filled with people. Seeing that our group was safely bedded down I gently moved the child's arm that had flopped in my face, and tried to go to sleep. Hit by the child's flopping arm again I woke up and became worried when I did not see Casey's form. His failure to return kept me awake until morning. We later learned that he spent the night conversing with members of the crew. When I heard their friendly expressions to Casey at our departure, I decided not to rebuke him for the worry he caused.

Wrong Train and Hasty Rerouting

There are train connections from Beppu that could take us more directly to Kanoya, where Yoshii Sensei was preparing for a youth rally. I included this route in our travel plans, but somehow missed the necessary transfer connection. I discovered too late that our train was going around Kagoshima Bay to the other side. Walter Maxey anticipated my mistake and met us in Kagoshima and told us that they were waiting in Kanoya. If we hurried we could catch the ferry across the bay and the bus on into Kanoya. This would, of course, get us there a couple of hours late. Upon arrival, Sheila and Kathy let me know they were not going to show up at the rally until they had showered and changed clothes. The guys used their body spray deodorant and showed up first, redeeming the time. The girls came later redeeming our U.S. reputation for cleanliness and well grooming.

My apologies for our lateness were brushed aside with an easy, "*Ii desho,*"(It's O.K.; no problem). We were then directed to the appetizing food placed on the picnic tables which had been set up in a lawn area behind the mission. The Maxey family was home on furlough, but just as Mark had written, Pastor Yoshii took care of all the planning. The young people surrounded our students, eager to practice their English. Watching the good natured interaction was rewarding. Meanwhile, Yoshii Sensei took a moment to explain to me the plans for the next day to take the bus and ferry back to the other side of the bay where we were to take part in a four day camp. He wanted me to know that the Christians would be one group of a number of others meeting in a prefectural health camp that included a commando course.

Chapter Thirty Four

WINDING UP THE 1979 TOUR

Commando Camp

The camp was reminiscent of my navy boot camp experience. Husky athletic directors were looking over your shoulders as you ran, climbed over barriers, swung from rung to rung over a chasm, and took a long down hill ride hanging on a pulley apparatus. They did shout encouragement at you as you huffed and puffed toward the finish line. The morning flag raising ceremonies contrasted my USA experience. Standing at attention was the same, but the flag was that of the Rising Sun. Casey Larsen felt uncomfortable with this early a.m. ritual and began to avoid it. I felt at peace that the war was over and the two countries were showing mutual respect.

Once this aspect of the prefecture health regimen was over, our Christian camp had separate well equipped rooms for classes and a general assembly hall for chapel. Announcements were made indicating that "the Christian band" had done well in the commando course ratings. But most of all it cheered my heart to see our SJBC gang being used in the classrooms. I caught glimpses of Kathy, Sheila, and Casey interacting with students. George and John were taking turns writing discussion points on the blackboard. Mike Huskey kept busy, in or out of classes, strumming his guitar and teaching choruses to gathered youth. It was a good opportunity for our students to teach the Japanese campers who appeared eager to learn English and Bible.

Even though it had been five years since I was last in Japan, they asked me to be the evening vespers speaker. There were opportunities to use Japanese in our San Jose College. Joseph Chae, an older Korean student applicant, was being turned down on the basis of insufficient fluency in English. When the dean heard Joseph and I conversing in Japanese he permitted him to enter provisionally if I would mentor him. Mr. Chae did gain in his English ability and graduated; during the interim he and I often spoke in Japanese. This helped prepare me for a return to Japan. Understanding that many of the students I would be speaking to in the camp chapel were not yet Christians, I stayed with simple messages from the parables in the gospels.

Camp Fire Drama Time

Japanese students recruited Mike Huskey and Casey Larsen for an elaborate skit they had planned for campfire time. Gifted in ad-libbing, Mike and Casey fit right into the role of the prophets of Baal, who had been challenged to a power encounter by Elijah, the prophet (I Kings 18:19-39). The staging was set with an altar upon which the oxen were to be placed. Robes and grotesque head gear were given to these volunteer prophets of Baal. Then the show began. With dramatized bodily gestures and a display of emotional pleading, using an ingenious mixed use of English and garbled Japanese, Mike and Casey put on a ludicrous but effective performance. The engineering skill of the students was timely for when Elijah's turn came we saw fire leap from the simulated altar as the Prophet called on Jehovah. This was Bible drama at its best for the O.T. message was made interesting and relevant through a highly enjoyable enactment that connected with youth.

By the time the closing night came friendships had solidified and camp morale was high. The singing was more participatory and enjoyed by all. The only note of sadness was that, as all camps do, it was coming to an end. I felt stress as I waited for my turn to bring the last message. My old colleagues, Pastor and Mrs. Ikeda were there in the camp, and Mrs. Ikeda approached me as the camp fire was dying down, "Sensei, isn't it too dark to read? Don't you need a flashlight? Since I had made the effort to

memorize my sermon outline, I responded, "It's O.K. thanks."
I brought a simple message followed by a gentle invitation for
those ready to make decisions.

Walter and Mary's Hospitality

Walter and Mary Maxey made room for all seven of us to
stay at their home following the camp. With the use of
borrowed Japanese futon they could bed us all down, and Mary
made sure that we ate well. Walter took pains to answer student
questions about missionary life and work in Kagoshima, Japan.
He also explained the suggested schedule for the five members
that would stay in Kagoshima. Since John Heberling had been
urged to go to Tanegashima by Doris Isbell, his grandmother,
he chose to go with me to the island. We were to board the ship
the following day.

Aware that we were all experiencing fatigue Walter made
a suggestion. "Why don't you go and see a movie tonight?
Superman is playing and it's in English with Japanese subtitles."
"Neat idea!" exclaimed one student; "Let's go," chimed in the
others. In less time than it takes for Clark Kent to slip into his
Superman costume we were entering a theater in Kagoshima
City that displayed signs showing Christopher Reeve playing
the role of Superman. Seeing the movie was thoroughly an
American experience that tickled our funny bones and made us
feel at home.

Back to Tanegashima

The Yakushima Maru was a much larger ship than the other
vessels on which I had previously traveled. There was much
less pitch and roll and therefore not as much sea sickness, but it
was still a tiring journey. Why did I feel that visiting the island
would be worthwhile for others as well as myself? During my
daughter Sharon's visit in 1974 she noticed the bright tropical
flowers and appreciated the cooling ocean breeze. During that

visit Pastor Ikeda guided us to the home of an illustrious person, Count Tanegashima. He was curator of the museum and taught us about the Portugese visit and the introduction of the flint rifle. Pointing to giant sea turtle shells mounted on the wall, he spoke of the day when these turtles were abundant. He also took us to the burial site of early Christian martyrs, and said that his family had cared for their graves. There was beauty, history, and mystery on the island and so little time.

Although they had only returned one day earlier, the Ikedas were there to meet us and extend hospitality for our overnight visit. I carried with me a number of small, wrapped Omiyage (gifts) and a set of colored slides that portrayed the earlier years when we lived on the island. The Japanese love to see photos that remind them of pleasant and nostalgic experiences. Although it was not Sunday, John and I both experienced loving fellowship, delicious food, and a memorable parting at the Nishinoomote pier the following day.

Okayama Stopover

Since our train pass only allowed for open seating and not reservations, Walter had sent some of his young people ahead to hold seats for us on the train bound for Okayama, our next stop. It gave us another chance to say "Sayonara," which they countered with smiles and the English, "Goodbye." After traversing the length of Kyushu we went through the undersea tunnel onto Honshu and eventually got off at Okayama City. While the group waited at the station, I inquired about which bus went to Hayashino, the home of Audrey West. With the help of friendly passengers we found places for our baggage, and seats to sit down for the winding three-hour ride up the mountain.

Audrey and Ando San, a coworker, met us and took us to her Christian Center; turned on the air conditioner and began to ply us with cool beverage. With motherly-like attention Audrey took care of our needs from Thursday to Sunday. With the help of Tarui Sensei, a high school teacher, and Ando San we were shown the beautiful sights in this mountain area, and given opportunities to shop in the rural villages. At the Center the youth could help with English classes or with music support for the church fellowships.

On one occasion we were taken to a nearby old folks home, which had pride in its modern facilities and the prolonged ages of their tenants. One of the directors served as guide and related the history of the home. Since our American young people were objects of curiosity and displayed open friendliness to the oldsters, they were warmly welcomed. We were introduced to a Japanese lady who was said to be 103 years old. We asked her how did she get to be that old? She responded, with a confident smile, "I didn't eat between meals." This was just before they served us some delicious treats.

Since this was the *Obon* season (Buddhist All Souls Festival) slow moving folk dances were popular for young and old alike. The elderly showed us how they danced as they moved about in a circle. It was humorous and a little disconcerting to see Mike Huskey get in the circle and imitate the movements of the hands and feet of the agile elderly dancer in front of him. I don't think he realized that he was sharing in a ritual that welcomed the return of departed ancestors. At the same time, it may be fair to say that similar to our Halloween, a great number don't really understand the full meaning of their holidays either.

On Sunday there was a joint service of several of the rural churches in the spacious hall at the Christian Center. It was reassuring to see the ministers and elders with their members exchanging warm greetings with one another. Once we were introduced, the arms of Christian fellowship were extended to us. Those I had known previously gave me an American handshake and a warm greeting, "Hamondo Sensei, Shibaraku deshita," (It's been a long time, Mister Hammond). Since it was almost three weeks since we had arrived in Japan, I was feeling more comfortable speaking in Japanese. I enjoyed the privilege of preaching and interacting with the receptive and patient audience at the Hayashino Christian Center.

Recovery of the Missing Camera

It was refreshing to watch the peaceful country scenery without the pressure of schedule as we traveled down the mountain to catch our train in Okayama bound for Tokyo. It felt a little like home when we returned to the Ichigaya Youth Hostel. We had time for a shower and a leisurely dinner. With a good night's sleep we would be ready to shop the next day for souvenirs for friends and family before returning.

We took a local train to Tokyo's Central station and from there we walked to the Bank of America to exchange dollars for yen. Then we headed toward the wholesale district where we had been told that top quality guitars could be purchased at a very low price. Both Mike Huskey and George Gardner, especially, were interested in pursuing this option. The others were quite willing to go along and window shop. Suddenly, Sheila woke from her reverie with a start and exclaimed, "I forgot my camera at the bank!" Since it was a Canon with a large special quality lens, and more importantly a gift from a special person, we understood her anxiety.

Postponing our shopping we went to the nearest public phone and I called the bank. The clerk who answered the phone said that they had discovered the camera, but they would be closing in less than an hour. He gave directions as to how to go to the back door of the closed bank to knock and pick up the camera. Since the way to the bank's rear door was a far different approach, we began to wonder if we were lost. Then I saw the door described over the phone and knocked. Almost immediately the door opened and a hand appeared with the camera. God is good!

Chapter Thirty Five

MISSIONS AT OUR DOORSTEP

Waves of New Immigrants

With the end of the Korean War (1950-1953) thousands of Koreans migrated to California. Two decades later the fall of Saigon (1975), ending the Vietnam War precipitated a flood of Southeast Asian immigrants to the U.S. Following this era, thousands of refugee Cambodians, fleeing from the oppressive measures of the Communist Khmer Rouge, overflowed Thailand refugee camps. Compassionate sponsors brought many of these refugees to American shores for another chance at life. The blood bath motivated by the vengeance of Ayatollah Khomeini after his return to Iran (1979) caused an exodus of many thousands of freedom-loving Iranians. Civil Wars in Central America in the late 1970's and early 1980's pressured increased numbers of Hispanic peoples to seek asylum in America. As a result of this swelling tide of newer immigrants, California's expanding population of ethnic minorities grew to over-forty five percent. It began to dawn on us that God had placed a mission field at our doorstep.

The Results of Teamwork

King Anderson, one of the directors of CityTeam Ministries in San Jose, inspired by his wife's efforts to teach Cambodian refugees in their home, initiated a cross-cultural training program for volunteer tutors in area churches. Central Christian Church, was one of the most responsive to this two-week training program. Some twenty of their members began helping ethnic families through English tutoring and friendship evangelism. Shortly after this, Bryce Jessup, minister at Central, accepted the call to be President of San Jose Bible College.

The Bible College had good rapport with CityTeam. Director Harry Brown had studied at SJBC; their Hispanic outreach was led by Wolfgang Fernandez and Ray Llovio; Paul Cummins led the black ministry – all were SJBC alumni. Anne Cooper, Nick Desmond, and Corky Riley, also SJBC graduates worked in CityTeam's Rescue Mission. General Director, Pat Robertson and other key personnel such as King Anderson, John Fuder, Chuck Starnes and Roy Thompson had been featured speakers in Bible College chapel and classrooms. Camp May Mac and youth outreach programs were assisted by students from the College.

For several years the faculty at SJBC had been experiencing difficulties with the growing number of students from refugee backgrounds who lacked skill in basic English. The increased use of visual aids and flexible approaches in testing were tried but unresolved problems remained. The idea of having a separate evening school to meet the specialized needs of ethnic students began to germinate at the College. Just at this time an article by Chuck Starnes advocating a training center for ethnic leadership appeared in **Vision,** a City Team publication. A copy of this article was given to President Jessup of SJBC with the suggestion that our school facilities and personnel be offered in a team effort. Approval was immediately given to contact City Team.

After several planning sessions held with SJBC mission personnel and City Team leaders in the summer of 1985, a decision to go ahead with a team effort to start the Multicultural Bible Institute (MCBI) was made. I recommended that Frank Schattner be the administrator of the evening school. Frank was a member of Central Church, had become an SJBC dorm dad, and was one of the key leaders in City Team's tutorial program. He and his wife Jan, had repeatedly hosted encouragement meetings for volunteer tutors. Their ethnic contacts along with those involved in City Team's training course were among the first students who applied for study in the proposed evening training program. The fall semester of the Multicultural Bible

Institute began with 37 students and continued to grow during the following decade. God had opened a window of opportunity that would prove to be very fruitful.

Strategic Church Planting

Realizing the need for follow up on the Cambodian families by a Christian leader who spoke their language, Bryce Jessup and Frank Schattner traveled to Southern California to see Moses Samol Seth. Moses was a dedicated Christian leader who had been successful in evangelism in the Kao I Dang refugee camp in Thailand. LaVerne Morse had sponsored him to come to the U.S. While adding to his education by taking studies at Cincinnati Bible Seminary and Pacific Christian College, he was active in church planting. Bryce and Frank hoped to have him recommend one of his trained leaders to help us in San Jose. To their happy surprise Moses offered to come himself to follow up on seekers and establish a Cambodian congregation. Events moved along quickly and on February 3, 1985, a new ethnic church was born in the spacious multipurpose building of San Jose Bible College. Leaders from CityTeam, SJBC, and participating area churches were there to celebrate this significant birth.

After only two short years new staff was added because of the pressures of growth. Dr. Roger Edrington, a former missionary to Britain, was invited to serve as Associate Director.[1] Ray Llovio, one of SJBC's bilingual graduates, was requested to lead the Spanish department and serve as the Associate Director of Ethnic Church Relations. The willingness of missionaries, such as Dr. Yoon Kwon Chae of Korea And Gil Contreras of Mexico to teach and share their rich cultural and first language experience attracted many students. It was a joy for me to teach in both day and evening classes and to co-edit "**All the People**," MCBI's quarterly newsletter.

Extension classes increased our outreach. Dr. Thomas Cooper taught African- American students in an extension in East Palo Alto. Moses Samol Seth began extensions for Cambodians in

Modesto and Stockton, and Don Byers, a former missionary to Thailand, recruited and taught Khmu refugees both in the Stockton area and Oakland. Lois and C.W. Callaway, missionaries from North Thailand, began extensions for Mien and other tribal students in Vallejo and Richmond. An Iranian pastor, Fereidoun Es-Haq, began teaching in the Farsi language in Los Gatos.

By networking with associated ministers and graduates the Multicultural Mission Department encouraged the planting of churches from the beginning. In the first five years twenty-two churches were planted among diverse ethnic groups: eleven churches among the dispersed Cambodians; five Korean churches in the Bay area; one Asian Indian, one Iranian, one new Hispanic congregation, and three Khmu churches.

Changing Student Statistics

As the foreign student advisor I experienced a dramatic increase in ethnic students on my counselee list. In 1985 I had almost an even balance of 10 American- born to 12 newer ethnic students. In 1986 it was 13 Euro-Americans to 16 of the newer immigrants. Three years later, I had 44 ethnic counselees and only 2 traditional Anglo students to counsel. In my daytime classes I was seeing the same shift during this five-year period. Traditional Anglo-Americans dominated my classes before 1985; five years later about 50% of my day classes were attended by the newer immigrants. At the 1974 commencement when I first saw students graduate that I had taught the full four years, there were seven ethnic names on the roster. In 1989, because of our intentional outreach to minority groups, there were 38 ethnic graduates ready to serve in their communities or return to minister in their country of origin.

7 Key Factors Ensuring Victory

1) **Providence** – Belief that the historical circumstances that placed thousands of receptive immigrants at our

doorstep were of God; and the realization that the preparation of key leaders had began decades earlier, convinced us that we were harvesting where others had labored (John 4:38).

2) **Prayer** - Overwhelmed by the sheer size of the task of reaching so many during the relatively short time of receptivity, leaders were driven to prayer.

3) **Vision** - Key individuals in administrative positions became convicted of the need to train ethnic leaders as the most effective way to overcome language and cultural barriers.

4) **Trans-denominational** - The fear of a loss of denominational distinctives can often prevent regional churches from working together. Fortunately God had convinced a number of key leaders that they could transcend party loyalties and cooperate without compromise for the good of the Kingdom.

5) **Networking** - By cooperating with churches and parachurch organizations that were involved in crosscultural communication, experience could be shared and diverse gifts utilized to advance the work of God.

6) **Teamwork** – The launching of MCBI was a team effort. Its rapid growth, so dependent upon parachurch agencies, pastors, missionaries, and widely spread extension classes, was a united effort. Continued success depended a great deal on our ability to resist the temptation to exclusive ownership of the program. By inviting others to identify with us and by appreciating their valuable contribution we could maintain the unity of the Spirit.

8) **Commitment** – Sacrificial serving and giving marked the first five years of this crosscultural training program. Busy administrators and teachers had to stretch in order to follow through with the demanding schedule of organizing details and teaching in both the day and night classes. Part-time volunteers continued

to play a strategic role in reaching and encouraging ethnic students.

The Japan Connection

Our readers may well ask, "What does all that have to do with your book title, *Stories From Japan, Past to Present*?" My answer is that God used my Japan experience to help mold me into a more humble servant and teach me insights in communication to people of diverse cultures. When I went to Japan in 1954, in spite of my Bible training, there was a residue of ethnocentric pride in my heart. Having served in the U.S. Navy (1943-45) I was part of the "G.I. generation" who were taught that they were part of the allied team that had defeated the enemies of freedom and had brought peace to the world. I needed to learn to love my former enemies and to understand their experiences and feelings.

Through my many mistakes I learned the lesson to listen more carefully to gain a more accurate understanding of cultural behavior. I came to appreciate the positive values in Asian, and more specifically Japanese, culture. It became evident that I could benefit by being on the receiving end of a cultural exchange. My simplistic judgments of character based on stereotypes were replaced by a deeper understanding of the conditions that produce behavioral patterns. Discovering that an organizer of a *Kamikaze* squadron in WWII was a sincere Christian caused me to stop and listen to his story. We both believed in the truth of the Scriptures, and we both had come to understand that the gospel, not war was the way to peace among men.

In keeping with my trans-denominational stance and a desire to network with faith churches, I kept continued contact with existing Japanese churches in San Jose. The Japanese Christian Church on Union Avenue in Cambell was founded by OMS International and is listed as evangelical and nondenominational. Nobumichi Murakami, a 1969 graduate of SJCC and a successful missionary in Japan, was from this congregation. Mitsuko Nishimura and Keiko Kuwajima, 1984 graduates, became leaders of Bethel Home for the elderly Japanese. George Gardner, an SJCC grad who had a taste of Japan on our 1979 short term trip, served as their youth director for a number of years. I found the leaders and members of this church to be warm and receptive, but also in need of reassuring acceptance by the dominant American culture because of their enforced internment during WWII.

Calstar Christian Church, a charismatic fellowship, was founded in San Jose by Pastor Masa Ishihara, a post-war immigrant. I found him to have an expressive but balanced faith. To follow up with linguistic help for the international students he sent to our evening MCBI program, we asked him to teach some courses in Japanese. This helped a number to accumulate credit until their English improved and they could enter the English day program and finish their studies for graduation. This proved fruitful. Seven Japanese finished their training and returned to Japan to serve.

---

[1] Edrington eventually replaced Director San Masilamoney, who moved on.

Chapter Thirty Six

1985 CULTURAL TOUR

Arrival in Haneda

The SJCC students traveling with me to Japan in the summer of 1985 were: Frank and Florence Winter, a retired I.B.M. technician and his wife; Chris and Tawndi Wohlwend, a young couple on the staff of the Fremont church, who are outstanding in piano and vocal music; Janel Butisbauch, a personable single student; and Richard Cutts, a recent graduate interested in missions.

Our China Airlines plane landed at Haneda on July 24. After clearing customs it was pleasant to be met by old friends and neighbors, Takekawa San and Omino San. They loaded our larger suitcases into Mr. Omino's truck so we could ride the trains with only our shoulder strap bags. We met them again at Higashi-nakano, where we had been offered a place to stay by veteran missionary, Leone Cole, who lived right behind the church in the former home of Andrew and Betty Patton.

Our location was convenient for traveling the next day into downtown Tokyo to exchange dollars to yen and to turn in our rail pass vouchers for wallet size tourist rail passes, saving considerably when traveling on any of the government lines. We then went to the travel office near the Tokyo station and made reservations to travel early the following day to Kyoto, the former capitol and cultural center of early Japan. Cameras were clicking as we spent the rest of the day sightseeing.

Visiting Ancient Nara

For the first time my group included married couples so I had reserved rooms in the modest priced Dai-Ni Tower Hotel near the Kyoto station. From there we went to Nara, 40 minutes away on a connecting line. Nara was the early court capitol before Kyoto, and here in a spacious park is located the **Todaiji**, the largest wooden building in the world, which houses the **Daibutsu**, one of the biggest bronze images of the Buddha. It was reassuring to meet Sakae Sensei at the Nara station. He was one of our earlier converts from Tanegashima, who now ministers in this ancient religious city. He had kindly offered to be our guide for the day.

The Daibutsu dates back to 746 A.D. Historians believe that Emperor Shomu ordered the building of this giant Buddha as a charm against smallpox and as a symbol that the ruler wielded over the country. Over the centuries the statue was broken up at times because of earthquakes and fires. The present figure was built during the Edo period and stands 16 meters high, consists of 437 tons of bronze and 139 kilograms of gold. It is huge, and yet it is only two-thirds the size of the original.[1]

It seemed evident that many of the Japanese visitors looked upon the image with a sense of awe; whereas to others it was only a cultural symbol of departed glory.

Sakae Sensei pointed out something that was very interesting. Not far behind this giant figure there is a wooden column with about a 14-inch wide diameter hole in the bottom. A legend states that, those who can squeeze through this hole, are ensured of enlightenment. After seeing that we hesitated to try, Sakae Sensei grinned at us and wriggled his way through the tight opening. It was apparent that for him this popular belief was more humorous than credible.

Hundreds of tame deer amble freely through the Nara park. Visitors can buy prepared food for them for 100 yen a sack. The deer are not shy but push in quickly for something to eat, and sometimes frighten children. In ancient times the deer were considered messengers of the gods, but are now merely considered a part of Japan's cultural treasures. Vendors line the walkways offering cultural souvenirs and religious charms as well as snacks of all kinds. The general atmosphere is more like that of a country fair than of a sacred religious site.

Kyoto's Cultural Highlights

A good night's rest in our Kyoto hotel prepared us for another day of cultural sight seeing and study. Kyoto is the religious and cultural center of Japan, filled with innumerable temples and shrines, so that it is best to pick out one or two of the better known sights when your time is limited. I first asked directions that would take us to **Nijo Castle**, the ancient residence of the first Tokugawa Shogun, Ieyasu. The very elaborate structure was built in 1603 and the style was designed to show the Shogun's power and prestige. The most interesting feature of the long wooden corridors of the castle is its "nightingale floors." The floor guards against the entrance of any treacherous intruder because it is designed to emit musical squeaks when anyone walks on it. Even when trying our best, we couldn't proceed down the hallways without making noise. Another safeguard, we are told, was concealed chambers where guards could stand watch. While deploring the cruel excesses of Ieyasu, one could not help but admire the workmanship of his carpenters. [2]

The **Ginkaku-ji Temple** was first a villa of the Shogun Ashikaga, who built it in 1482. The name means, "Silver Pavilion" and it was intended to have been covered with silver but never was quite finished. It was converted into a temple after the death of the Shogun. When we were there it appeared to be weather-worn and did not live up to its reputation as a breath-taking sight.

We checked out of our Kyoto hotel in time to catch the bullet train at 12:29 p.m. to Okayama City. We then took the bus to Hayashino, the home of my former college English teacher, Audrey West, and enjoyed a fellowship dinner at the Christian Center. In the morning we shared in the service with the local church and in the afternoon took part in a combined church fellowship at the Center. Chris and Tawndi blessed us with their special music during the worship. I preached in my somewhat rusty Japanese. Typically, I saw smiles where I had not intended humor. We ate lunch at a restaurant in the area and prepared for the *Shinboku-kai* (informal fellowship meeting) that evening. Each of the team members had a chance to share and interact with those who came. All too soon, our short visit was over.

Visit in Hiroshima

On Monday we descended the mountain in time to catch the 1:12 p.m. train to Hiroshima, arriving there at 2:08 p.m. Single missionary Carolyn Barricklow and friends met us. That very evening Carrolyn asked us to share a word of greeting or testimony at the Community Center where they were having a cultural heritage program. We heard kind words of welcome and saw a demonstration by a martial arts expert. Most of those in attendance were lively young people. I was impressed by Carrolyn's free use of the Japanese language and her composed demeanor.

After introducing us to the group we were each asked to share. Frank Winter's testimony of long years of service with I.B.M. after which he entered Bible College to better serve the Lord was challenging. Chris and Tawndi expressed appreciation for what they were experiencing in Japanese culture. Janel and Richard did the same. Carolyn did a good job of interpreting. I spoke in Japanese but felt unsure if I was connecting with these non-Christian youth. But, thanks to Carrolyn, the spirit of the meeting was cordial and there was a warm enthusiastic exhange.

On Tuesday we took time for laundry and careful repacking. Wednesday's schedule included a visit to the Peace Memorial Museum and later a ferry boat trip to a nearby island. Having previously seen the graphic photos of the aftermath of the WWII atom bombing of Hiroshima, I was more braced for the shock. Our team members grimaced at the scenes and felt the full horror of such total warfare. Yet, they were glad that they had shared this experience with their new Japanese friends and joined them for a group photo.

That afternoon the ferry boat took us to a nearby island called, Miyajima that had a mountain with a commanding view. Lydia Kishi, a former friend and translator from Kagoshima, was our guide. What I didn't know was that Janel Butisbauch had a fear of heights, but was bravely trying to overcome it. What to us was a beautiful view from a cable car, was a very terrifying experience for Janel. Going up that mountain in a tightly packed closed space was a real test for her. After the strenuous experiences of the day, it was quite relaxing to share in an informal fellowship and watch fireworks, which were set off more for fun than to celebrate any particular occasion.

The Shimabara Rebellion

At 10:08 a.m. we were once more aboard the Shinkansen (bullet train) heading south to north Kyushu. Arriving at Hakata at 11:45 a.m. we pushed out of the station and met Ben Hirotaka, who was our host for the next few days. Ben had come to the U.S. from Japan when a youngster. After receiving training he and his wife, Nobuko, returned to Japan to serve as missionaries. We were made to feel at home in their care and were introduced to their friendly church folk during a fellowship dinner.

The next day we loaded into Ben's van and went on a long drive to Amakusa and the historic site of the Shimabara Rebellion. Shimabara is located on a peninsula adjacent to Nagasaki, the second city to be atom bombed. The historic significance of Shimabara is closely associated with the rejection of early Catholic Christianity in Japan. The initial reason for the rebellion of the peasants in Shimabara was excessive taxation enforced by an oppressive *daimyo* (feudal lord). But the fact that most of the peasants were Christians made them the brunt of the already existent anti-Christian policy of the Tokugawa Shogun, who feared the western political connections of the Catholic priests.

After 3,000 of Nagasaki's best fighting *samurai* were defeated by the peasants, the governor called for aid from the Shogun, who sent 200,000 soldiers to stamp out the 30,000 resistant rebels. Entrenched in the Hara fortress the rebel forces held out for months, but then ran out of food and ammunition. In April of 1638 the shogunate forces defeated the peasants and then proceeded to behead an estimated 37,000 of the recalcitrant and their sympathizers. From that time on until the 1860's the ban on Christianity was strictly enforced.[3] As we walked the pathways that displayed short legends of those who had been slain on the spot, we wondered to what extent this history restrained the Japanese from accepting the Christian faith in our day.

Camp Fun and Travel Fears

Sharing in the new Christian camp in the cool mountains of Nagano Prefecture was refreshing after the heavy cultural lessons of Hiroshima and Shimabara. Harold Sims and Mark Pratt were directors, and Andrew and Betty Patton were managers. Yokomizo Sensei and other Japanese leaders were their hands-on associates. With such a capable team that included an excellent cook, camp was bound to be good.

Tawndi Wohlwend had her chance to demonstrate what she had learned in my one-unit language class. Harold Sims expressed genuine surprise as she directed the evening song services, using Japanese to give song page numbers, request the crowd to sit or stand, and select men or women for certain stanzas. Chris accompanied her on the piano with the same relaxed confidence. The other young students on the team also mixed well with the Japanese youth which gave me a feeling of pride.

Our retired couple, Frank and Florence, showed what good sports they were by joining the youth in the evening skits. Portraying an updated Prodigal Son story they went through the routine of the foreigners in a far away land dancing in a disco. Their twirling bodies and waving hands timed with a background of beat music produced outbursts of laughter. With the able help of Mark Pratt the daytime Bible classes went well and I felt like I connected with the youth in my chapel message. Harold and I had both turned 60, but during a softball game we managed to connect our bats with the ball and get around the bases. This too, was an expression of culture.

During the weekend following camp the team split up. Part of the group went with Harold to his church in west Tokyo; the rest were guided to Paul and Kathleen Pratt's place in the southern part of the city. I was scheduled to preach in Kumegawa. We all came together again Sunday afternoon at an informal youth rally at the Pratt home and shared our experiences. Paul put in a video of, "The Ten Commandments," which stimulated interaction with the Japanese youth. After a strengthening fellowship time, Paul loaded us in his van and drove us to an economy hotel located near the train line where we could travel to the Haneda airport the next day.

That last night in Tokyo, August 12, 1985, I turned on the television in my hotel room to watch the news and learned of the major tragedy in which Japan Airlines, Flight 123, had crashed into a mountain only 100 km from Tokyo. All 15 crew members and 505 of the 509 passengers were killed. I was hoping that the students did not watch the news in their rooms. We were scheduled to leave the following day on the same model plane, a Boeing 747. But I underestimated their faith; they had heard the news and were still trusting in the Lord's watch care as we headed for the airport by train and monorail that morning.

Once again the fear of heights did attack Janel after we were in the air. Chris prayed as Tawndy massaged her shoulders until she calmed down. Fatigue brought the release of sleep, and the rest of the trip was uneventful. The moment the plane's wheels touched down safely, a greatly relieved Janel shouted, "**Praise the Lord!**" Her exclamation broke the tension and produced a burst of spontaneous laughter from the passengers. Later, I learned that Janel had conquered her fear and was again flying to distant points to serve.

[1] JAPAN, pp. 456-57, Published by The Lonely Planet, 1997 edition.
2 Ibid., JAPAN, pp. 383, 392, The Lonely Planet, 1997 edition.
3 Wikipedia, the Free Encyclopedia, Shimobara Rebellion.

Chapter Thirty Seven

ALL JAPAN CONVENTION

A Special Invitation

"Hamondo Sensei, for the first time the All Japan Convention of the Christian Churches will be held on Tanegashima, and we want you to bring a message for us." I felt unprepared to accept Pastor Ikeda's invitation in his letter, but sensing that God's hand was in it, my emotions quieted and I felt a sense of peace. It had been 38 years since I first visited the island of Tanegashima, and 7 years since I had last been to Japan; yet mentally there had not been a disconnection. In my college classes and church messages I often referred to my mission experiences. However, I realized that I would have to work to revive my speaking ability in Japanese. Circumstances had interrupted my pattern of returning periodically to my former field of service.

Earthquake Shakeup

The Loma Prieta earthquake of October 17, 1989, measured 7.1 on the Richter scale, and caused havoc as far as 70 miles away from its center in the Santa Cruz Mountains. There were 63 deaths, 3,757 injuries, and 6 billion dollars in property damage.[1] Standing in the kitchen in our San Jose home, when it began to shake at 5:04 p.m., I saw dishes fall from the cupboards and a large wall mirror that hung in the entrance way come crashing down. I learned later that my wife, who was working on a four storied office floor, had been knocked off her feet. Because of the resultant pain in her chest and shoulders I urged her to get an x-ray.

It was November before she could schedule the x-ray and December 8 before she learned the results. Our college Christmas celebration was scheduled on that very evening. Without letting me know what she had learned about the results of the x-ray, Eleanor urged me to go to the festivities without her because she was not feeling well. After returning from the party I learned the alarming truth - the x-ray showed that her lungs were opaque. The breast cancer discovered 8 years earlier, that we thought she had fought and won, had returned with vengeance. The prognosis of the doctor was that she had only about 3 months to live!

It had been a year since my wife passed on to her heavenly reward when Pastor Ikeda's letter came. She had defied the odds and lived a year and three months before the cancer took her life. From her hospital style-bed in our front room she could view the play of colors the refracted sunlight created on the row of large glass blocks I had installed in the patio at her request. With her new portable phone she frequently called family members, especially the grandchildren, and her many friends. The Kaiser Hospice workers had coached me how to administer morphine to ease the pain. On March 12, 1991, she was freed from all her pain and went home to the Lord.

Closing The Gaps

It was apparent to my family and friends that my speech and behavior revealed that I was still grieving. Returning to Japan might be the experience I needed to regain healing and a sense of renewal. To do so I must close some gaps, the foremost of which was the language gap. To revive my ability to hear and comprehend I resumed attending the Japanese language section of the Japanese Christian Church in San Jose. To regain my understanding of the written ideographs, I plunged into study of the Japanese texts assigned to me. Now living alone, I spent most of my free time in preparing my message for the convention, and in reviewing the basics of Japan's complex language.

Although Asians respect older people, I felt that I needed to find youthful student volunteers to take with me. In previous visits the students were the ones who closed the gap and interacted freely with other youth who make up the larger portion of the younger churches. Perhaps because of rising travel costs, I ended up with just two very unique volunteers. John Alpoyanis was Greek and retained his ability to speak his parent's first language. Sin Yon Pak, was Korean, who I learned later, had a striking ability in vocal music. More than it being my calculated choice, I believed the Lord had His hand in selecting these companions.

A Warm Up Strategy

From the start I planned our itinerary in Japan so that I could preach portions of my convention message as we traveled from **Tokyo** to stops between, on to **Kagoshima** and finally **Tanegashima.** My strategy was based on my growing belief that "practice makes perfect" and my feeling that John and Sin Yon would not be offended by the repetition of a message they did not understand. I was first invited to preach at the Machida Church in south Tokyo since the founders were on furlough.

When I saw that old friends and former members of churches in which I had served had come to Machida, it made it easier to speak. Domen San, who had made his decision to accept Christ years previously when I preached in Tanabe, was there in the morning to lead and interpret for John and Sin Yon. That afternoon in a scheduled rally, Harold Sims was present to translate for the two young men as they brought short messages. Hearing this bilingual exchange helped revive my language skills.

Ben Hirotaka gave us red carpet treatment when we got off at **Hakata** in northern Kyushu. He insisted on taking time out to guide us to **Nagasaki**, known for being the second city to be atom bombed. John and SinYon were getting cultural exposure as well as opportunities to meet the Christian Japanese. That evening after returning I learned of Sin Yon's special gift. When asked at a church gathering if he could sing, he brought himself erect and spontaneously sang a hymn boldly and clearly without any instrumental accompaniment. Later I came to understand that Sin Yon's fear of the Japanese was overcome during this trip. He had been brought up listening to stories of the harsh treatment of Koreans by the Japanese. The warm hospitality of the Christians had put his fears to rest.

Nostalgic Visit In Kagoshima

Finally we arrived in Kagoshima, the southernmost prefecture, the place where we began our Japan ministry. As we had done on previous visits we divided our efforts so that we could serve on both the Satsuma and Osumi sides of the peninsula. John and Sin Yon stayed under the guidance of Walter and Mary Maxey and I moved on across the bay and took the bus to Kanoya where I was scheduled to speak. Mark Maxey was busy preparing for his part in the convention. I stayed up late to study through my convention notes and prepare for my Sunday morning message as well. Gradually I was becoming more assured that the rust was being removed from my former Japanese fluency.

My visit to the Kanoya congregation was pleasant. But I couldn't help notice that people I knew were getting older. During the lunch time fellowship the members of the former youth group that I had known, jokingly referred to themselves as, "the old youth group." In my memory, Pastor Yoshii was a young man, but his touch of grey hair and dignified manner affirmed the reality of the passage of time.

A big change that I enthusiastically welcomed was that in place of the six-hour journey to Tanegashima on the older ships you could now travel on the fast "Toppy" or hover-craft that sped to the island in less than two hours. When I rejoined John and Sin Yon, Walter helped get our tickets for travel on this new sleek craft. The young students seemed to take the fast ride for granted. But I remembered well the queasiness I felt on the older vessels and therefore immensely enjoyed the trip.

Convention Memories

After they permitted us to unfasten our seat belts, I could stand and look out and observe the many changes in Nishinoomote's harbor and pier. Among the throng of people who were waiting for friends and family members to disembark, it was not hard to pick out Pastor Ikeda's white hair. He greeted us warmly and then straightway took us to the New Tanegashima Hotel which was finished just in time to host the convention. Beautiful bouquets of flowers surrounded the registration desk. We were helped by courteous convention personnel who were registering guests and assigning rooms. I learned that Pastor Ikeda had already paid for all three of us. Since I was scheduled to bring the first message at 7:30 that evening, I went to my assigned room and spent the rest of the day in study and prayer.

It was clear from the evening preliminaries that there was careful planning in the organizational details of the convention. Mrs. Sadako Tanoue, a lady of senior years, who headed the convention planning committee, made the opening remarks and welcomed the guests. Mark Maxey, representing the Christian ministers of Kagoshima Prefecture, gave warm words of welcome on behalf of the churches. After extensive introduction, Mayor Enokimoto, reassured the gathered assembly that the City of Nishinoomote was delighted that they had come to their historic island.

The theme of the convention displayed on a large banner above the speaker's stand was based on **John 14:16, "And I will ask the Father and He will give you another Comforter that He may be with you forever"** (NASV). Pastor Ikeda introduced me by relating how our family including two small children had come to live on the island, during which time a third child was born. He went on to say that I was currently a teacher at San Jose Christian College and had repeatedly returned to Japan with students. Finally he mentioned that my wife had passed away the previous year.

Wanting to accustom the Japanese audience to my manner of speaking I began by describing how it had taken me six hours by ship when I first came to the island, but today it took us less than two hours on the Toppy. Then I went on to describe how Mr. Maxey had first introduced us to the island in 1954. To add a touch of humor I told how I was impressed by Mr. Maxey's humility when he dropped heavily to his knees on the floor of the old two-story Japanese Inn in a formal bow to our hosts with the result that the building shook. I went on to sincerely thank Mark for his guidance and suggestion that we make Tanegashima our place of service.

Then I spoke of the occasion of Ikeda's first visit when we rode on my motor-cycle up to Number 16 bus stop in the mountains to answer the call of Mr. Sakae when his wife died. I described the dramatic circumstances in which Ikeda, who was yet a seminary student, conducted a memorial service and boldly sang, "The Love of God," in a clear voice that had great impact on the gathered mourners. There was a strong feeling that God's Spirit was with us. Later, Yoshiyuki, Sakae San's son, was to become a Christian and enter the ministry. This gave some background for Sakae Sensei who brought an enthusiastic message the following day.

In the course of my remarks I announced how Bill Jessup, the founder of our college, had spoken in our chapel and declared that he wanted to preach the gospel until he died. Three months later, after speaking in a local congregation, he sat down in the pew, had a heart attack and went home to the Lord at age 86. My point with each of the above examples was that the Lord was there in each instance. He was there in our choice of service on Tanegashima. He was there to comfort at Sakae San's cottage during the memorial service for his wife. And the Lord was there in the life of William Jessup giving guidance and purpose right up until the day he died.

Among us three speakers, Professor Oda from the Osaka Bible Seminary was the scholar. He was known among church leaders nation wide for his editing of the widely published Japanese-Greek Lexicon. He had not only studied Biblical Greek but in his graduate studies in Athens had become fluent in the contemporary language. He and John Alpoyanis had several

Greek conversational exchanges. John fell asleep during Oda Sensei's message. However, he awoke with a start when the professor facetiously addressed him directly from the platform in his mother tongue.

In his introductory remarks, Sakae Sensei mentioned that Tanegashima is known as "The Island of the Gun." Portuguese vessels, blown off course, landed on Tanegashima in 1543 and introduced western technology to Japan including their ancient rifle. The local ruler bought two of the firearms and had them copied. Six years after the Portuguese introduced the gun, Francis Xavier introduced salvation through the cross in Kagoshima. In 1575 Oda Nobunaga used the gun to unify Japan's warring clans.[2] The message of the cross is being used to bring Japanese believers out of isolation and unify them with the worldwide community of the Kingdom of God.

---

[1] Wikipedia Free Encyclopedia, The Loma Prieta Earthquake, October 17, 1989.

[2] Wikipedia Free Encyclopedia, under Musket.

Chapter Thirty Eight

MEETING THE JAPAN FAMILY

Finding a New Partner

During an area-wide prayer meeting held in the college cafeteria, we sat by round tables facing toward the prayer leader in the front. A graceful, middle-aged lady took the chair beside mine. During a time of self-introductions I learned that her name was Beverly Wynia, a widow. At a point in the prayer meeting, the leader asked for the names of countries for which people were particularly burdened. Beverly raised her hand for China. I spoke up for Japan. Then the leader asked people to separate and start their own table for that particular country. I surprised Beverly and myself by saying, "Let's not separate. Let's start an Asian table." Which we did.

After hearing Beverly's challenging account of her visit to China with the English Language Institute of China (ELIC), I asked her if she could show her slides in my Introduction to Missions class. She agreed. Beverly came as scheduled and did a good job of talking up short term missions with ELIC. To thank her for her contribution I later invited her to a Japanese dinner at Minato's restaurant in San Jose's Japan town. This led to a reciprocal exchange in which I was invited to dinner at her house and an opportunity to meet her family and friends. Both the delicious roast beef dinner and the sweet disposition of her son and his fiancee convinced me that I should get better acquainted with the cook.

To make a not so long story shorter, after an extended pattern of weekly dating I proposed marriage to Beverly. The date was set for June 26, 1993, and her two sons and my five youngsters were all invited to take part in the ceremony. Following the piano prelude by Christopher Luthi, an accomplished pianist who began his training with Beverly, youngest son, Bill Hammond, opened the service with two special guitar numbers. The lighting of candles was by Kristy and Laura Zinsmaster, Beverly's nieces. My son, Jim, minister of the Verde Valley Christian Church in Arizona, presided over the service. Alternating with the message and vows, eldest son Tim Hammond sang, "The Lord's Prayer," and, "I Love You Truly." A trio made up of Tim, Mary, and Bill Hammond, sang the beautiful Gaither chorus, "Gentle Shepherd."

Everyone available in our extended families had a part. Arlene Williamson, Beverly's sister, was the Matron of Honor; my daughters, Sharon and Mary were bridesmaids. Beverly's two sons, Duane and Jim, served as groomsmen. My brother, Don, was Best Man. Beverly's brother, Jim Zinsmaster, escorted the bride and served as usher along with my brother, Chuck, and son-in-law, Curt Lueck. Seven-year old granddaughter, Karissa Hammond, served as a flower girl. During the closing of the ceremony everyone in the bridal party, including the grandchildren, sang, "Bind Us Together."

Reunion With Japan Friends

After our first wedding anniversary we boarded the plane from San Francisco bound for Tokyo. I wanted Beverly to meet my friends in Japan. Our first stop after arriving at the Narita airport was Yokohama, the new home of the very hospitable Domen family. From there we were scheduled to visit a dozen other cities. Our airline standby privilege (a courtesy of Beverly's oldest son) and Japan Rail Pass helped to make it economically possible. Christian hospitality made it physically and socially enjoyable.

One of our purposes was to make contact with SJCC graduates and other friends. Tetsuo and Hideko Domen opened their home to those in the Tokyo and Yokohama area. Among the college alumni who came were Cathy Heatlie of LIFE Ministries,

Mayumi Takahashi, and Masaaki Minoguchi, accompanied by his lovely new bride. Other U.S. contacts who attended included Keiko Arai, a former SJSU classmate of Beverly's, and Jonathan Hammond, my nephew, who was teaching English in Tokyo. We joined with other Japanese friends in sharing a time of praise and fellowship. The inspirational highlight was when Hideko Domen, our beautiful blind hostess, sang heart warming hymns, accompanied by Beverly at the piano.

Veteran missionaries, Audrey West and Daynise Holloway, are also SJCC graduates. Along with Keith Summers they make up our missionary friends who serve in the small mountain towns of Okayama prefecture. Audrey and Keith, who serve with the Christian Center in Yunogo, gave us a tour of the area, put sumptuous feasts before us, joined us in singing old favorites and hand delivered us to our train for a tender farewell.

Yoshiaki Fukushima is another former SJCC student that came to see us when we visited with Paul and Rickie Clark, also alumni, in Osaka. Yoshi shared his dreams with us, and revisited on Sunday with his mother to hear me preach. In spite of the highest recorded heat wave in 100 years, the Clarks gave us a tour of the Osaka Bible Seminary of which he was president, and also drove us through congested traffic to visit Sakae Sensei, a convert from Tanegashima, who heads up the Ikoma Bible Institute in Nara.

Service Opportunities

In addition to various opportunities for Beverly to play the piano, she shared in English Bible Classes in Okayama with Audrey West, and in Osaka with Rickie Clark. Also, we were hosted to a delicious dinner by the members of one of Ben and Nobuko Hirotaka's Bible classes who wanted to use their English in the relaxed atmosphere of a restaurant in Fukuoka.

Perhaps our greatest contribution was in listening to battle worn soldiers on the front lines of the kingdom. After forty three years of faithful service Mark and Pauline Maxey's one prayer request was that they could stay longer. Tetsuo and Hideko Domen wanted prayer for wider and more effective unity among God's people. Both prayers were focused on finishing the task.

I was asked to preach on each of the three Sundays we were in Japan. In my introductory remarks in the Nishinoomote church I remarked that the work began to do much better when Pastor Ikeda came to help me after his graduation. Hearing a chuckle and noticing hands covering the smiles, I was not surprised to hear later that instead of the Japanese word for "graduation," (sotsugyoshiki), I had used the term for "funeral," (soshiki). One of the members, with a twinkle in her eyes asked, "How did Pastor Ikeda manage to do so much after his funeral?"

Serendipty Surprises

Always the charming host, Pastor Ikeda wanted to show us the improvements on the island of Tanegashima. He took us to the **Tanegashima Development Center** that was housed in a unique building designed like an ancient Portuguese sailing ship. Much like a museum the enclosed display items gave a pictorial overview of the history of the island. Of principal interest was the story of the flintlock rifle that the Portuguese introduced. Both the Portuguese original rifle and the copies made by the Japanese smiths were exhibited. Life-like mannequins were posed in different positions in the production of this historical weapon that changed the history of Japan.

A bigger surprise awaited us when we visited the **Tanegashima Space Center** on the southern tip of the island. Here was a series of modern buildings that take up 8,600,000 square meters. It is known as the most beautiful rocket-launch complex in the world. The main role of the Space Center is the management of satellites at every stage of flight.[1] I couldn't help but recall my reference to the Soviet's first man made satellite in a sermon illustration 37 years previously. Before our eyes were the evidence of the dramatic changes that time had brought.

After our return to the port town, on a pretext of making a home visit, Pastor Ikeda ushered us into a taxi which drove us to a viewing point on top of a hill. There a scene appeared below us of a recently completed well-designed building complex surrounded by spacious grounds which were in process of being attractively landscaped. Colorful playground equipment stood beckoning from every corner. An ornate sign above the entrance is translated as, "Zion Early Childhood Educational Center."

We hastened to get a closer look; kicked off our shoes and entered a full size gymnasium with a glistening wood floor. The smiling minister led us past the young people playing badminton, greeted teachers and smaller children nearby, and began to show us the many specialized rooms that circled the central multi-purpose auditorium. Well equipped offices for the staff, a kitchen that would be a chef's delight, class-rooms designed for little tykes, an adult training center with stacks of yet unboxed computers, and immaculate modern restrooms – all this and more greeted our eyes.

The next day we joined a session for parents. They were listening to a taped program by a skilled Japanese minister who had a good sense of humor. As I watched the expressive faces of the parents I recalled that 36 years previously I had objected to Ikeda's plan to build a kindergarten. Reluctantly, I had finally conceded and set up a sister church program with the Green Valley Church in San Jose. A wise missionary had advised me that our role is similar to that of John the Baptist. We must decrease in order for the national leader to increase in the eyes of his people.

Mission aid had ceased more than 25 years previous to our visit. Now I was observing an indigenous ministry in which parents were being reached and hundreds of kindergartners were being taught to praise and honor Jesus Christ. As Brother Ikeda walked down the streets he was honored and greeted by young and old alike. Over three decades of gently cultivating the resistant soil had produced an environment that shows promise for the future of the church.

This revisit to the place of my earlier ministry with my new wife gave me a feeling of peace and reconciliation with God. The hurts of earlier days of our disagreement about whether or not to build a kindergarten or focus only on direct evangelism were healed. Our wedding anniversary trip was a door opener for more ventures of short term service in Japan and other Asian countries, and a discovery that more reconciliation was needed closer to home.

Tensions with my coworkers in those early years were due to my misunderstanding of their feelings and my own personal pride. My new marriage relationship was tested because of these same blind spots. Pride in my missionary experience and a condescending attitude toward what I deemed was my wife's lack of exposure produced conflicts that led to tears. Gradually I became more familiar with my bride's tender sensitivities and her marvelous gifts for service. The Lord has been giving me a fresh appreciation for Beverly's rich contribution to my life and ministry.

---

[1] JAXA Japan Aerospace Exploration, Tanegashima Space Center (www. jaxa.jp/about/centers/tnsc)

Chapter Thirty Nine

CHANGING PATTERNS IN JAPAN

The Misfits of Japan

The term "Yakuza" is used to describe the underworld equivalent of the Mafia in Japan. The term comes from the numbers in a Japanese card game. **Ya** means 8, **ku** stands for 9, and **za** refers to 3, which makes a total of 20, a number which has no worth in the Japanese card game of *Oicho-kabu*. The term Yakuza therefore refers to those without any worth, or preferably, society's misfits. The term originated as far back as 1610 when undisciplined samurai harassed and terrorized any in their areas of influence. However, they protected the members of their own band with a remarkable loyalty. From the mid 17th century the gamblers and street vendors made up the bulk of Yakuza membership.

As Japan began to industrialize in the modern period the Yakuza made efforts to operate behind legitimate business fronts and to take an interest in politics. They learned that as they sympathized with certain politicians and officials they could avoid harassment from the police. Under the guise of patriotism the Yakuza had a role in the ultra-nationalist terror of the 1930's. Two liberal prime ministers and two finance ministers were murdered at their hands. They supplied the muscle and the men to further the jingoistic ends of the political right.

During the Allied occupation the Yakuza enriched themselves with black market dealings, even channeling the rationed out food from the American troops to their advantage. Influenced by the American gangster movies they began to dress in black suits, wear sunglasses and crop their hair short. By the 1960's the Yakuza had grown to 184,000 members. They began marking out territories and full scale wars erupted between the various gangs. Yoshio Kodama asserted leadership similar to the Mafia "godfather" style and settled the gang wars. Yakuza offers its members loyal comrades, money, status and authority under the guise of service to the community by offering protection. However, in present day Japan citizens are learning that problems are solved in a far less brutal manner if they turn first to the police.[1]

Converted Yakuza

During our 2001 summer visit to Japan our SJCC team ran across an amazing documentary video. On the cover was a photo of a tough looking group of former Yakuza members who had become Christians. Their shirtless torsos displayed large colorful tattoos, a symbol of their former identity. The title of the video given in Japanese idiom was, *Oyabun wa Iesusama* (My Boss is Jesus). How did such an amazing transformation come about?

The beginning place for change we learned was the concession of a Yakuza member to attend the church of the attractive Korean Christian lady he wanted to marry. She knew nothing of his means of livelihood, but let him know that she would not marry anyone who did not believe in God and go to church. Reassured by his popular stereotypes of the church the gangster thought it would be easy to go along with her request. He would be laughing inside as the minister spoke of the good people in contrast to the bad.

To this roughneck's complete surprise, the pastor declared that all men were sinners and that we could only be saved by grace. He also gave examples, such as the thief on the cross, where society's worst criminals could be forgiven through their faith in the shed blood of Christ. A stigma that would never be forgiven in traditional society could be removed by entrance into the kingdom of God. Once convinced of this truth the repentant gangster became a follower of Jesus and began witnessing to his comrades.

A Team of Former Misfits

"Former misfits" would describe the team of four men that accompanied me in my 2001 visit to Japan. Jason Ma is an energetic youth leader serving with Youth for Christ, but he honestly confesses of the time when he should have been put in jail for stealing. Jim Matteri, also an effective and compassionate youth minister, testifies of his traumatic experiences in a dysfunctional family. David Molchan, is the son of a banker, a top student and a youth minister, yet admits his former vulnerability to drugs. Steve Salazar was a drug dealer since age 16 and became a member of a violent Hispanic gang, but now he is a gentle Christian and pastor of the Sunrise Bible Church. Each of these fellows had considered themselves "misfits" but now give spontaneous testimonies of God's grace.

Because Eddie and Wendy Buchanan, Canadian Baptist missionaries in Iwaki, Japan, asked for help, we went there first. On two different days we passed out tracts that contained a Christian message and an invitation to the Iwaki Hope Church. It was an interesting experience in a rural area nearby the mountains. The fellows learned to imitate me and give a brief word of invitation in Japanese. Eddie reassured us that each year they had visitors drop in who came with the invitational tracts in hand.

On Friday evening at the local Christian Coffee House ministry Jason Ma gave his shocking testimony of stealing and apprehension by the police which led to a wakeup call and conversion to Christ. From the gathered young people's reactions I learned that Jason's experience was relevant to the current Japanese youth culture. It was becoming more apparent that large numbers of Japanese youth were rebelling against the extreme competition in the school system and the rigid conformity of traditional society. From reactions that led to dying one's hair green to the extreme of suicide many youth in twenty-first century Japan were crying for help. [2]

Unlike other teams I had brought to Japan, our group of four guys and their white-haired leader were not gifted musically. Before coming we had practiced singing choruses in Japanese and English. We were more humorous and entertaining than inspirational. Seeing a group of roughnecks singing, "He's Got the Whole World in His Hands," while we made circular arm motions ending with open hands, produced a joyful response from children and adults alike. Singing, "Everybody Ought to Know," and "Heavenly Sunshine" in Japanese triggered instant applause.

Creations For Children

When Eddie Buchanan sent an earlier written request that we come up with some creative ideas for the children, I contacted my daughter Sharon for help. I recalled how she had used long slender balloons to shape forms to illustrate biblical messages. She went through Ephesians 6 on the armor of God and fashioned the different parts of the armor. When she put the different parts of the balloon armor on me in the motel lobby where she met us, it drew the rapt attention of the clerks and the motel guests who were present. "The kids," Sharon said, "get really excited and want to try it themselves, and they do get the application of the biblical truth." Sold on the idea I acquired several packages of the long, slender balloons, and two hand air pumps and packed them in my baggage.

During the Saturday when the children in Iwaki gathered, the balloon armor created quite a stir. When the fellows saw me fashioning a balloon sword, they tried it themselves with success. My brief directions were: "First inflate the long tubular balloon, then a fold here, a pinch there, and then twist to form the handle." Before long numbers of the youngsters were battling one another with their spongy weapons, and making noisy battle sounds. We did leave the church that Sunday in a state of peace and Eddie confided in me that the testimonies and fun presentations of the fellows gave convincing evidence of their changed lives.

It was at our next stop, the Shinshu Bible Camp, that the balloon creations became a major manufacturing event. Missionary and Japanese staff members had brought their families with them. A couple of their children discovered our creative balloon class and were immediately attracted to balloon creations such as bees and wiener dogs. The word got around to the other children and we were kept busy the following three days of camp industriously making balloon creations. I believe that the fellows enjoyed the experience as much as the kids. It is questionable as to how much Bible they learned, but the children's parents assured us that our class was a big hit and we had freed up the parent's time for their camp duties. Second generation missionaries, Tim and Lisa Turner together with David and Rika Cole were doing a super job in leading the camp.

Planting New Churches

After seeing Jason Ma and Jim Matteri off at Narita airport because of commitments stateside, David Molchan, Steve Salazar and I boarded the express train for Nara, the home of Sakae Sensei. Pastor Sakae again offered his services as guide and host. We saw the cultural attractions of this ancient religious city and were treated to a dinner in a nearby restaurant. The next day, we attended a lively midweek morning fellowship in the church he pastored in Nara, and then went on to visit his new church plant in Osaka. This newer venture appeared to be an outreach to the less fortunate and was located in a part of town that showed signs of urban decay. For the first time I learned that Sakae Sensei's brother had been involved in a major food program for the poor.

Pastor Sakae requested that Steve give his testimony and that I bring the evening message. In his humble, unassuming manner, Steve gave his testimony of a life that took him downhill. Then he related how, when he ended up in jail and arrived at a place of complete despair, he learned of God's saving grace and forgiveness through Christ. After interpreting Steve's convicting remarks I brought a message that included a description of how God's presence was felt in the mountain cottage in Tanegashima from which Yoshiyuki Sakae was called. Sakae Sensei told me later that there were those in the service that made decisions for Christ.

We journeyed further southward to Hiroshima where Joseph Chae, an SJCC graduate, had planted a new church not far from the central station. Although Pastor Chae was Korean, he spoke fluent Japanese and appeared to be successful in his church planting efforts. Under the auspices of the Korean Holiness Church he had purchased a three-story building which was walking distance from the train station.

The fact that Christian Koreans have been successful missionaries in Japan points to the power of God's love to overcome years of traditional animosity.

The Freeing of the Lepers

Our journey took us south to Kanoya where we were welcomed by Pastor Yoshii and taken at my request to visit Mark and Pauline Maxey. Sadly we learned that Mark Maxey's Alzheimer's had progressed to the place where he did not recognize old friends. Pauline kept him feeling peaceful by playing music of his favorite hymns. In a short time that brave lady would be alone but insisted on staying on in Kanoya, which had become her home. Fortunately, her missionary son and daughter-in-law, Walter and Mary Maxey, are only a couple of hours away.

Early Sunday morning we left for the leper colony. I had prepared a message in which I thanked all my old friends for the help and guidance they had given me in my first years in Japan. I didn't realize at the time that a new law regarding the treatment of Japan's lepers had been passed on May 23, 2001. In effect the government was apologizing to the lepers for keeping them confined after their Hansen's disease had been cured.[3] Now, free from many restrictive rules, they could socialize with people and permit bodily contact. Sensing a change in demeanor when one of the leper Christians extended the stumps that had once been his hands, I grabbed them and exchanged greetings. David Molchan did the same and later in SJCC's chapel he testified that the experience moved him deeply.

---

[1] Yakuza, The Japanese Mafia,
   http://www2.gol.com/users/coynerhm/yakuza_the_Japanese_mafia.him
[2] Makoto Watabe, "Youth Problems and Japanese Society," The Japan Foundation Newsletter, June 2001.
[3] Harvard Asian Quarterly,
   http://www.asianquarterly.com/content/view/122/40/

Chapter Forty

INSIGHTS FOR MISSIONS

Incarnational Involvement

When Jesus, who in his very nature is divine, left the beauty and security of heaven to become man, he gave us our best example for missionary service. As God enables us we are to identify with the people to whom He sends us. This means that we are to adapt to their lifestyle and learn their language. Becoming accustomed to a different diet may not be difficult, but adjusting to the underlying world view of another culture will most likely take many years of effort. Language is the key to understanding how people think and the more time the missionary puts into his effort to master the vernacular of his newly adopted neighbors the more completely he will understand their behavior.

As we learn the idiom of the people we learn more about their culture, which represents the totality of their learned behavior. Another basic lesson of Jesus is that we love and respect every person regardless of society's biased evaluation of gender, race, or social status (John 4:1-26). A prideful, ethnocentric approach to a diverse culture is doomed to failure. People respond only to those who respect them. Words alone are not convincing. To convince others that we are concerned about them we must take time to build relationships. Memorable bonding experiences build bridges of understanding.

The above foundational truths I was taught in theory prior to going to Japan to serve. In applying these principles in daily life I learned that, at times, my spirit was willing but my flesh was weak. Those times when the gap between my professed ideals and my actual practice became too great I experienced culture shock. I discovered that acknowledging my vulnerability paved the way for understanding.

I learned that one's greatest asset can be the ability to laugh at oneself. I hope the reader understands as he reads the numerous comments about language mistakes and trying experiences of cultural adjustment that I have learned to share these stories so that others can laugh with me. A healthy sense of humor reflects recognition of the vulnerability of man in contrast to the power and glory of His Creator. As we mature we learn to laugh at ourselves and not poke fun at others.

Understanding Field Conditions

Matthew's account of the parable of the sower points to three factors that relate to the degree of fruitfulness: **the sower, the seed, and the soil** (Matt 13:3-8). Mark adds **the unknown factor** in growth that points to God's sovereignty (Mark 4:26-27). We are taught to anticipate that if the sower is faithful, and the seed is pure, the soil should produce. But we tend to overlook the conditioning of the soil – the historical and cultural background of a given field. We need to learn how to better adapt the message in order to penetrate the hardened soil.

We wonder why only one percent of the Japanese population has publicly accepted the Christian faith, while just across the narrow straits of the Sea of Japan, over thirty percent of the South Koreans are declared Christians. Why such a large difference? Were the missionaries that went to Korea more dedicated? Was the message they preached more pure? Were their methods more effective? After reading Roy Shearer's book, *"Wildfire: Church Growth in Korea,"* [1] and reflecting on my own first hand experiences I came to answer the above questions with, "none of the above." Church growth in Korea was most rapid during the times when the staunch Christians resisted the persecution of *outside invaders* such as the Japanese imperialists and the Chinese communists of those periods.

The persecution against 16th century Japanese Catholic Christians came from *ruling forces within* Japan that claimed loyalty to their Emperor. This same ploy of loyalty to the Emperor was used by the initiation of the 1890 Rescript on Education which restricted the response to Protestant missions. Awareness of this background history helps one to understand Japanese apprehension about change. At the same time it helps us to appreciate the admiration that many Japanese Christians have for Kanzo Uchimura, the Christian high school teacher who refused to bow to the Emperor's picture at the reading of the Rescript. We need to understand also why these same Japanese Christians agree with the criticisms Uchimura had against western church forms, which did not separate the message from its westernized package.

A unique factor in Korean culture made it easier to communicate the concept of a transcendent Creator. An indigenous word for a high God was already existent. The Protestants wisely appropriated this term (*Hananim*) in referring to the God of the Bible. In Japan the term for God or gods (*kami*) had a diffused polytheistic meaning and was in use with reference to the Emperor as divine. Missionaries have to spend much time in clarifying their intended meaning. The Apostle Paul had the same difficulty with the Greek word for God (*theos*) which in general speech would refer to the Greco-Roman pantheon, so the problem is not insurmountable.

Beyond cause and effect factors of national behavior that we learn from our study of history and culture, there are unique areas of individual motivation that are unknown to us. Judgments of personal behavior based on generalized stereotypes often miss the mark. All Japanese are not the same. The appeal of the gospel is that God knows each one of us, and while being fully aware of our areas of pride and shame, still loves us (Romans 5:8). The missionary is most effective when he withholds judgment and accepts individuals as they are. God has a way of choosing the most unlikely individuals to bring glory to His Name (I Corinthians 1:26-31).

Cross Cultural Communication

During the modern period Japan was the first Asian nation to industrialize, which meant that along with the technical developments she accepted the scientific assumptions of biological evolution and materialistic naturalism. This is one more field condition that puts restraint toward the supernatural posture of the Christian faith in the minds of her millions of students. Students who came to me had many questions which reflected this humanistic scientific background.

I have suggested in chapter 12 that rather than a direct attack of an either/or position on every point of difference, it works better to offer available options that show the basic harmony between general and special revelation. The same God who created the cosmos also gave us the Bible. We need to humbly admit that we do not have all the answers. Balanced biblical interpretation seeks to sort out the core essentials from those things which even the Apostle Peter acknowledged were hard to understand (II Peter 3:16).

When the Apostle Paul came to Athens he could have made a blistering attack against the Stoic and Epicurean philosophers. Instead he found a *point of contact* in the altar to the Unknown God. Showing respect to their religious propensity he used this opening to set forth the truth about the Creator. He went further in order to point out *common ground* areas that related to all men. All men have a drive to know, to seek God, for Paul points out that even one of their Stoic poets said, "For we also are his offspring," which is in basic agreement with Scripture (Acts 17:22-30).

We are puzzled at the assurance that Paul and Silas gave to the Philippian jailer, "Believe in the Lord Jesus, and you shall be saved, you and your household" (Acts 16:31). In our individualistic thinking we question how they could assure the jailer of the decisions of the members of his household. We are not familiar with the group orientation of oriental culture. We are reassured when we read that Paul and Silas spoke the word of the Lord to the jailer "together with all who were in his house" (v.32). The unity of the extended family is sacred in many cultures. If the head of the house makes a decision that affects them all, they are moved to go along with it, especially if the reasons are shared.

I've acknowledged the weakness of "extraction evangelism" and have tried to be more inclusive of the whole family in our invitations. However, there are examples of those who have first made individual decisions for Christ, and then eventually won their families over time. From my own failures using western methods and from the self-admissions of others, I have come to have second thoughts about mass evangelism and the urging of on-the-spot decisions. A growing awareness of the complexity of Japanese culture made me more cautious to make sure that a decision to accept Christ was based on understanding and not the emotions of the moment.

To lighten up our writing I have enjoyed including such stories as my wife, Eleanor's, popcorn party. She had discovered an approach that would unite her ladies in a very worthwhile Christmas project. Making popcorn balls and delivering them to the orphanage was a very successful venture. She had discovered a "functional substitute" for the making of *omochi* (rice cakes) which are placed on home altars at New Year's time. Creative thinking could discover many things in a religious culture which could be turned around and given Christian meaning. Going back in time, the Christmas tree is one example. However, we learned that the well-known *Hakata* pottery craftsmen had fashioned dolls that typify the manger scene of the Christmas story. The wise men and shepherds were given Oriental faces which made it more appropriate for Japanese culture and gave us a natural setting for relating Christ's birth.

Adapting to Cultural Change

In our observations of Japan covering almost a half a century we have noticed the rapid rate of change. Industrialization has led to modernization and materialism. The rapid pace of urbanization has led to a growing secularism which contrasts to the reactionary growth of the so called "New Religions." The homogeneity of Japanese traditional values has been eroding. The flow of youth from the conservative rural base to the sea of change experienced in the mushrooming cities keeps the population in a state of flux. Conservative forces in government agencies, especially in the school system, attempt to retain conformity for the sake of control.

In today's world Japan's experience is not that different from other industrial nations. In the United States the educational efforts to bring excellence into the class-room have created pressures that have led to a 30% dropout rate from high school. In Japan the continued efforts to enforce student conformity have led to cliquish clubs and the bullying of students who appear different. Increasing incidences of suicide even among middle school students appear connected to the bullying in the school which made them feel alienated.[2]

Japan's material gains have been impressive. Their rapid transit system in the cities and their bullet trains on the major intercity trunk lines are marvels of modern convenience. The Tanegashima Space Center constructed on the southern tip of the island where we worked is a striking example of modern innovation. The fact that there is available electric power 24 hours a day and air conditioning in restaurants and hotels contrasts to the less developed conditions of our experience. Today the sea sickness experienced during the six-hour trip to the island has been replaced, for those who can afford it, by a pleasurable two-hour trip on the hovercraft.

But the conveniences of this modern Japan come with a price. The cost of living is higher in Tokyo than in most cities of the world. Office workers put in twelve-hour days, six days a week. Because housing in the inner city is cost prohibitive, one- and two-hour commutes from the suburbs are necessary. Because education is so expensive, one child families are becoming the norm. Marriage is delayed indefinitely for many young people who want to use their earnings for their personal use while they continue to live with their parents. Cross-cultural marriages are increasing, especially in rural areas, as men, failing to find an available Japanese wife, marry immigrant aliens from other Asian countries. [3]

One example of missionary adaptation to the changing economic reality which prohibits the construction of expensive church buildings is the establishing of house churches. Chad and Jennifer Huddleston, an energetic couple in the Osaka area, have first built up a fellowship in their apartment and then have gone on to foster other house churches. Jennifer is a third generation missionary, the daughter of Paul and Rickie Clark and quite at home in Japan. Chad is a keenly focused missionary with a vision for growth. Lay leadership is developed by special training sessions in seminars and camps. Prayer for the individual and community needs is stressed. After young people come to a place of faith they are challenged to really make Christ the Lord of their lives, to become His disciple and begin to share His love with their friends and family. They continue to have teams of students from stateside Christian colleges visit in the summers to strengthen their outreach.

Yet the expectation to house the fellowship in a church building still goes on, especially when this has been the pattern in older missions. A second generation missionary, Walter Maxey rejoices that a recent graduate of Osaka Bible Seminary has returned to Kyushu to become the pastor of the Kagoshima Church. Although housed in a strategically located building that includes a second-story parsonage the members have been without a pastor for some years. The ongoing needs for informed Bible knowledge, Christian counseling and formal marriage and funeral services, precipitate requests for qualified clergy. This surely indicates that the role of the Bible College or seminary continues to have a strategic place in preparing trained church leadership for the future needs in Japan.

Summing Up With Ten Nuggets

Digging into the life experiences represented in our stories we came up with ten nuggets, or mission insights, that can serve as guidelines for the missionary. I believe that, although they were learned in Japan, they can be applied to most fields.

1) **We should have respect and appreciation for past laborers.** John reminds us that "others have labored, and you have entered into their labor" (John 4: 38). I recall the belated time of harvest of the dormant seed that resided in the heart of the matriarch on Shikoku who had been helped by an English missionary lady after the 1923 Tokyo earthquake (Chapter 13). I am grateful to Mark and Pauline Maxey for the initiation of the work we entered, and for Isabel, Mark's sister, for her role in winning one of our key coworkers. Also, I realize that Pastor Hideo Yoshii had made successful trips to Tanegashima before we arrived. We are indebted to these dedicated predecessors.

2) **There is a correlation between the missionary's attempt to identify with the culture and the establishing of indigenous churches.** As we do our very best to learn the language and customs of the people we show respect for their culture and discourage copy-cat imitation that leads to the westernization of the church. It is essential that the Japanese embrace Christ as their own Savior, not a western import.

3) **It is important to set aside our proud self-reliance and learn the grace of receiving, thereby bestowing dignity on others.** We are rewarded by giving a listening ear to those who have something to teach us about their insights on life. As we learn to relax and appreciate the hospitality and fellowship of the native people we become more a part of their community. As we open our hearts to the people, they open their hearts to us (II Corinthians 6: 11-13).

4) **We must believe in the presence of God and anticipate His working in providence if there are to be any significant changes for good.** We see His hand in turning our mistakes into blessings as when I mispronounced the word for satellite, disrupting a strategic evangelistic meeting (Chapter 5). He brings unexpected encounters into our schedules that get us

back on track as when an Obaasan showed up on our doorstep with a desire to worship God (Chapter 8).

5) **It is essential that the missionary have a non-adversarial approach toward people.** Paul was in prison because of his many enemies when he wrote, "For our struggle is *not against flesh and blood,* but against...the spiritual forces of wickedness in the heavenly places" (Ephesians 6:12). Rather than making adversaries of those in the world religions, we should look for points of contact (Chapter 23). Instead of assuming an antagonistic posture toward the science community, we'll find it more fruitful to look for areas of common ground (Chapter 12). The Lord restrained my negative impulses so that my positive approach to the town's politically influential wine merchant opened the door to our using the public hall in Onta for church services (Chapter 10).

6) **Never lose sight of the importance of interpersonal relationships.** Satan's attacks are designed to divide us. Missionaries leaving the field because of interpersonal conflicts is the subject of frequent reports. Prayer meetings, area rallies, and regional or national conventions do much to "preserve the unity of the Spirit in the bond of peace" (Ephesians 4:3).

7) **Recognize the power of family witness.** Dr.Yasuo Furuya of International Christian University (ICU), states with conviction that if Japanese Christian parents passed their faith on to their children, the church would move beyond a mere one percent, and become a more effective witness at 10 percent.[4] The value of the Protestant missionary family cannot be over estimated. A family has a built-in witness to different ages, and, as God chooses, is a source for 2nd generation missionaries who are natural communication bridge builders.

8) **There is an ongoing need to pray and work for church unity.** It takes humility and focused effort to bring

about the spirit of oneness for which the Lord prayed. While not advocating the compromise of essential truth in order to have togetherness, we must come to acknowledge that much disunity is from cultural conditioning, unquestioned assumptions in biblical interpretation, and polarized opinions enforced by one's group loyalty. Progress has been made in some areas but gaps remain between social classes, diverse styles of worship, and between evangelical and charismatic perspectives.

9) **Affirmation of the freedom of means, and the free expression of culture, and of spiritual gifts, can release the power of the gospel.** Paul's fervent declaration that, *"I have become all things to all men, that I may by all means save some"* (I Cor. 9:22) should prevent us from giving undue attention to methods or from restricting cultural worship styles. His charge that, "There is neither Jew nor Greek, there is neither slave nor free man, there is neither male nor female, for you are all one in Christ Jesus" (Galatians 3:28), should remove the barriers to the free expression of our Spirit-given gifts. Chapters 25 and 27 discuss how gospel freedom permits diverse methods in missions and creative leadership roles for women.

10) **Praying and working for new laborers for the world harvest is a part of   missions** (Matthew 9:37-38). In Japan the pastors and missionaries are aging and realize the need for youthful replacements. Churches and parachurch organizations such as Youth With A Mission (YWAM) have used short-term missions to recruit youth. Their programs encourage short-term *courtships* with the culture, leading to long-term commitment for some.[5] Since youth attract youth, missionaries who mentor young mission interns are needed.

Meaningful Choices

In the final analysis, the choices that the indigenous church leaders make are critical for the future. Sakae Sensei has not followed a pattern of hovering over one congregation which has reached optimum size, instead, challenged by the unreached population in urban Japan, he has planted churches in other needy areas. Recently he requested that one of the graduates of Ikoma Bible College together with his coworker, Chad Huddleston, hold a seminar in his school on church planting and house churches. His vision has also inspired him to teach the members of his congregations of worldwide needs. For a number of years he and some of his coworkers have gone to serve in Africa in the summers.

Akada Sensei, pastor of the Onta Church in Higashimurayama, Tokyo, has made himself available to fill the many requests for Christian weddings. Through this means he supplemented his income in order to pay the bills and send his son, Naoki, to college and seminary. As Christian parents pass their faith on to their children the church will grow faster than the one percent of population growth. It is interesting that Naoki is serving as an associate pastor in a Disciples Church that began in 1884. In making this choice the young pastor has crossed a divide produced by the choices and circumstances of an earlier generation.

At a time when Pastor Ikeda's work had become self supporting through the kindergarten outreach, and the number of enrolled children had risen close to 300, he quietly announced that he and his wife were going to China. His daughter would continue to manage the kindergarten; the aging church was turned over to a young seminary graduate who had been one of his converts from Tanegashima.

When he returned to Kyushu for a short furlough his demeanor impressed missionary, Al Juve, who wrote: "We got to see Pastor Ikeda and his wife, at the convention last summer. We had not seen them in years. It was also the first time we had seen Motonobu (his minister son) in a long time. They told us about their missionary work in China. They seemed very different from the rest of the Japanese at the convention. What they had experienced God do in China filled them with a joy and a fire that were stunning! It was neat to see."[6]

This handful of national leaders that I partnered with were motivated to make their own diverse choices. Beyond them could be added a long list of faithful Japanese pastors and evangelists that have weathered the storms that come to struggling minority religious groups. Notable among these many Christian soldiers is nationally-known **Akira Hatori**, who apologized to the Koreans during Explo '74 for previous Japanese belligerency (Chapter 32). His testimony at the Urbana Conference in Illinois honored an English missionary lady, Miss Burnett, who had not only won him to Christ, but had mentored him in Bible study and evangelism. He credits her prayers for his family that all of them came to know the Lord.[7]

Hatori received further education and experience and became Japan's premier TV evangelist speaking to six million people at a time. In extensive three-day campaigns held all over the nation, he averaged 200 decisions for Christ a month. He goes on to testify that Miss Burnett also gave him a missionary vision. He began by sending out his staff workers to South America and organized missionary conferences all over Japan.

Akira Hatori was chosen to be Billy Graham's interpreter during the 1967 Tokyo Crusade. Although his meteoric rise in evangelistic effectiveness some years ago was exceptional, his experience of being won and mentored through a missionary who demonstrated the love of Christ is not unique. God continues to use those with servant hearts to come alongside potential national leaders and pass on the vision for winning a lost world.

Hope for the Future

Jesus taught us to pray for laborers for the harvest (Matthew 9:37-38). This follows his affirmation that, "the harvest is plentiful," which, at first glance, doesn't seem to apply to Japan. He also reminded his disciples that, "others have labored," and this would explain why they could anticipate a waiting harvest (John 4:35-38). Would not the biblical context refer to the many prophetic seed sowers, that labored prior to the first arrival of the Messiah "in the fullness of time" (Galatians 4:4)? *What evidence indicates that Japan's fields are being readied for harvesting in our day?*

Professor Harold Netland of Trinity Evangelical Divinity School, who spent much of his life in Japan, reminds us that the sales of Bibles in post-WWII Japan rose from 400,000 in the 1960's to over one million between 1971 and 1990. He quotes a Japanese authority who affirms that one in two or three Japanese homes has a Bible. Dr. Netland also reminds us that a significant number of Japanese have been influenced by Christian kindergartens or Sunday Schools. Many also have been impacted by studying conversational English with missionaries or by attending mission schools.[8] *Can we not anticipate fruit from these sown seeds in the future?*

Drawing on his experience in 35 years of successful cross cultural church planting in Japan, Stan Conrad suggests that the problem may not be Japanese aversion to the gospel but the packaging in which it was presented. He documents the historical and cultural factors which restrained the growth of the church, but still feels that the label, "resistant," applied to Japan is more derived from misunderstandings than from facts. He cites Donald McGavran as saying, "Sometimes unresponsiveness is due to hardness of heart, pride, or aloofness, but more often than we like to think, it is due to neglect." By neglect he is referring to the failure of the missionaries to learn the language and make more adequate efforts to present the gospel in a manner that is more sensitive to the culture.[9] We feel there is some truth in this conclusion, yet to simply do things in "a Japanese way" does not seem to resolve the communication problems. The enigmatic behavior of the Japanese still leaves us with questions.

Why, in present day Japan, are thousands of educated Japanese being won to Christ through listening to the words and music of Johann Sebastian Bach, the 18th century German composer? A contemporary historian tells us that, "After two failed attempts to popularize Bach's music in Japan since the late 19th century, a veritable Bach boom has been sweeping that country for the last 16 years." During the Christian Holy Week, eager enthusiasts pay over $600 to hear Masaaki Suzuki's organ performance of Bach's sacred music. Why is this? Is it, according to one analyst, "because Bach's music reflects the perfect beauty of created order to which the Japanese mind is receptive?"[10] Or is it because the beauty of the gospel comes through in an acceptable form to those with preferences for the classics? What about those who are more attracted to the music of popular culture?

God may have given a communication key to Ken and Bola Taylor, who have been serving in Japan since 1997. Their unusual ministry has been in the field of popular music, developing "Black gospel choirs" among Japanese vocalists. In the summer of 2007 we visited the Twin Lakes church in Capitola, California and learned that they were supporters of the Taylors. A number of their members had just returned from visiting Ken and Bola in Japan. They reported with enthusiasm that twenty-five "Black gospel choirs" had been formed and these gathered into one mass choir twice a year. Moreover, some of the Japanese singers, 80% of whom are not yet believers, had become Christians! The participation of the Japanese choir members was leading them to accept the reality behind the words.

This refreshing, innovative approach comes at a crucial time in Japan's social history. The straight-jacket restrictions that produced Japan's phenomenal economic success up until the bubble burst in 1989, have apparently led to Japan's present day lethargy. Prolonged repressive restraint on individual expression has created a new social illness, which Japanese psychologists call *hikikomori* (withdrawal retirement). Over a million young people, 80% of them men, have dropped out from society and seldom leave the isolation of their rooms. Parallel to this new epidemic is the climbing suicide rate – 660 every week, 94 persons per day! [11]

My wife and I met the Taylors when they visited San Jose Christian College a number of years ago, and were thrilled by their inspirational music. We learned of the enthusiastic involvement of the reserved Japanese in the singing style of Whoopi Goldberg, as portrayed in the film, "Sister Act." Because of their professional music background, Ken and Bola felt they could use this Japanese infatuation for the Black singing style by organizing groups singing Black Spirituals in Japan.

This summer we learned that their vision had become a reality. Not only were they helping the reserved Japanese find release in singing Black spirituals, they also were encouraging creative indigenous music expression. In their own words they are involved in evangelism, equipping, encouraging, and exploring. Their focus is "to share the gospel of Jesus Christ in Japan through church planting strategies with a focus on music and creative arts."[12] It has caught on! It seems to reinforce the view that if the gospel is presented in a culturally sensitive way, its natural beauty will have a life changing impact that causes believers to make it their own.

Conclusion: The overlapping questions I've raised about the growth of the Christian faith in Japan; whether there is enough evidence that the field is being readied, and whether it is justifiable to anticipate fruit from past labors, can be answered with an unequivocal "Yes!" (II Corinthians 1:19). Three factors give me this hope for the future destiny of the kingdom of Christ in Japan: (1) the current signs of diversity of those who have broken with the traditional "stay in your box" conformity; (2) the faithful standby Christian leaders with their well established institutions; and (3) the creative innovations and enthusiasm of newcomers. The cement that can prevent the polarization of these complementary building blocks is the love of Jesus.

> And I pray that you, being rooted and established in love, may have power, together with all the saints, to grasp how wide and long and high and deep is the love of Christ, and to know this love that surpasses knowledge.

> (Ephesians 3:17-19 NIV)

[1] Roy Shearer, "Wildfire: Church Growth in Korea," Grand Rapids: W.B. Eerdmans, 1966.

[2] Makoto Watabe, "Youth Problems and Japanese Society," The Japan Foundation Newsletter, June 2001.

[3] "More Japanese finding wedded bliss with foreigners," The Japan Times, February 8, 2004.

[4] Dr. Yasuo Furuya's convictions on Japanese church growth appeared in Dendo Shinshu, Series #1, published by Nihon Kirisuto Dendo Kai, Tokyo, November 20, 1987.

[5] A number of students in our Guatemala band returned for longer service.

[6] Email from Al Juve, February 17, 2006.

[7] Urbana.org web site copyright by InterVarsity Christian Fellowship.

[8] Harold Netland, "Missions and Jesus in a Globalizing World," EMS Journal, Number 12, William Carey Library, 2005. p.135.

[9] Stan Conrad, "Encountering Japanese Resistance," EMS Journal, Number 6, William Carey Library, 1998, pp. 117-131.

[10] Uwe Simon-Netto, "Bach in Japan," Christian History & Biography, Issue 95, Summer 2007, p. 42

[11] Michael Zielenziger, "Shutting Out the Sun, How Japan Created Its Own Lost Generation," Vintage Books, Septemper 2007, pp. 16-19. and p. 190.

[12] http://www.kenandbola.com

1: CULTURAL ADJUSTMENTS

Typhoon survivor Grandmother Kudo

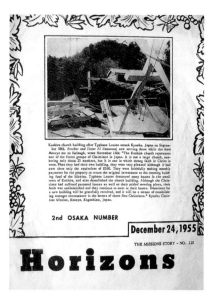

Photo: Destruction of Kushira Church

Island Church and Parsonage

Tim & Sharon Found Friends on Island

Kids received lots of hugs from islanders

Tim shows Curiosity about Shinto Festival

Trying out Dad's Motorcycle

2: ISLAND FELLOWSHIP

Tim and Sharon with Youth Leaders

Sakae San's Early Cottage Meeting

Nishinoomote Church, Christmas, 1957

Sharon visiting Sakae San's Home,1974

Tanoue's Home Fellowship in Noma,

The Nishinoomote Sunday School
1957 Jonohama Church

3: NEW BEGINNINGS

Born in Kagoshima, Mary was a novelty.

A fresh start in return to language school

Seki San assists us in starting a church. She gave wise counsel and mentored the youth. A family spirit developed.

We began an Open Forum magazine in 1960

A church begins in our Kumegawa home. Akada Sensei eventually became the Pastor. At times the church outgrew the home so we began to meet in the Onta Public hall.

Yoichi and Tomiko Muto, dedicated workers in the Kingdom. Yoichi is proficient in Bible teaching and in writing. Tomiko is gifted in social work.

Stephen Lijima, author of the Pastoral Song journal, is a popular speaker in churches, conventions, and camps.

Rev and Mrs. Phil Foxwell. He worked his way through Wheaton College doing magic shows, followed by a convincing testimony of faith.

Hideo Yoshii, has been the pastor of the Kanoya Church of Christ for decades. Known for his emphasis on the love of Christ, he gives grace-filled messages as he visits and serves other congregations.

5: STUDENT ENCOUNTERS

Fellowship with visiting SJCC friends.

Yoshi Sensei speaking to youth at camp.

Vivian Lemmon mentored Tetsuo Domen, who married Hideko Yabiku, who has a beautiful singing voice. They raised their family of five although Hideko is blind.

Domen San leading at a church rally. He accepted Christ when in high school, and went on to graduate from a top college, giving him more credibility to witness.

Receptive youth at Shinshu Bible Camp.

Our team found it easy to make friends.

6: QUESTIONING RELIGION

Ujigami, a field deity to
help produce more rice.

Harold Sims studying a temple's history

Nio, Guardian of the Gate
to keep evil spirits away.

Dr. David Filbeck of Thailand
gives helpful cues about demons
in chapter nineteen.

Passing on traditions to son

A ten million dollar "new religion" temple

Joe Garman preaching at Kumegawa Church in Tokyo Suburb

Fish Eye photo: 1967 Tokyo Billy Graham Crusade in Budokan

Early English Speaking Church Service Led by Bill and Lois Walker

The Hayama Seminar Welcomes all Missionaries to Share in its annual Open Forum

Parental Joy at the Birth of Billy in 1963

Helping Dad mail FECM magazines

Mary & Jim taking care of Blacky

Al & Eleanor Hammond
Family in 1963

Annual Camp was part of family life.

Hammonds on a park horse in 1965

10: READJUSTMENT TO THE U.S.A.

Jim and Jean Francis became ministers of the Martinez church when Al and Eleanor felt called to Japan. For over fifty years Jim led the young church, establishing it firmly in the community. The term that is used to describe the life style and labors of the Francis family is "Builders." Today, in 2008, their son, Bill, is ably leading the church on firm foundations.

Jim and Jean Francis and Family in Martinez, California

"Secularization has been accomplished in the mistaken belief that it meant 'religious liberty'. That great ideal has been largely nullified by this negative interpretation. To the Fathers it meant liberty in religion, not immunity from it. There can be no religious liberty if the basic faith of our people is destroyed by the 'acids of modernity' in a secular society."

Earnest Johnson
Columbia University

Although Al was strengthened in his understanding of Japanese language and culture in his graduate studies at Cal-Berkeley, he was saddened at the lapses in morality and the sharp divisions in U.S. society reflected in the views of the student body. The quote above encouraged him, and made him all the more appreciative for the builders in society.

Al at home in the classroom at SJBC

11: MISSIONS AT OUR DOORSTEP

Mayumi Returned to Tokyo, Japan

Professors at San Jose Christian College

Pastor in Yokohama, Japan

Sabu Abraham and Family represent the many graduates who have returned to Asian countries to serve.

Yoshi is a hospital worker in Osaka

Graduates: Top left- Mayumi Takahashi with Al and Beverly; Center- Masaki Minoguchi with his new wife. Lower left-Yoshiaki Fukushima with his mother.
Professors: Top right- Each one shared, but some who focused on international student needs were: Nam Soo Woo, Moses Samol Seth, Clay Baek, Don Byers, Roger Edrington, and Stanley Friesen.

12 SJCC VISITS TO EAST ASIA

Welcomed in Korea to attend Explo '74

1979 Team visiting Osaka Castle

SICC team at Japan's Supreme Court

1985 Team included retired couple

Macao and China visit in 2000

John cooling off Sin Yon Pak, 1992

1992 Convention Banquet

Yoshiyuki Sakae Preaching

John speaking Greek with Professor Oda

Cultural Demo of the Ancient Gun

Gathering in the park for a photo where outdoor breakfasts were served.

Sin Yon poses with ancient rifle in hand.

Family Support for Our 1993 Wedding

Welcomed by Mark & Pauline Maxey

Instant Friendship of Beverly & Audrey

New Kindergarten Complex: a Surprise!

Walter and Mary Maxey and Family

Fellowship with John & Mary Muto

Steve's changed life is beautiful testimony

Former *Yakuza* crime members have converted to christ. The video title is, "My Boss is Jesus." At the bottom are photos of two who became Christian ministers.

Many Japanese prefer a "Christian style" ceremony

Wedding Coach of the Crown Prince with Michiko Shoda in 1959

Chad & Jennifer Huddleston & Family, Focus on Home Churches

Ken and Bola Taylor and Family, Focus on Creative Arts

The youthful enthusiasm o the Huddlestons and Taylor give us hope for mission in Japan. The Lord can giv continuity to their outreacl through their families. Pau and Rickie Clark, (abov photo), now serving in Japan and Mongolia, are the parent of Jennifer. Paul is the so of Martin Clark, long tim President of the Osaka Bibl Seminary. Solid foundation plus freshness of approacl give promise for the future.